T0121798

Season of
Deceit

Robin Timmerman

Order this book online at www.trafford.com
or email orders@trafford.com

Most Trafford titles are also available at major online book retailers.

© Copyright 2013 Robin Timmerman.
All rights reserved. No part of this publication may be reproduced, stored in a retrieval
system, or transmitted, in any form or by any means, electronic, mechanical, photocopying,
recording, or otherwise, without the written prior permission of the author.

Printed in the United States of America.

ISBN: 978-1-4669-8721-0 (sc)
ISBN: 978-1-4669-8722-7 (hc)
ISBN: 978-1-4669-8737-1 (e)

Library of Congress Control Number: 2013905391

Trafford rev. 04/02/2013

 www.trafford.com

North America & international
toll-free: 1 888 232 4444 (USA & Canada)
phone: 250 383 6864 ♦ fax: 812 355 4082

This book is a work of fiction. Any resemblance to actual events, locales or persons is entirely coincidental

For Bess

PROLOGUE

She lay on the floor where she had fallen. Sprawled like a broken beetle between the upturned stepstool and the cupboard where she'd been reaching. One old split heeled slipper, the culprit, by her bleeding nose. And in her hair, the oily smell of sardines joined with the other sour smells in the room.

She couldn't move but it didn't seem to matter. Another old woman gone, that wouldn't matter much either in the scheme of things. Oddly, she felt no pain. Maybe that was the final gift.

She felt badly for her darling kitties though, a small regret to add to the long list of a long lifetime.

The furry ones, confounded at the sight, had scattered. But after a bit, one braver than the rest, came creeping back to sniff at the fish. Others followed and when they'd eaten, they leapt up to their perches by the window. They preened themselves while the pale winter sun advanced slowly across the crumpled form on the floor.

The room was growing colder.

1

"Looks like another break-in," Chief Halstead told Officer Pete Jakes.

"That cottage where the old lady died last week. You'd better take Poitras and check it out. A neighbour reported seeing a light in the place last night."

He frowned at Jane's post-it note.

"Look for anything that might indicate they're the same thieves who hit the Bay Road places last week. Though I doubt they'd get anything of much value from the old lady's place. From what social services said, it was hardly a luxury home."

Every winter there was a rash of smash and grabs on the Island. This year it was worse than usual. The weird snowless winter had the whole Middle Island population in a flap. The farmers were complaining that there wouldn't be enough melt in the spring. (Other years they complained that there was too much). The snowmobile clubbers were upset because they'd hardly had their machines out. And the doomsayers were confirmed in their warnings that global warming would be the end of life as we know it.

Bored teenagers who would normally vent their energy in winter sports and snowmobiling had taken to pilfering, chiefly at cottages left empty for the season. A bottle of booze here, maybe a VCR. Often it seemed that they didn't even want the stuff, the looting was more a rite of passage and the police would find the items tossed in a nearby ditch.

Pete drove the cruiser along bare road. Even the winter-fallow fields were only thinly streaked with snow, echoing the brown markings of the sparrows that clustered on the dry hawthorne twigs. The old-timers at the Island Grill spoke of the snowstorms of their youth, that had left huge drifts piled up to the top of the telephone poles. Of the blocked causeway to the mainland, of being shut in for days at the farms on the various Island points, only struggling out through the drifts to feed the livestock. Of babies being delivered by the father because the doctor or midwife couldn't get there. And times when there was no news from the outside world for nearly a week.

Stories told with great pride and ever-growing embellishment.

But this year, only four inches of snow had fallen in January instead of eighteen, virtually none of the white stuff in February and here it was already March. Pete had developed the Island habit of checking the sky, today the color of dirty cotton batten. Not winter, not spring, just dreary.

The cottage was on in inland road, on a scruffier part of the island where the soil was rocky and never had been good farmland. There were no big old houses, and no fancy new ones either. The area was now mainly used as rough grazing for a small herd of beef cows. The farmer would leave them to wander, then round them up in the winter. The original farmhouse of the property had been placed back on the better, more travelled road on the bay side of the property.

Akantha Samos' little house was a rude structure, a storey and a half, its brick exterior now covered in crumbling yellow stucco. The place crouched on the edge of the bare fields that stretched behind to a line of spindly lombardy poplars. There were no trees by the house, only a couple of winter bare lilac bushes indicating the entrance from the road.

A lonely spot. This was Jakes' second winter on the Island, and he was appreciative of the beauty of some of its more isolated spots. Still, it was hard to see any charm here even for thieves, who generally preferred to target the homes of the wealthy along the lake front, where there would be easily lifted booze and electronics.

Officer Nick Poitras echoed his thoughts. "Geez, how dumb do you have to be to want to rob this place?"

Poitras, this year's rookie cop (as Jakes had been last year) pretty much thought anyone would have to be dumb to live in the countryside at all. It was a typical attitude of the young newbie cops from the city who had been sent on assignment to the tiny four-man Middle Island police force, under the provincial police training program. Unlike Pete who with his wife Ali, had succumbed to the Island's rural charm and decided to stay.

Pete parked the cruiser on the road, though he doubted there would be any useful information to be gleaned from the driveway. In this strange and disturbing winter, there had been no fresh snow yet this month. So, no handy footprints or tire tracks. The two policemen ignored the front door of the house, which obviously hadn't been cracked open for years, and went straight round to the back. Shards of shattered glass lay on the ground.

"Here's the broken window," Nick said. "But I don't know why they bothered, look at this door." A flimsy thing, hanging loosely on its hinges. He pushed it open with his foot.

The opening was almost blocked with crowding, heavy furniture.

"Watch it," Nick warned. "You could break a leg, trying to get through this junk."

Pete pushed his way in. "See if you can find a light that works."

"Geez!" Poitras yelped, as something yowled and dashed past his boots. "What the heck was that?"

"Not the old lady's ghost," Pete said dryly. "Just a cat. She had a bunch of them and the humane society's been trying to catch them."

The place was cavelike and cold as a freezer inside.

"At least the lawyer had someone turn the water off," Pete said.

They picked their way gingerly past a chrome-legged kitchen table and chairs with split plastic seats. The table was overflowing with empty cat dishes, the sink enamel streaked with a dirty rainbow of stains.

Pete pictured the old woman lying helplessly on the cold linoleum flooring. She had died there, not to be discovered till the next day by the visiting home help. The unfortunate fate of many an elderly shut-in. He stopped in grim contemplation at the door to the main room of the cottage.

"Holy crap," Nick said.

The room was crammed with an ancient, patterned couch and chair, several teetering standing lamps and end tables overflowing with china cat ornaments. Cheap hangings and framed prints from the dollar store decorated the walls.

Cats are just small people in fur coats.

A home is not a home without a cat.

The feline smell was stale and cold rather than rank, for which Pete was grateful.

There was a bed in an alcove and a bathroom. The old woman probably hadn't been upstairs for some time.

"Look at that TV," Nick marvelled. "It must be from the seventies or something. I wonder if it works."

"Probably," Pete said. He'd noticed a rusty aerial on the roof.

Nick looked around. "I don't see the remote."

"Try the dials on the set."

After a couple of false starts, Nick found the power button. "Yep it works," he said. "I bet she didn't get too many channels though."

He started switching the round dial as if he was in a sci-fi movie, discovering an artifact from an ancient civilization. A few blurred pictures appeared, then the familiar backdrop of the Bonville station newsroom.

Pete looked at the decrepit furniture. So she'd sat there in the saggy cushioned black chair, with cats on her lap and watched her TV shows. For how many years? No visitors except the home help lady. A cold, depressing picture of old age. The whole place was overpoweringly depressing. Perhaps not though, when the old lady was alive. She would have had the heat on, would have made tea. He hoped she had been happy with her ornaments and her pets.

Nick stood up, bored with the novelty of the old television set, and looked disgustedly around the room. "Like I said, what's to steal here? You couldn't even give this stuff to the Good Will."

Pete agreed. That left sheer vandalism as a motive, but though the place was undeniably crammed to the rafters, the scene was not what he would describe as complete chaos. There were definite pathways through the junk to the kitchen, the bedroom and the bathroom. The stacks of yellowing newspapers for instance, looked as if they hadn't been disturbed for decades. He looked at the name and date of the papers on the top of the pile. The Toronto Star, September 1965. More than forty years ago.

A couple of framed pictures. A young man in army uniform, a tall dark-haired girl on each arm. Perhaps the dead woman and her sister. Under their pretty, piled-up hairstyles, they each had the same long, bony face. He climbed the narrow staircase and found two cramped rooms under a sloping ceiling. Grimed windows that he doubted had been opened for a decade and an unusable cot, buried under garbage bags full of clothing. As Nick had said, what would a thief hope to find here? What could be the temptation?

Impossible to tell whether anything had been taken. He doubted that the lawyer's office or anyone else had yet attempted to sort through the contents of the place, or to make an inventory. And how would it read?

Kitchen, ten bags of junk.

Living room, twenty bags of junk.

But perhaps an inventory of some sort should be done now. The broken window should be boarded up and the door lock replaced to discourage further vandalism. That might work, until the next time anyway.

"Let's go," he said to Nick. "Whoever broke in, I doubt they found anything much here."

He stopped at the end of the walk to look back. The cottage looked lonely and abandoned. And something else. Something secretive and unresolved. But he shook off the melancholy feeling and returned to the cruiser. The afternoon was chilling down. He was glad he had someone to go home to that night.

2

Doctor Baird's instructions had been precise and strict. Ali Jakes had listened in disbelief.

"I've let you work a lighter schedule at the school for the past few months but the toxemia isn't going away. You're now six months pregnant and the threat is too great for both you and the baby. You're going to have to stop working."

"But the blood pressure reading simply must be wrong," she protested. "I've never had any problems with my blood pressure. I feel wonderful. I'm calm, happy, ask my husband Pete. In the ultrasound, the baby looks perfect."

Dr. Baird looked pointedly at her swollen ankles, rising like ugly sausages out of her sneakers.

"Most women's ankles swell up in pregnancy," she said defensively. "I read about that in my *What to Expect* book."

Doctor Baird nodded. "Yes they do, but in about seven percent of cases, including yours, the swelling occurs all over the body." He pressed a finger into the honey-coloured skin of her upper arm, leaving a sizeable dimple.

Ali coloured. "Water retention. I read about that too."

Dr. Baird smiled, "Abnormal water retention."

"But I've been good as gold, I've followed your orders to the letter."

"I know you have. And I'm certain you'll continue to do so."

He reached for his prescription pad. "I can write it out for you if you insist. *Quit your job, take your maternity leave now. Stay home. Don't exert yourself. No housework, no heavy lifting . . . .*"

He smiled at her dismay, then said seriously. "Remember, we're watching out for any bleeding, any premature erratic contractions. Doctors don't know why this happens but research shows that a relaxed schedule with little exertion is the best course."

He wagged his finger at her, "And I mean *no* exertion. I want you to take a nap in bed at least twice a day for an hour or more."

"Can I read?" she asked drily.

"You can read. Just keep in mind that if your symptoms get any worse, you'll be spending the next ten weeks resting in Bonville General."

The doctor was referring to the hospital in Bonville, the city on the other side of the Bay. With a population of some thirty-thousand, it was a bustling metropolis compared to Island life and provided for Island residents such necessities as a hospital, a district school for highschool aged students and an impressive shopping mall.

Ali sighed. Of course she would comply with Doctor Baird's orders for the baby's sake, whatever the difficulties, but her thoughts raced in a kind of panic. The school would likely have no problem finding a substitute teacher, she would just be taking her maternity leave a little earlier than expected. And she and Pete had already decorated the baby's room. But what on earth would she do with herself? She was normally such an active person.

Dr. Baird saw her to the door. "Think of it as a vacation, Ali. After your baby arrives, you probably won't get another holiday for some time."

That was two weeks ago. Now she tossed her book, *Knitting for Your Baby,* to the floor and held up a clump of something that looked vaguely like a sweater for an octopus.

"Guess what this is," she demanded of Pete. "I dare you."

He knew better, and didn't even look up from the coffee table where he was putting together a bird house kit.

Ali threw the clump of wool after the book.

"I need Miranda to show me how," she said crankily, speaking of her elderly neighbour who was away for a few months in Costa Rica visiting a former student. "I *miss* Miranda. I bet she can turn out a baby sweater in an afternoon."

She twisted impatiently on the couch, which she shared with a feathery-tailed black and white border collie, Miranda's dog Emily.

"I refuse to just sit here and get enormous. Poor Emily just sits and looks beseechingly at me all day."

"Don't listen to her," Pete muttered absently, as he scanned the direction sheet.

"She's fine, I walk her morning and evening and she seems quite happy to loll around with you on the couch. Why don't you open up one of those jigsaw puzzles I brought you?"

Sparks flew from her wonderful coal-black eyes.

"Jigsaws! This from the man who used to kiss my toes and call me his Turkish princess."

"You're still my princess and I still kiss your toes."

"Yes, but now I can't feel them. Or see them."

"What about the courses on the Net?" he asked. She had looked for some teaching upgrading courses but it was the wrong time of year, too late to register.

"Besides, I hate Net courses. There's no dialogue, no interchange of ideas. No *conversation*."

He'd bought her a bird-watching guide too. She hadn't opened it.

"What good is that to me?" she had complained. "Bird watchers *walk*. They hike and trek. That's the very nature of birdwatching."

"I guess you'll just have to watch the birds that come to you," he said mildly.

Now he was gluing the sides of the birdhouse together. He looked so sweet, with his hunky former soldier's frame bent over the fussy task. Then again, *he* was just as gorgeous as when they'd met two years ago at the Afghanistan reconstruction project where she'd been teaching a class of elementary students. Even more handsome really, since he'd let his blonde crew cut grow out a couple of inches. She felt contrite though, and picked up the bird watchers guide.

"Darn it, you're just too nice these days," she said. "You have to say something rotten so I won't feel so guilty."

"Maybe we should ask your mother to come earlier," Pete suggested cautiously. "She could be company for you." Then he had to laugh at Ali's pained look.

"O.K. That's pretty rotten. You think my blood pressure is up now!"

"Seriously," he said. "I'd feel better if there was someone here with you. And you say that you're starved for conversation."

Ali shook her head vigourously. "Not that starved. Besides, Nuran wouldn't last two days on the Island, she'd perish from boredom out here in the country."

"*We* like it here," he said mildly

"We have each other," she said reasonably. "We have our lovely little house that we're fixing up just the way we like it. We like to walk and spoon in the country moonlight – or we used to anyway." She groaned and threw up her hands, "But what on earth could we do with Nuran for a whole month? Oh, it would be impossible."

And it wasn't as if the village could provide much excitement. She tried to picture elegant, cerebral, world-traveller Nuran attending the Kiwanis winter barbeque or the policemen's easter egg hunt. Unthinkable. And far too easy to imagine how Nuran with her feminist socialist eye, would categorize the local women's monthly quilting meeting. She'd likely use the subject for her next best-selling book on the voluntary subjugation of North American women.

"Trust me darling, it's a foolish idea. She says she's put my due date on her calendar. So I suppose we can expect a card. Luckily we're having a daughter or I'd probably never hear from my mother again. It was bad enough that I got married."

But Pete didn't smile. "I can't believe your mother would refuse to help. Let's give her the benefit of the doubt and at least ask her."

Ali was firm. "N. O. spells NO. Besides we've already got the home help coming in three mornings a week."

She ruffled Emily's fur. "Now tell me about your day. It's *got* to have been more exciting than mine."

He put the birdhouse aside to allow the glue to dry, wishing he could put a more cheerful spin on the day's events. But Ali had already seen the CKAS news, they watched it every night with their dinner.

The coronor's report had now been filed on Akantha Samos, eighty-eight years old. Death had resulted from complications arising from a fall. Ms. Samos had apparently slipped off a stepstool while reaching for something in a cupboard. Unfortunately Ms. Samos had been unable to call for help and had not been discovered until her home helper came round the next morning for her regular visit. By that time, the old woman was dead.

An employee for Bonville Social Services, sounding defensive, said that Ms. Samos had moved to Middle Island about ten years earlier, had never been very friendly, had rejected neighbours' offers of help and friendship and had gradually become a total recluse. The employee then reminded viewers that the service ran a 24 hour hotline for emergency calls. The number flashed on the screen.

"Lina was Ms. Samos' home helper too," Ali said sympathetically, speaking of the woman who came in to help her three mornings a week, as per Doctor Baird's orders. "She told me how shocking it was to find the old lady lying there on the kitchen floor."

She shifted uncomfortably on the couch. "How was it out there today at the cottage. Was there much damage?"

Pete grimaced. "Hard to tell. The place was so crammed with junk."

"Lina said that the Humane Society had managed to round up most of the cats."

"There was one there today."

"Poor thing!" Ali said. "Couldn't you catch him?"

"It didn't look too bad. He's probably sleeping in some nearby barn."

"Better off than her. To think she lay there and died all alone!"

"She was an old lady, darling. Her time had come."

"Lina said that Ms. Samos wasn't in that bad shape, that she could have lived another ten years." She frowned. "Apparently she didn't like baths, though."

11

Pete made a face. "That must have made the visits kind of tough."

Ali nodded. "Lina said she only suffered the home help because social services said they would bring her into the county home if she didn't allow it. It's all such a shame! Lina said that the father once owned a wonderful big house on the bay side and he brought his family here in the summers. But it's long gone now, burnt down."

"It's a sad end darling. And a common one, try not to worry yourself too much over it." He pasted a decal of some flowers awkwardly on the side of the bird house.

"There, do you think they'll like it?"

She blew him a kiss. "They'll love it. I'd move in tomorrow if I could fit through the door."

He picked up the bird-watching guide and opened it at random. "Some of these birds are kind of cute. Here's one called the rufous-sided towhee. "

"I'll towhee you," she threatened. "Don't forget, I've got these long, sharp knitting needles to get rid of."

3

If seasons all were summers, and leaves would never fall.

Chief Bud Halstead pulled his Ford F150 pick-up into the parking lot of the Middle Island Police Station, narrowly missing Jane. His secretary, dispatcher and general manager of the station, was struggling vainly to close a large red umbrella. The fabric was patterned with yellow ducks, the umbrella no doubt the property of her small granddaughter.

Halstead got out and moved to help her. Rain at the beginning of March, ridiculous! And unnerving. Like most Canadians, Halstead was made uneasy by the signs of drastic climate change. Christmas Eve there'd been a faint dusting of the white stuff but the rest of the time, even on cold days, the skies remained stubbornly stingy. In his fifty years and more on the Island, he couldn't remember a winter like this. No fun, like a birthday cake without frosting. This year's crop of kindergarten students wouldn't even know how to make a snowman.

"Morning, Jane," he greeted her. He took the umbrella from her and straightened it out.

"Thanks, Chief."

She followed him into the station. Neither made any comment as they threaded their way past a row of green plastic buckets that stood like sentinels in the station lobby.

Jane picked up the coffee carafe and headed for the sink. "That report you wanted is on my desk."

"You've called Sammy?" Halstead asked, scowling up at the brown-stained ceiling tiles.

"Of course. I told his wife it was the second time this week we've had the drip. That you think the new roof he put on isn't sealed properly around the chimney."

But then nobody would ever have expected all the rain they'd had this winter. Normally Canadian roofs were built to handle heavy loads of snow.

"You didn't talk to him?"

A foolish question. Sam the roofer never answered a telephone. But sometimes his missus actually relayed a message to him. There was always hope.

After a couple of months of working in noise and clouds of drywall dust and sanding grit, Jane, like Halstead, had become philosophical about the station renovation project. And truth to tell, the one-story brick bunker on the west end of the Island's one town, didn't look any different outwardly. This time of year, there weren't even any petunias in the pots out front. But the wiring was no longer hazardous and the new bathroom was a treat.

Now Jane set about organizing the day, which she did with an easy efficiency. At sixty, she was a youngish-looking grandmother, hair greying blonde but still bouncy, wearing black stretch trousers and a cardigan sweater she'd knitted herself. Her desk in the lobby was the nerve centre of station operations. There was also the chief's office, a common room with a couple of desks for the officers, an interview room and a small, rarely-used holding cell.

Halstead took his yellow mug from the shelf above the coffee maker and poured himself a cup. As he stirred in cream, he looked appreciatively out the back window of his office. He'd told the contractor that he didn't want to lose the view of the field. He liked watching the changing seasons unfold on the land, the sight had often helped his thought processes when he was working through a knotty case.

Only this year, it looked as if the country was experiencing an endless dreary November. No ice fishing huts out on the Bay because there was no ice. The February snow festival cancelled because there was no snow. The area conservation officer was reporting nature's confusion as well. Normally hibernating critters were awakening too early. The creatures like the land itself, weren't getting their rest, their fallow time. Trees were in danger of sending out new shoots too soon, huge snowy owls were coming down from the north because of low lemming counts and starving and dazed, were wandering the roadsides. Everywhere were the signs of disturbance, unsettling and uncertainty.

Vern Byers the Island County Clerk was happy though, with his barely-touched snowplowing budget. And overall, Halstead had to admit, the snowless winter had made life easier for cops. Fewer emergency calls, no driving out in blizzards to rescue folks.

He turned from the scene of squawking crows wheeling above the muddy ruts of the field, "So, what's the headache of the day, Jane?"

She dropped a couple of OPP circulars on his desk. This month, several bulletins warning of fraud artists preying on seniors. Promises of prizes and sweepstakes. Non-existent life insurance policies. Transient businesses selling home repairs that often required an advance deposit, such as roof repairs, driveway resurfacing, pest control.

Some schemes involved even larger amounts of money, perhaps a senior's entire life savings. Or the loss of a home, put up for collateral on a bogus loan.

Cut your mortgage payments in half!

Special investment offer. Must be kept confidential, don't even tell family members.

He put the sheets aside with a scowl. Scum of the earth. The Island was perhaps not as good pickings as the towns and cities, because strangers tended to stand out from the locals, but it was still necessary to keep a close watch.

"What else?" he asked Jane.

"Same as yesterday, chief. The provincial emergency preparedness plan. The deadline is only a few months away and Council is getting antsy, wanting to know how we're going to tackle it. "

He scowled at the offending four-inch thick manual that had dominated his desktop for the past week.

"Did you have a look at it?" he asked her. "Instructions on how to cope with tsunamis, earthquakes, chemical spills, even a nuclear meltdown. Not much applicable to Middle Island."

Jane raised her brows. "I certainly hope not."

There were other more sobering elements. Information on new border regulations and guarding against terrorists. A different world than the one he'd grown up in. Since Halstead's bailiwick also encompassed several small islands, much of his border was liquid. In fact one of his officers, Art Storms was currently attending a four month's course in lake crossing contol techniques in the States.

The reviving smell of coffee filled the station as the two other officers of the Middle Island police force, smallest autonomous force in the province, arrived to start their day. There was young Pete Jakes, who came to the Island as a trainee a year and a half ago. Jakes had been serving in the Canadian military, but after a serious brush with a roadside explosive in Afghanistan, he decided to switch careers. He and his wife Ali, took to life on the Island and decided to stay. In Halstead's opinion, a good deal for all concerned. He was always glad to see new settlers on the Island, especially young ones. The Island needed new energy, new ideas. Jakes, army trained, had all the makings of a good, smart cop.

He wasn't as sure yet about this year's trainee, Nick Poitras. Unike Jakes, who at twenty-nine was more mature, most of the city kids sent to the Island to train were openly scornful of the 'hick' surroundings. Halstead supposed that country kids who wanted to be cops, also yearned to be in the city, busting drug gangs and catching bank robbers.

That made it tough to recruit new cops to serve in rural areas. If it wasn't for the provincial training programs, he'd probably get no one at all, so he'd better just hope that Poitras got over his attitude and settled in for the year. The kid was tall and lanky and fit enough, though he lacked Jake's natural athletic coordination. Maybe it was his freckles but he looked like a kid altogether and he had a sort of a spacey look about him too, as if he was easily bored with details. And for a cop, noticing details could save your life or someone else's.

Jakes reported on what they'd found at the Samos cottage.

"The lawyer is going to get someone to board up the doors and windows."

Halstead nodded. "Let's hope he finds a relative sometime soon. An empty house can be a magnet for vandals."

Jane handed Halstead a note. "I've got a call from that artist lady, Penny Loo, who lives down on Snake Point. She says some hunters have been shooting too close to her house and that they've shot up her mailbox."

Halstead sighed. The hunting issue was a contentious one. No one objected to a farmer or other Island resident taking a deer, and there were venison steaks in many a Middle Island freezer, but the annual influx of weekend city hunters was a concern. Usually mailbox and other careless shooting incidents ended in mid-December with the wrap up of deer hunting season. By then, the hunters who had descended on the Island like a plague of winter locusts, had mostly gone back to their condos in the city.

But there was a hundred acre hunk of private property down at Snake Point, where the owner rented cabins out to weekend hunters. The guests could hike around and shoot at rabbits and coyotes, both open season targets, but deer and wild turkey hunting on the property was technically governed by the same seasonal restrictions laid on the rest of the the Island. Practically speaking though, it was a long drive even in a police cruiser from one end of the island to the other. And the guests got bored at times. There had been complaints before.

"I guess those city weekend hunters don't want to get their boots wet going out into the fields and they're taking out their frustrations on mailboxes. They're worse then the local teenagers. "The locals even had a special term for these unwelcome guests –*Cidiots*.

"And Ms. Loo isn't the only one," Jane said. "Doug Guardian at the Rowan Tree Retirement Home left a message that they heard shots and saw lights out in their back field last night."

"Jack-lighting."

Jane nodded.

That *was* serious. Blinding deer with powerful flashlights or car headlights, so that the animals stood dumb and helpless to be shot. The practice was strictly illegal, in or out of season. It was also dangerous even for other humans in the vicinity because the hunters couldn't see far enough beyond the targeted animal.

'Sound shooters,' Halstead said disgustedly. "They shoot before looking, at every twig cracking in the bush."

Jane looked at her notes, "Doug's worried that one of these cidiots will send a stray shot through a window and injure one of his residents."

Halstead spoke to Jakes. "You'd better get out there and have a look. Talk to the woman and Guardian, then drop in on the hunting camp. You can take Nick with you."

"I thought deer hunting season was over," Nick said. "I wanted to try it but thought that I'd missed it."

"You did miss it, kid," Halstead said. "The season is long over, it's just that some of these fellers think the regulations don't apply to them. One year we caught one of them trying to sneak a buck off the island in his car trunk. But I'm afraid if you want to hunt deer, you'll have to come back next December. Or sign up with the Island force permanently."

He laughed at the look of horror on the kid's face. *Another year in the boonies? No way.*

4

"It says here that wild turkeys have five thousand feathers," Nick read aloud. "Males can weigh up to twenty-five pounds and the biggest turkey ever recorded weighed thirty-eight pounds."

"Big birds," Pete agreed.

Nick flipped the page of his Outdoor Man magazine, "That would just about do my family for Thanksgiving dinner. And all the relatives."

He had bought himself a gun at Christmas and he couldn't wait to try it out. The birds had been re-introduced on the island five years ago and the season started at the end of April. Now he looked frustratedly out at the section of woods passing by the cruiser window. The Island was dotted with smaller farm woodlots but 'Turkey Woods' as the locals now called it, was a ten kilometer stretch of scrub maples and cedar trees that ran practically back to the Bay.

"It says here the birds are out there breeding right now, gobbling away. If there was snow, you could see the tracks, but there's no point in going out in that mess."

Pete drove silently. Personally, he was glad that the provincial wildlife might be getting a break. He had become sickened by killing in his military experiences. He could live with killing for food but not the abuse and cruelty he had seen in the behaviour of some hunters.

Snake Point was one of four rocky island points that jutted out into the lake. The others were Lighthouse Point, Collier Bluff, and notably Hawks Nest Point, where a murder at a proposed wind turbine site had been the site of Pete's first big case on the Island. The Island geography wasn't tough to figure out, not even for a new recruit. The half-mile causeway that joined the island to the mainland and the neighbouring city of Bonville, ended at Middle Island Village, (pop. 850) the only major centre of commerce. The rest of the island's 3200 residents were scattered over farms and a couple of small hamlets.

From the village, Route 1 led around the island to the east, while Route 2 led west. A few secondary routes crisscrossed the Island, mostly unpaved. Bumpy dirt roads, little better than paths, fanned off to lead to cottages either on the Bay Shore in the north or the open waters of Lake Ontario in the south. Snake Point was on Route 2, on the Bay Side.

Penny Loo, the artist lady as the locals called her, was standing on the front steps of her bungalow, with her jacket wrapped around her shoulders. She barely waited for the officers to get out of the cruiser, before running down the steps. A petite young woman, with Eurasian features, she was quivering and her voice shook with anger and shock.

"I heard the bullet hit the mailbox. Look." It was a bright blue metal mailbox, painted with vines and flowers. There was a big hole in one of the daisies.

"There were some other shots too." She pointed up the road towards the lake. "And they roar around back in the woods all the time on those all-terrain vehicles. It's very disturbing when I am there trying to paint."

Pete examined the mailbox, noted the details of the times she had heard the shots and thanked her.

"But what are you going to *do*?" she demanded, pulling at his arm like a little girl, with surprising insistence. "This used to be such a peaceful spot before that man bought the land for his hunting camp."

The police could probably bring a nuisance charge for the mailbox shooting but there wasn't much they could do if people wanted to joyride on private property. There weren't even any noise bylaws this far out from town.

"We're going to talk to the people across the road first," he said. "I'll get back to you."

She stared worriedly after them, her little flower of a face pale above her purple coat. One thing he could do for sure, was investigate whether the miscreants were breaking any of the provincial hunting regulations. There were heavy fines for that.

"She's cute," Nick said, as they drove away. "I wonder what kind of pictures she paints."

"Local stuff," Pete said. "The lake, fields, trees, sometimes a barn. Beautiful skies. She's really good." There was an amazing picture of peony flowers that he was saving to buy for Ali's birthday. "I think she's having a show at the Main Street Gallery this spring, you could see the paintings there. If you're not out shooting turkeys, of course."

* * *

Rowan Tree Retirement Home read the letters on the big metal mailbox. The two Rs were shot out and the rest of the surface was a pockmarked twin to Penny Loos' box. Pete turned through the gateposts and drove up the circular drive, passing not one but two of the mountain ash trees that had given the place its name. The home was a handsome old frame farmhouse with a large modern addition grafted to one side. Although the windows and design were modern, the work had been tastefully done and carefully integrated with the original structure. There was a large wrap-around porch that would be a pleasant place where residents could sit in the summertime.

The owner, a big-framed man wearing jeans and an expensive looking yellow parka, the kind you could wear to climb Everest, came down the porch steps to meet them. Near sixty, Pete judged, but in good shape, face tanned either from a holiday or a sunlamp.

He extended his hand, and said with a friendly though not overbearing heartiness, "Doug Guardian. I'm the one who called the station."

Pete shook hands. "Officer Jakes. I understand you've had some trouble from hunters trespassing on your property. We saw the mailbox on our way in."

Guardian shrugged impatiently. "I don't care about the mailbox. Mail boxes are fair game on the Island. Like clockwork, the first day of summer holidays, the kids go on a spree bashing mailboxes with a baseball bat. And in winter the city hunters use them for target practise."

He turned to look back out over his fields, "But I do mind about dangerous nonsense in my woods. Sounded like a rifle too, which means they were after deer and it's way, way out of season."

"How close to the house do you think?"

Guardian waved his arm, encompassing the property. "I've got four and a half acres out there, backing on the woods. Our residents never wander too far but we do have paths and benches in back of the house. If these fellers had been shooting at some critters in the summertime, they could have hit one of the residents.

"I'm fond of the deer myself," he added. "I put out a bale of hay in the really bad weather and the residents get a kick out of watching them come to feed. They can see the woods from the common room window. I'd hate to think of the shock if they saw a wounded animal run out on the lawn. We'd probably be looking at a couple of heart attacks. And my wife doesn't like it at all. She was quite frightened."

"So, what did you hear exactly," Pete asked. "And what time was this?"

"It was my wife Dawn, who heard them, she was in the kitchen around dusk, making some tea. She even dropped the pot. But here she comes now," Guardian said. "You can ask her."

Pete had pictured a sixty-year old woman, feminine and more than a little reliant on her big husband's protection. But the woman striding towards them was about forty, tall and athletic looking, dressed in well-fitting jeans and a zippered jacket. Her short blonde hair was cut in a functional but not unattractive style.

She didn't shake hands, seemed abstracted and still thinking of whatever domestic detail she'd been discussing with her staff. When she shifted her attention to the policemen, Pete saw that her eyes were denim blue.

"I hope you catch and charge those monsters," she said without preamble. "It's terribly upsetting for the residents. It's bad enough when the season's on but this . . . ."

Pete nodded towards the road. "We're going to the camp to talk to them now."

"I'd hate for this to escalate," Guardian said. "One year someone tossed a pile of bloody deer guts in the driveway. That wasn't very pleasant."

Dawn Guardian nodded, wrapping her arms around herself in a shiver and not from the weather. "It was sickening. Why do you allow it?"

"Hunting is legal in season, ma'am," Pete felt obliged to point out.

"It shouldn't be," she said heatedly. "It's a barbaric sport, like something from the middle ages. Haven't these goons ever heard of supermarkets?"

And where do you think supermarkets get their meat, lady? He said nothing though, no point in getting into that argument. Besides, she seemed genuinely upset.

Guardian saw them to the cruiser, chatting expansively about his new extension, apparently added only last summer.

"Those big windows there, that's the new common room where we show movies, have bingo nights, that sort of thing. Then there's the exercise room and once a week, a lady from the beauty parlour comes to do hair and manicures."

"How many residents live here?" Pete asked, to be polite.

"We have twelve singles and four couples suites," Guardian said proudly. "Four full-time staff and six temporary, such as cleaners. Medical visits can be arranged, either here or we arrange a drive for the resident."

He looked at Pete with an assessing professional eye. `Got an oldster in the family? Grandma or Grandpa, Mom or Pop?"

"No, no one," Pete said tersely. No one who wanted his help at any rate.

5

S nake Point Hunting Camp. Private. Keep Out.
Two pillars of piled up stones framed a six-foot chain link gate, with a set of antlers mounted on it. An open padlock hung on the chain.

Nick got out of the cruiser and pulled open the gate. "Looks like a neat place," he said admiringly.

The gravel track lead to three rustic-style wood frame cabins, arranged in a sem-circle around a larger A-frame structure, built of glossily varnished logs. There was nothing rustic about the vehicles parked in front of the buildings. An expensive green current model SUV, and a maroon Cherokee Jeep with a trailer big enough to haul two snowmobiles. Although this winter, an ATV might be more useful.

"Approach with caution," Pete warned Nick. "Sounds as if these guys shoot first and look later."

No one seemed to have noticed or paid any attention to their arrival. Pete knocked on the door where a plastic wrapped copy of the provincial hunting regulations was nailed to the door. The paper under the plastic was yellowed and dated two years earlier.

Pete called loudly. "Anybody home?" When there was still no answer, he pushed open the door. They saw a large main room with raised ceiling above the log walls. Sturdy furniture around a stone fireplace. Doors, probably to bedrooms. The kitchen area was open, all the basic appliances and a big slab of a table. On the counter, a couple of boxes of beer and a rye bottle. A real men's playhouse. The men were apparently out.

"That must have been a big sucker," Nick said, pointing to a deer head trophy, mounted on the wall above the fireplace. "Look at those antlers, a ten-pointer." He'd been studying the terms. "Symmetry counts too," he said knowledgeably. "So they're the same on both sides."

Pete thought the head looked years old, the hide faded and dusty, the glass eyes dull. As if the owner of the place had bought it at a pawn shop. Beneath the trophy there was a much smaller plaque, with just the twelve inch white flagged tail.

Got him coming and going, the plaque said.

Yuk, yuk.

Another wall held mounted gun racks, some empty. He checked out the guns that were there. Several shotguns, a rifle. Boxes of ammunition on another shelf. Not a reassuring sight, especially if you were a cop. He picked up a magazine, similar to the one that Nick had been reading. One article described expensive hunting tours to the B.C. Rockies and the Arctic to pursue animals from helicopters and snowmobiles.

Come to Nature's Playground – Your Perfect Hunt Awaits

Let Us Help You Plan Your Trip

Other pages advertised firearms, crossbows and semi-automatics.

Check Out These New Products For Your Bow.

And just so the reader would have something to do on those long stretches between hunting seasons — *Create Memories—Start Filming Your Hunt Today!*

"Someone's coming," Nick said.

Three someones, three men crossing the parking lot, all in camouflage clothing and carrying rifles. They could have stepped right out of the pages of their glossy catalogue.

Pete opened the door to the porch. He felt his stomach muscles tighten, in automatic reaction to a perceived threat, the psychologists would say. A soldier might say the same thing. Or a cop. A gun is a gun is a gun, whether carried in peacetime or war. The presence of a gun always altered any situation.

'Lo officers," said the man at the front of the group, as he came up the porch steps. Small and wiry, with what looked like dark hair under his cap. In his thirties, Pete guessed. "What's up? Or did you just come by for coffee? I see you've already made yourself at home."

"Just calling to see if you folks were around." Pete said easily.

The wiry man pushed past him through the door. "We can still offer you that coffee."

His two bigger pals followed him in. All three wore caps and no one doffed the headgear when they came inside. They did prop their rifles against the cabin wall.

"Aron Hawrie," said the smaller man, putting out his hand. "The big bearded guy is Bob Boone and the quiet guy is Terry Walsh. We've got a time share in this place, come up on weekends when we can get away from the city."

Pete jerked his chin towards the weathered notice on the door. "You are aware that deer hunting season is over for the year?"

"Yessir," Hawrie said. Apparently he was the spokesman for the trio. "We've just been out in the back forty taking practise shots. Tin cans, targets, that sort of stuff. Practising up for the spring Wild Turkey hunt next month."

"You don't need any rifles to shoot at turkeys," Pete pointed out.

"We've got shotguns too," Hawrie said.

It sure looked as if they had all the gear and ammunition they needed to eliminate every living creature on the property. Pete privately wished they could all work their aggressive energy off on a paintball course. There would be far less headaches for law enforcers that way.

"Taken any practise shots at mailboxes, lately?" he asked.

Hawrie creased his forehead in exaggerated thought. "Nope. No mailboxes. I didn't know there was a season. "He looked at his companions for confirmation. Boone guffawed, his big red face splitting open like a cut melon.

Hawrie shrugged. "Sometimes we scare up a rabbit. With the shotguns," he added hastily.

"Ever wander off the property?" Pete continued. "Maybe over near the little white house just up the road. Or the retirement home that backs on the woods bordering this property? You know, the one with the *No Trespassing, No Hunting* signs all along the fences. Apparently there was some activity in the woods behind the building around dusk last night. The owner's wife heard some shots."

"Nope, it wasn't us. There's a hundred acres here to roam around in. All the way down to the Bay."

"As long as you keep in mind that the provincial hunting regulations apply to private property too."

Pete asked to see their firearms permits. Hawrie had to paw through the junk on the kitchen counter but he eventually found the permits and they were all up to date.

Two .30 rifles, a .22 and three shotguns. Boxes of ammunition for all.

"When's the owner coming back?" Pete asked.

Hawrie shrugged. "He's got a boat down in Florida. He's usually out on the ocean this time of year."

"Got an e-mail address for him, a cell-phone number?" Pete asked.

Hawrie looked stumped.

"Who do you call for emergencies about the place?" Pete suggested. "Plumbing, power failure." *Ammunition blow-ups.* "Or just to book your time-share."

Walsh chipped in. "There's his office in Toronto. You could try that."

*　　*　　*

"I bet it was them out shooting last night," Nick said.

Pete nodded. "Luckily they didn't hurt anyone or themselves."

Two kilometers along the road, Pete hit the brakes as a whitetail deer leapt out of a woodlot and bounded across the road in front of the car. A doe, probably about two hundred pounds and enough to cause a nasty accident for both car and animal. The animals were plentiful this year, actually benefiting from the absence of the snow that usually blanketed their forage.

"Aways slow right down," he told Nick. "There are usually a couple of others behind the first one."

And here they came. Two more of the graceful leapers, their distinctive tails standing up like white flags behind their tan rumps.

"Ka-boom, ka-boom, ka-boom," Nick pretended to take a bead on the last disappearing rump. "And there's venison for supper."

"You can't shoot them from a vehicle," Pete reminded him. "We fine people big dollars for that, even in season."

"I remember. Just kidding."

"Besides, those does are likely pregnant. You shoot them now and there won't be any fawns for you to shoot next year."

Nick still looked yearningly out the window.

"Well at least I've got that turkey hunt coming up in the spring. The old timers at the Island Grill say there's a real big one out there. They call him Old Tom. He's over ten years old and nobody's ever been able to get him. They say he's a forty pounder at least and cagey as hell."

There was always an Old Tom, Pete thought. Or old Spike the pike. The legendary fish, fabled bear or moose seemed an integral part of hunting lore.

"Good luck," he said drily. "I hear those turkeys are pretty smart."

And those cidiot hunters back at the camp were pretty dumb. Especially if you considered that the legal limit was only one bird a year. Taking into account the hundreds if not thousands of dollars they probably spent on clothes, hunting equipment and weekend accommodation, he figured that worked out to one pricey turkey dinner.

Ali stuck a happy face sticker on the notebook page and wrote *Good work, Brandi* in the margin. She stacked the notebook on the 'done' pile and sighed as she flopped back on the couch. Ten down, only twenty more to mark. Normally, she didn't mind marking and noting the progress of her young students, but now that she was stuck at home and marking papers was her *only* contact with the teaching profession, she was feeling pretty frustrated.

Now she looked restlessly around the living room. The vacuum cleaner roared like a banshee in the hallway. When it stopped, she called out eagerly.

"It's tea time Lina. Come and have a break."

Ten minutes later, a sturdily built woman about forty, wearing jeans and a bright blue sweatshirt, entered the room bearing a tray of tea things and a plate of cookies. Her short red hair topped a round face, now flushed with her work.

At first Ali had felt terribly guilty lounging around on the couch while another woman did the household chores but lately not so much. Lina was a good cook and on a cold winter day like this, it was lovely to smell supper warming in the oven. Nicer for Pete too, to have something to come home to, other than a crabby, pent-up wife.

She patted the couch beside her. "Sit, Lina," she invited. "Tell the poor forgotten prisoner what's going on in the outside world this week."

"I thought that husband of yours would keep you up to date. He phones you twenty times a day to check on you."

"Not any more. I told him I'm not a clock! Besides, he was waking me up all the time from the naps the doctor ordered me to take, so I told him he has to wait till I call him."

"That should work."

"So what's up Lina? What's the scoop?"

With her intricate network of relatives and clients, Lina was usually a more reliable source of news than the Bonville Record, the local newspaper.

"Let's see. Somebody shot up some mailboxes on Route 2, but Pete will tell you all about that tonight. Everybody's mad at Council because of the property tax increase and with this crazy weather my forsythia is trying to bloom – in March if you can believe it. Oh yes, and I popped into the funeral home yesterday to sign the book for Akantha Samos."

"Was anybody else there?"

Lina shook her head.

"Couldn't the Social Services find any relatives?" Ali asked.

"Akantha mentioned a sister a couple of times but I think she passed on a few years back," Lina said. "I guess the lawyer will put a notice in the Hamilton newspaper. That's where she was living before she came to the Island."

She sipped her tea, face uncharacteristically sad and thoughtful. "I should have listened more closely to the old lady but I just never had the time. She'd natter on while I was soaking the kitty dishes and trying to make a dent in the kitchen mess. It's like that with a lot of my elderly clients. They're all so lonely. It's terrible when you think of it, how they must all have had family once. But they've just been left behind and forgotten."

Ali looked round the cozy room and shivered. She thought of something. "Maybe she left a will. "

Lina snorted. "If she did, good luck finding such a thing in that mess. One of those hoarders she was, like that program on television. And what did she have to leave? The cottage is falling over, there's only a quarter acre of that useless scrubland around it." She put down her cup reluctantly and Ali quickly refilled it.

"You said her family once owned a house here."

"Yes, that whole chunk of land. My granny said there was a fine house on the Bay side and he brought his family here in the summers. But that was sometime when my granny was young, back in the 1940's."

"But that's not where Akantha lived?"

"No, the house burned down long ago. Like folks say around here, if you live in the country, the firemen save a lot of basements." Lina sipped her tea appreciatively. "I guess Akantha remembered the place though and she moved back. She's always been alone there in the cottage."

"That's sad"

Lina nodded. "I think the sister might even have committed suicide. There was some story connected with that but as I said, I didn't pay much attention. I work around old, rambling people every day. I just say uh huh and go on with my cleaning."

"And now they're all dead and gone."

Lina groaned and wriggled her purple-stockinged toes. "Yep, a sad end to a sad story."

"What will happen to the place, to her things?"

Lina shrugged. "I imagine they'll just hire a truck and haul the stuff to the dump. That's what I'd do."

*   *   *

Pete came home at supper time, smelling of cold and stamping his feet. He gave Ali a kiss that left her breathless.

"How was your day, gorgeous?"

"Oh, nothing much. I cleaned out the basement, carried the television upstairs, and took Emily for a three mile hike." Yeah right.

"Great!" he said. "Now we can watch movies in bed."

Joking aside, that was about all Pete was up to after walking Emily and eating Lina's casserole – tuna this time. But after dozing all day, Ali often wasn't tired at bedtime. Pete did his best to stay awake and chat. He told her about the peppered up mailbox and the shooting incident at the Rowan Tree Home.

"Of course my gung-ho sidekick, was taking it all in. He can't wait to bag something feathered or furred."

"Nick?" Ali thought of the gangly fellow she'd met several times at the police station. "He doesn't look like the mighty hunter type."

Pete laughed. "No, but he wants to be."

Ali's feelings regarding hunting were mixed. "It's hard to judge." she said. "I've always had enough to eat but there are so many people in the world who don't."

She'd read in the paper that the New Zealand Parliament was currently debating whether animals had rights—specifically the great apes and primates used in research—and considering a Parliamentary amendment to that effect.

She patted her bump, "I think I'd kill to feed my baby."

He embraced them both. "And so would I. But if you saw these guys out at the camp and their arsenal of equipment, you'd have to think that here in North America today, it seems a spectacularly unequal contest against the wildlife. It's not about food any more when you're blowing some animal apart."

Or people. He'd seen enough visual evidence in Bosnia and Afghanistan of what an AK 47 could do to the human body.

"These guys are like dangerous kids playing army," he said. "They even wear the same clothes. The jackets, the pants, the caps, all in the camouflage pattern."

She kissed him, "I bet they don't look nearly as handsome as you did in your army gear. And I'm sure your lecture today will have some effect. Those hunters will be more careful from now on."

"Maybe." He subsided against the pillow, closed his eyes.

Changing the subject, she said, "Lina told me that Akantha Samos' family once had a summer place on the Island."

"Hmmm. That's nice."

That noncommittal hum. After a day in the cold air, he was already dozing off. She thought of Akantha Samos and her ramblings that nobody listened to. Apparently nobody listened to pregnant people either.

But that was hardly fair. She was only restless because she'd been dozing off and on all day. She lay awake awhile longer, listening to the rise and fall of his gentle breathing. He hardly ever had the nightmares about the landmines anymore, as the sweet spirit of the Island enveloped them. Of course life moved on through its allotted course, even here. Babies were born, old people like Akantha Samos died. But life on the Island seemed closer to the natural rhythm of things. Perhaps it was the effect of living so near to the wildlife, knowing that the birds and creatures on the the land were going through their natural cycles as well.

Still, it was sad about Akantha's lonely end. Pete said the authorities hadn't been able to find a will registered anywhere. The lawyer had put notices in the local newspaper and also in the city where she had come from, to see if a relative would come out of the woodwork.

"Maybe no one will show up," Pete had said. "The place could actually be more of a liability for a relative and might just revert to the council for taxes owed."

She looked out the window at the cold, bare fields and hoped that the humane inspector had been able to catch Akantha's frightened cat and take it to the shelter. She would ask Lina about it tomorrow.

She sighed and tried to feel sleepy. Some dumb reality show was starting on the television and the remote was halfway across the room.

"Please turn it off," she begged Emily but the dog only burrowed her nose in the carpet and wagged her tail.

7

"Mornin' Jane."

"Mornin' Chief."

Halstead didn't have to ask what headaches there were today. He already knew the line-up and there were several. And here came the biggest one now, County clerk, Vern Byers, his dour mug looking more doleful than ever. He sank wearily into the chair in front of Halstead's desk. Vern was somehow always weary.

"I hate to even ask how the emergency preparedness report is coming along," he sighed.

Halstead wanted to sigh too. Instead, he went on the attack. "I hope you and your councillor pals have been practising. Last time we held a drill at the Town Hall, it took you fellows ten minutes just to get the fire extinguisher out of the case and then we had to show you how to use it."

"That was new equipment," Vern protested. "Somebody had misfiled the instructions. Anyhow, that's just small potatoes." He reached for the brick-sized manual on Halstead's desk and opened to a page. "What about this?"

He read out: "*The aim of this plan is to protect the health, safety, welfare and property of our citizens.* Then, with heavy emphasis. "*It is imperative to recognize that local police forces are the front line defense in the war against terror.*"

He looked accusingly at Halstead. "The Council want to know what kind of network have you set up against terrorists trying to get from Canada to the States?"

Halstead snorted. "Gee, Vern. I kind of thought we'd leave that up to the Coast Guard."

"You know what I mean, Bud. Our network on the shoreline."

"I thought I'd leave that up to the gossips who live there. You know as well as I do Vern, that no one can put a damn rowboat out on the water without somebody noticing, let alone a terrorist's fancy speedboat. The only terrorists likely to descend on Middle Island are the tourists in the summer."

"Ha, ha." The clerk didn't look as if he appreciated the joke. "But really Bud, what are we going to come up with? This is serious stuff, do you think we can handle this sort of thing? There's nutcases everywhere nowadays. Remember that movie about Russians taking over a small town. That could happen to us."

Halstead didn't bother pointing out that the man's fears were at least two terrorist nationalities out of date. "Then you'd better keep a good look-out," he advised.

He saw the clerk out, patting his shoulder.

"Relax Vern. Let's wait till Art comes back from the course. He'll be able to fill us in on our responsibilities on the water. In the meantime, we're going to go on with the emergency drills, so get your fellow councillors to start practising up."

He could have pointed out that despite the dire language of the manual, it was not so easy to disrupt a rural area. There were no central water systems for instance, except in the village. People had their own wells, a terrorist would be kept busy trying to spike every one with cyanide or LSD for that matter.

But he doubted the news would comfort Vern. Poor guy should never have taken on the job of acting Mayor of the Island. He was happier running his gas station.

*   *   *

Halstead used his own knuckles to rap on the door of *YourSpace Retreat,* he was always uncomfortable gripping the metal nude goddess knocker. Stephanie Bind opened the door. She was fully dressed in classy-looking jeans and a scoop-necked mauve sweater, but Halstead had no problem remembering what she looked like last night when she kissed him goodbye.

"Good morning, Chief," she teased. "Long time, no see."

He'd been yearning for her for eight months, had been wildly happy for a consummated two but still wouldn't stay overnight. He was a widower of a thirty-year marriage, hardly a naïve kid, and he and his wife Kathleen had fooled around before tying the knot of course. But even so, he had never lived in an unmarried state with a woman before.

"I feel as if I'm sneaking around," he'd said at first. "And I'm the chief of police."

"Then walk in here openly," she said, kissing his cheek.

She laughed at his look. "Let's just ride the wave for awhile, Bud. We don't want to smother each other. Maybe this is better anyway." She gestured at her face, her hair. "I turned forty-eight last week, I'm at an age where it takes *work* to look presentable. You don't want to see me in the morning."

He wouldn't mind at all, dreamed of waking up with her as his wife in their own house. He supposed he was lucky to be a male. His face was more rumpled than an unironed shirt but at least he looked the same all the time. What you saw was what you got.

On this weekday in March, Steph had no guests at the Retreat. They ate their lunch in the big room before the fireplace, under a large Penny Loo painting of the country roadside sprinkled with purple and white fall asters. Today, the view leading down to the water was the muted grey and brown palette of the strange winter weather, the lake open only a hundred yards off shore.

"The ducks will be back soon at this rate," Steph said. "Good thing I didn't put cross-country skiing in my Retreat brochure."

He asked about her seventeen-year old daughter Livy who was spending the school year in Vancouver with her father.

"She sounds good," Steph said. "Really good. She's taking some science courses and is hoping to get a job planting trees in the summer. That means she'll be away even longer but I have to tell myself it's worth it."

She rose to put another log on the fire and they moved to the butter-smooth leather couch. "It's good that I've got my work here at the Retreat. My poetess is coming in a couple of weeks and I've got eight clients signed up to attend. They'll be doing their own readings too. I can always book you in for a session," she added slyly, then laughed at the expression on his face.

He opted to change the subject. "And how is the campaign going?"

"Very exciting!" she said. "I'm going to be interviewed for a special supplement in the Saturday Record."

Steph had recently been nominated for the Business Woman of the Year award by the Professional Women's Association of Eastern Ontario. And the Retreat was up for the Best New Business Award.

"Wow." Halstead said. "I'll buy ten copies. And you know you've got my vote."

"Why thank you kind sir, I'll need it."

Dawn Guardian of the Rowan Tree had been nominated as well.

"That's two of us from Middle Island in a field of ten. Of course Dawn owns and operates the Rowan Tree with Doug but he sent in the nomination himself, outlining all the changes she's made to the place. She set up the seniors gym classes, for instance and made the facility available to everyone in the community, not just residents at the Rowan Tree."

He stretched luxiouriously into the couch cushions. "The Rowan Tree is a nice place I guess, but I'll be lobbying for you, of course. Just tell me where to send the bribes."

Steph laughed. "Don't be silly. Part of the purpose of the award is to generate awareness of all the great women and businesses in the area. It's an honour just to be nominated."

He grabbed her in a hug. "I know you're going to win, Steph, you've done a terrific job with the Retreat. And don't give me that baloney about how it's an honour to be nominated."

She squirmed in his arms. "O.K. of course it would be nice to win but it's not the be all and end all it is for you testosteroned guys. Women aren't as competitive. I met Dawn on the street the other day and we just had a laugh about being rivals."

"Hooey," he teased. "Women are just as competitive as men. I seem to remember a good-looking kid sister of a friend of mine who wanted pretty badly to be a cheerleader. She practised for weeks. You looked real cute in those pom poms too."

Steph managed to free herself. "That was for the good of the school," she said primly, pulling down her sweater. "The team deserved the best."

She laughed at his look. "But enough about me. How is it going with the Island Emergency Defence Plan, are our borders secure?"

"Safe as houses," he promised, holding up two fingers in the Boy Scout's salute. "Nobody wants to come here this winter anyway. We've got no cross country skiing or snowmobiling, just the Saturday euchre game at the town hall. There would be nothing for a terrorist to *do*."

"Sounds as if you'll have some time on your hands, chief." she said, with a minxish look. "How dull."

"Doesn't have to be."

Later, he stood on the doorstep, cap back on. "I'll be back on Friday ma'am, to check those fire extinguishers."

"You do that, chief." Then she smiled that killer smile. "Remember, we don't have to own each other Bud, we can just enjoy each other."

So far he'd managed to do that. The enjoyment part was easy. A nice, uneventful winter, with lots of pleasant suppers at the Retreat, that he could welcome. But the conundrum was never far from his mind. The agony and the ecstasy. He didn't want to do the wrong thing by pushing Steph into a decision that she didn't want to make.

The problem was he had no one to consult for advice. His late wife Kathleen had been his sage advisor in all things, especially dicey social situations. *Wonder what she would have made of this!*

His former police partner had retired to Arizona and he couldn't see discussing matters of the heart with his curling buddies. He could easily imagine the guffaws at the tavern if he ever brought up a discussion of open 'relationships'. He'd never hear the end of it. Better to just go with the flow, ride the wave or however the lingo went these days, and enjoy the sheen of the moonlight on the empty road. He liked to think of his Island folk settling down peacefully for the night, it gladdened his policeman's heart.

* * *

Lina Russell yawned and gave herself a little shake as she passed the deer crossing warning by Little Swamp. It had been another long day, but Thursdays were always fun. Once a week, she conducted a foot massage clinic at the Rowan Tree Home and then stayed to have supper in the common room with her grandmother and some of the other residents. The old dears got a kick out of seeing a young person (by comparison anyway, Lina was forty-two) and Lina got a kick out of them. She usually brought some special treats for dessert which the old ladies fell on like a pack of starlings.

The scene aways reminded her a bit of her own giddy dorm room days when she was taking her nurse's training. If she blurred her vision, that is. The youngest of her dinner companions was in her eighties and instead of wearing baby-doll pyjamas, they all wore baggy sweat pant suits (easier to mop up accidents, said the staff.). But a hen party nevertheless, with all the attendant giggling and cheerful gossip.

Juicy speculation about romances between different members of the staff, vitriolic though groundless complaints about the food, comments on recent disasters at the hands of the hairstylist. Sometimes Lina wondered how much Gran took in. She was a bit deaf but more than that, a little spacey these days and prone to relate any topic to her pet canaries. Then, after listening quietly and apart for ages, she'd startle them all by piping up with a comment.

The ladies had been surprisingly heartless about the death of Akantha Samos, or maybe unmoved would be a better word. The Samos sisters had only visited the Island in those long-ago summers and had never attended the local school, so none of the group actually knew Akantha. There even seemed to be a general feeling that she had deserved her lonely end as she was too snooty to have gone into a 'home'. Though she had nothing to be snooty about, all agreed. The family money had been long gone, no one could remember how.

The conversation finished up with a dire natter about the most recent senior scam story on the television news. An elderly woman had given a ten thousand dollar deposit to a home repair firm representative who said that her roof needed reshingling. Two weeks later, after the cheque had been cashed and no shingles or workmen were forthcoming, the woman's daughter found the representative had never worked for the home repair firm. The victim's face briefly filled the television screen, almost child-like in hurt bewilderment.

The Rowan Tree ladies clucked their sympathy. Then Gran grabbed the last cupcake. Near the end of life, as at the beginning, it seemed that life was all about the essentials.

The road through the swamp was a dark tunnel, lit only by the steady beam of her car headlights. The car was new, a chirpy little red Fiesta. Lina had been working hard and felt she deserved it. She shivered a little, thinking of the elderly women she had just left. Most of them had been widowed for a decade or more, but somehow they seemed to have found fun and companionship even in a senior's home, their last stop on the journey. She wondered how well she would do in the same situation.

Best not to seek things to worry about, mother used to say. There's plenty enough to think about right now. And good advice too.

Such as this strange snowless winter, must be that global warming stuff you heard about. Hard on the polar bears she'd heard, but what could a person do? There had always been change in the world. Look at the changes Gran and the other old ladies had seen. From the Model A to the internet. Some of the old dears were even learning how to use e-mail. Not Gran of course, she hadn't the concentration. These days her memory was like a grab bag of woolen bits, all mixed up. She would delve in and you never knew what she was going to come up with.

Which reminded her, there was something the ladies had been talking about, something interesting one of them had said.

Was it Gran – when they were all talking about the Samos sisters?

She thought back over the evening, but the teasing memory eluded her, staying just out of reach. Like her car headlights, only briefly illuminating the dark and not penetrating the woods behind the road. Never mind Gran's memory, what of her own these days? She was always forgetting things and she was barely more than forty. Best just to wait and the thought usually popped up later, sometimes after a night's sleep.

Emerging from the swamp, she was glad to see the lights of the neighbour's farmhouse. Soon she was home and Paddy her golden retriever was running up to give her his exuberant, sloppy greeting. The niggling thought like so many others, was shelved in the familiar avalanche of domestic detail.

The night was dark, but that was not the frightening part.
You were the hunted or the hunter
Always, only the one or the other
It was always the same.

You could feel safe sometimes for a little while
But then the danger came back
You could never get far enough away.

This strange winter, with no snow for shelter
And now the past was seeping up out of the ground
It wouldn't stay buried
It wouldn't keep away.

You were the hunted or the hunter
It was always the same
There was never any other way.

Creatures can tolerate periodic stretches of unusual weather but too extreme changes too often will start to show an impact.

Ali looked glumly out at the bird feeder. Pete had put the pole where she could see the birds easily from the kitchen but it was such a gloomy morning, even the breakfast crowd of juncos were hiding. The sky was heavy and oppressive, a lowering bank of metallic-grey clouds. The hibernating farmers' fields shrank from the dry static cold, lying flat and dull.

Ali was feeling pretty heavy and oppressed herself. All gobbled up and disappearing, as if her entire former self had been subsumed in her enormous pregnancy.

How long since she'd had an intelligent thought? She missed Miranda, couldn't bear looking over at the empty house. And Miranda was away for another whole month yet!

She opened the laptop and read her neighbour's latest e-mail.

Dear Ali:

How are my chickens? I hope Stella's boy is taking good care of them and that you are taking good care of yourself and your little one to be.

I am still looking for a decent 'motherhood' quotation to send you. Most of them are as soppy as a cheap greeting card and Shakespeare my stalwart, is too grim. Besides, many of his characters were most ungrateful to their parents!

'How sharper than a serpent's tooth' and all that. Will keep looking.

The weather here continues hot and lovely. I wake up to the chatter of parrots and the smell of the sea. Elinor's young students are delightful. They have that same zest for learning I remember so well from my classes in the Arctic. And so polite too — they even pretend to like listening to an ancient crone like myself.

Soon Elinor will be taking me into the interior to visit her other school. She says that the transmitting signal isn't very good there so don't expect an e-mail from me until we get back.

Give Emily a pat for me and tell her to be a good girl. I hope she isn't being too much of a bother.

Ali typed,
Dear Miranda:

Emily is no bother at all. She's good and faithful company – I'm surprised that she can bear being around me!

I am so bored, crabby and ungrateful. I'm ashamed of myself and don't deserve such a sweet husband as Pete. But I'm so jealous of his darn sauntering freedom. Poor sweet baby, too! I'm trying to stay calm and unfrustrated and unworried for her sake. Today I sat in the rocker in the nursery and read aloud some of the children's books we've bought. A is for Apple, B is for baby and so on. Nursery rhymes and lovely pictures of baby animals and birds. Very soothing for the both of us

Just as well you aren't here, I am reduced to babbling!

Enjoy your adventure in the jungle, and when you come back, please write me every detail.

Love, Ali

She felt guilty, even Emily seemed to eye her with disapproval.

"I know, Emily, but I can't *help* it. If only I could even go for a walk."

For a moment, she allowed herself to dream of putting on her boots and coat. Striding along the road. *Moving*, instead of the prospect of another day of sitting and vegetating on the couch.

Thank goodness it was a Lina day. There would be chatter and news and another voice in the house. Although maybe she had the day wrong. But no, it was Wednesday. Lina had an earlier client in the village who she helped with a morning bath, but she was usually at the Jakes' by nine o'clock. Ali checked that the coffee was still hot and moved restlessly to the window. The driveway remained stubbornly empty, no little red car in sight.

By nine-thirty she called the agency dispatcher. Not to complain of course but just to inquire if Lina had reported in that morning.

The dispatcher immediately rang Lina's pager.

"That's odd, she's not answering. But Lina always has her cell phone turned on when she's working. I'll try to track her down for you Mrs. Jakes and get back to you."

As Ali was putting the phone down, there came a knock at the door. She had raised a fuss for nothing. Just add anxiety to her list of failings at the moment.

But it was Jane Carell from the station, her face grave.

"Pete asked me to come," she said. "Lina's been in an accident. He was afraid you'd be upset."

"Is she hurt? Is it serious?" Ali asked faintly, sinking down to the couch.

Jane nodded. "Brace yourself, dear."

*   *   *

Halstead stood at the side of the road, his jacket soaked in frigid morning mist. The area beyond the ditch was a swamp in spring, now the spindly trees stuck up like white bones from the gelid black mud. He had stood on this road at this spot before, attending at accidents. The curve had always been a bad spot. There was swamp on both sides of the road and when there was a warm day and melting began, the water leaked across the road. Only to freeze by evening.

So he knew where they were headed when they got the call. A driver on his way to work in Bonville had seen the car in the ditch. Halstead and Jakes had sped out of town in the cruiser, arriving just moments before the ambulance. The man who had reported the accident was waiting ashen-faced beside his sedan. He pointed to the ditch but there was no need. The little cherry red car lay like a stranded ladybug in the shallow, water-choked ditch. From the angle, it was only too obvious that the driver, even if alive, would be in dire straits.

"I called down there," the man said. "But no one answered. I couldn't see much and I didn't want to do the wrong thing, so I left my car lights on and called 911."

It was a grim, grey morning. The sky was barely lightening now at eight o'clock.

One of the paramedics had already scrambled down into the ditch, Jakes right after him. The two young men wrenched open the passenger door and looked in, while Halstead stood silently at the top, waiting for the bad news. And it came. The paramedic who had slipped partly into the car, emerged, shaking his head.

"It's a woman. She's gone."

He signalled to his workmate, to lower down the gurney. It was a complicated manoeuvre to move the woman as gently as possible out of the car.

Jakes helped, looking pale. "I know her," he called to Halstead, as they were struggling up the slope. "It's Lina Russell, she's been helping Ali at the house."

Halstead looked reluctantly at the woman who would now be officially labelled a body. He swore. "I know her too, and her family. They're good folks."

"She was supposed to be coming to our place today. She must have been on her way into the Village."

Halstead nodded. "She was likely on the road by 6:30. It would still have been dark. This fellow here says he didn't see anybody else out then."

He watched the paramedics lift the gurney into the ambulance. He could get the details of the accident later. Unfortunately, there was no rush.

"What were her actual injuries?" he asked the paramedic.

"She had her seatbelt on but still knocked her head pretty bad," the man said sympathetically. "Looks like she hit a tree and then went into the ditch. Somebody will have to call her folks."

"Her husband Guy's probably out cutting brush," Halstead said. "Jane will get ahold of someone to roust him out."

He wasn't looking forward to the call. "See if her purse is down there in the car will you, Pete. As you're already wet."

Jakes' boots squelched in the icy water. Adrenalin had carried him so far but any minute now he would become aware of the bone-chilling cold.

"We'll get you back in the cruiser in a minute," Halstead said. "And turn the heater on."

Jakes' head and shoulders appeared from behind the car. "Chief, I don't think we'll be going anywhere anytime soon. There's some cracks in the driver's side window."

"So? I'd kinda expect that."

"Looks as if they might have been made by a bullet."

"What the hell?"

"Yeah, that's what it looks like. A hole with cracks all around it. I've seen that kind of pattern before, overseas."

The paramedic spat angrily onto the road. "Probably one of them cidiot hunters fooling around, firing off pot shots any which way. Then they didn't even stop when she went off the road. What kind of a bastard is that?"

"Any sign of a bullet?" Halstead called down.

Pete shook his head. "The floor of the car is mostly under water. We'll have to wait till they pull the car out. Even then, it's doubtful. She had the passenger window open a few inches – if the bullet kept going, it could be anywhere in the swamp."

"Poitras!" Halstead called to Nick who was standing in the other lane directing what traffic there was. "We're going to leave you here for awhile. I'm calling Bonville to ask them to send you another officer to help secure the site. Don't let anybody else stop and mess around here. Just keep them moving."

They left him, looking young and nervous and alone in the swamp.

1 ◻

Off—kilter – not right, out of alignment, aberrant.

Jakes pulled into the driveway at the hunting camp, scattering gravel from the cruiser's tires. Halstead noted his tense features, his rigid arms.

"Better stay calm, lad. I'm angry too, but we don't know that it's these fellows who fired that shot."

"I'm calm," Jakes said.

"Sure you are."

The green SUV and the Cherokee were there, but there was no reaction from inside at their arrival. Halstead thumped up the couple of steps of the cabin and banged heavily on the door.

"Yo," called a voice. "Come on in."

The hunters were at lunch. A big manly lunch, steak and eggs and bacon slices. The sight of the jolly threesome sitting and laughing and tucking into the meal made Pete want to puke. They hadn't bothered to get up from the table, though they would have seen and heard the cruiser pull into the yard.

Hawrie, the smooth one, looked up from his food. "Afternoon officers. What can we do for you?" Walsh and Boone didn't even look up.

Halstead took his cap off and slapped away the wet. "We were just wondering where you fellows were early this morning."

"How early?"

"Just early."

Hawrie reached for a piece of toast. "We slept in," he said disgustedly. "Crappy weather, too wet to be out looking for anything."

"Yeah, some winter you've got here," the skinny one chimed in, as if the policemen had ordered up the unseasonable weather just to tick him off. "We've only had the snowmobiles out once this whole winter. We should go further north next time," he said to his buddies.

And good riddance to you, Pete thought.

Halstead took a chair, though nobody had asked him to sit. Pete stayed standing against the door, his gaze scanning the armoury.

"So you were all here," Halstead said. "All together, all the time."

Hawrie scowled. "Boone was here that's for sure. I could hear his snoring. Shakes the goddamn rafters." He pushed back his plate, the food unfinished. "Why all the questions anyway? You're ruining my appetite."

"A woman was killed on Island Road Two this morning," Halstead said tersely. "Car skidded into the ditch."

"Sorry to hear it," said Hawrie. "The radio said the roads were slippery this morning. But what's that got to do with us?"

"Somebody took a shot at her. The driver's window was all cracked up."

All three looked up at that.

"Somebody killed the woman?" gulped Walsh, his thin face whitening. "Jeezus."

Halstead was unmoved by this show of concern. "Looks like the shot scared her so bad she drove off the road." No need for these fellows to know that so far they'd found no bullet.

"Sorry," Hawrie said again. "But what's that got to do with us? We don't know any of the local people except that nutty artist dame down the road who comes out and yells at us all the time."

Boone laughed and started to say, "Yeah and if we were going to shoot anybody . . . ." but Hawrie froze him with a look.

Halstead scanned the three faces. "We're thinking maybe some careless somebodies were taking a shot at something else. Like a deer for instance. Maybe one of those shots went astray."

Boone reddened. "Hey wait a minute. We didn't shoot anybody."

Hawrie made a shushing motion with his hand. "What road did you say?"

"This road, this one right here. A couple of miles up, at the big curve through the swamp. "

Hawrie shrugged. "Like we said. We were all here."

"How do you know nobody left?"

"Why would we?" Hawrie said. "We're looking to shoot rabbits and coyotes, not people in their cars for chrissake."

Halstead nodded to Pete. "We're just going to have a gander at those rifles if you don't mind."

"Hey wait a minute," Boone said belligerently. "We've got rights here. Where's your warrant?"

Hawrie stared him down. "Never mind, Boone. We've got nothing to hide."

He watched as Pete took a gun from the rack. "They've all been fired recently, so that won't tell you much. We've been shooting out back at targets all week."

"Just checking the gauges for future reference," Halstead said easily, as Pete made notes.

"How long are you staying?" he asked Hawrie.

"Over the weekend, going home Monday. But we'll be back weekends through April."

Halstead nodded. "Then you won't mind giving Officer Jakes here, your city addresses and phone numbers. And who owns what vehicle."

"Mine's the Cherokee," Hawrie said resignedly. "Walsh came with me, the green SUV is Boone's."

Halstead nodded. "And I'm warning you right now, I'd better not ever find you fellers wandering off the property with your guns in hand. I don't want to hear a single complaint from your neighbours about potshots either. The way you fellows shoot, you're bound to injure somebody eventually. But not on my Island."

He reached for the yellowed paper on the door, ripped it down and jammed a new sheet on the nail.

"I'm giving you a new door decoration. This year's hunting seasons and regulations. Something for you to study up on in the quiet country evenings. Cause you don't want to be going outside at night with all this dangerous activity going on."

As they drove away, Halstead looked somberly out at the grey, soggy landscape.

"Did it seem to you that those guys were hiding something? Covering for the Boone feller maybe?"

Pete nodded. "Yep, I got the same feeling. Hawrie didn't exactly say that he'd opened the bedroom door and checked that Boone was there."

"So maybe the snoring story is just a story and big hunter Boone was out and about early on his own, taking potshots."

"What do you think he was trying to shoot?"

"I think that one's determined to get a deer this trip. Even if he has to sneak it out in his trunk."

He sighed. "But there's not much we can do without a bullet. And there's not much chance we can find a bullet in a swamp. Not unless the thing hit a handy tree. So I guess you can figure what you and Nick will be looking for all afternoon. That bullet in a haystack. Meanwhile, I'll be giving the husband the bad news."

He wasn't looking forward to the visit.

"What's he like?" Pete asked. "Ali told me he and Lina were separated."

Halstead nodded. "People wondered why she didn't leave sooner. They met in high school and were quite the cute couple. She was a cheerleader and he was a well set-up young farmboy. But Guy turned out to be a drinking man and he's never done much of any account. Lina made the living and Guy worked odd jobs. A bit of logging, wood-chopping for others. He has a truck and hauls things for people in the summer. He was supposed to haul away the old shingles from the station roof job but he somehow never got around to that either."

"Sounds like a real winner."

"Now he lives in a shack by the swamp on his dad's property. He's not a bad feller, he was never abusive to Lina or their daughter. He's just sort of useless."

"Has he got a rifle?"

"I imagine. Most of these Island boys do." He reached for the speaker on the dash to check with Jane.

"I don't think Guy's got a phone anymore chief," she said. "Likely hasn't paid his bill."

"I'm on my way."

He looked at Jakes, it seemed a long time since breakfast. "Why don't you drive to the Grill first," he said. "And we'll pick up some burgers, something for Nick too. We've still got a long cold day ahead of us."

Pete took the road to town. He'd learned in the army not to feel guilty about hunger. You had to eat, no matter the traumatic event. And there had been some doozies. At the diner, he ordered extra fries. He figured he and Nick would need the fuel.

*　　*　　*

Though it was noon, Guy Russell was still abed or acouch as it turned out, an old hounddog at his feet. The dog hadn't barked at the knock on the door and now thumped his tail as Halstead entered the shack. The one-room dwelling was meagerly furnished with a woodstove, a hotplate, the couch and a turquoise coloured bar size fridge covered with various beer company stickers. There was a rifle though, propped up carelessly against the wall.

Russell, a lanky man in jeans and a ripped brown parka, was snoring. The place was filled with beer and gassy fumes, probably not all from the dog.

Halstead leaned over the couch and gave Russell a shake.

"Hey Guy. You've got a visitor. Wakey, wakey."

The man on the couch stayed prone.

Halstead shook him again, more roughly.

"Come on Guy. Upsy, daisy."

Russell groaned and pulled the coat up over his face.

Halstead rose and turned on the hotplate under the kettle. He saw no coffee but found a box of tea and put two bags into the least filthy mug on the battered table. He poured in the steaming water and hacked off some sugar from an encrusted dish.

The dog had lumbered to the door and now wuffed to be let out. Halstead left the door open for the air. Back at the couch, he grabbed hold of Russell's coat collar and hauled him up roughly to a sitting position. "Come on Guy. Time to get up."

It took another couple of minutes before Russell opened one bleary eye. He rubbed his brow aggrievedly.

"Give me a beer. There's one in the fridge."

"Sorry Guy. Tea's all you get. I've got something to tell you."

"Hey Bud, give a man a break. I tied one on last night."

"You tie one on every night."

Russell took the cup reluctantly, swore at the heat of the liquid but gulped some down. When he looked up, at least both eyes were open. There wasn't much left of his cute high school looks. His hair was still black but his features were blurred and puffy with the constant deluge of booze. He seemed to be registering the fact that Bud was there, that he was a cop.

"You got bad news for me, Bud?" he asked warily. "Did I tear up the bar last night, wreck something?"

Halstead looked over at the rifle.

Yeah, you might have wrecked something. But Christ, I hope not.

"Yes I've got some bad news, Guy. Lina's been in an accident. Her car went off the road at the big curve up the road."

It took the man a minute to absorb the news. Then he shook his head like a deer warding off flies. "How bad, Bud? Is she hurt?"

"Real bad. She's gone, Guy. I'm sorry."

Russell's hand began to shake and he dropped the cup. Hot tea spilled over his leg but he didn't notice.

"Jeesus, no, Bud!" He put his hands over his face and rocked in a spasm of sobs.

Halstead walked over to the door and stood looking out. The old dog sat in the yard, scratching himself in a patch of weak sunlight. A bluejay screeched somewhere in the woodlot where Russell had been gradually clearing a road for the truck.

When Russell was quiet again, he returned and picked up the cup.

"Want some fresh?" he asked.

Russell shook his head. "Who's gonna tell Alison?" The Russell's daughter, away at university. He seemed overwhelmed at the task.

"Maybe your sister, her aunt?" Halstead said. Russell seemed relieved at the suggestion. He wiped his face with his sleeve and stood up, looking dazed.

"Gotta take a leak."

There was plumbing in the shack. Halstead heard water running in the sink too and when Russell came back he was cleaning his face further with a dirty towel. He went straight to the fridge.

"Gotta have a beer, Bud. At a time like this."

He proffered a can to Halstead who waved it away.

"Someone spotted the car in the ditch at seven this morning, Guy. We figure Lina must have been on her way to work for six. That means she would have gone off the road around five forty-five, when it was still dark."

Russell took a swig from the can and shook his head again, as if hoping to push the picture out of his mind.

"We figure there must have been some noise when the car went off the road and hit the ditch. You didn't hear anything I guess. When did you come home by the way?"

And how? Even the Island good old boys were wary these days of the stringent alcohol restrictions. You could lose your license if driving after consuming only two beers.

"I didn't hear nothing. We took a cab to Gary Johnson's place, had a couple more pops and passed out. I woke up in the morning and walked home."

About a mile. Probably nothing to Guy, even drunk. He'd been walking and hitchhiking the Island roads since he was a teenager.

"About what time was that?"

Russell seemed to have exhausted his befuddled powers of memory.

"I don't know," he said vaguely. "You should ask Gary. I wanted to get home to the dog."

So Guy could have been coming along the swamp road as late or early as five o'clock. Halstead had already noticed that his jean cuffs were still damp.

He'd have to check with Gary Johnson.

Russell drained the can and reached for another. "Jeezus, Lina gone. That just tears me up. We had our differences, sure but . . . . Jeezus."

Halstead walked across the room and picked up the rifle. "You ought to be more careful with this Guy. I hope you don't get it out when you're in your cups. You could hurt yourself or the pooch. Or somebody else. "

"Ah I just sit on the step sometimes and pop a rabbit. There's a bunch of them that hang around here."

Halstead checked the barrel. "Shot any rabbits lately?"

"Ask Henry. He gets to fetch them."

Russell's words were already getting slurred, from tiredness or possibly from shock.

Halstead placed the rifle up on the rack above the bathroom door.

"Stay and have a beer," Guy pleaded. "You can't just come and give me news like that and leave."

"The beer's all gone," Halstead said. "You've run out."

Looks as if you might have run out of everything. "You'd better go talk to your sister."

11

In nature's infinite book of secrecy, a little I can read

Late afternoon. The ambulance and paramedics were long gone. Callan's tow truck had come and winched out the smashed ladybug car, its bright paint lashed with streaks of ugly black mud. The sun, which seemed to have never really risen more than a few degrees above the horizon, was now preparing to give up altogether. In the swamp, the skimpy trees cast thin fingers of shadow across the opaque patches of water.

The two policemen, clad in waisthigh hipwaders, slogged their way through the deepening dusk. Pete could feel the icy water even through his trousers and the thick rubber waders. His legs felt numb. Beside him, Nick plodded along halfheartedly, obviously just as exhausted and cold. And dispirited, because they were getting absolutely nowhere.

Now Nick turned and threw his arms up dramatically, taking in the entire grey, dripping surroundings. "I give up. You'd need a miracle to find a bullet here. Or tracks of anybody."

Pete straightened, his neck aching from looking down at the soaked ground. What had they found, what had they learned? Not much. The swamp had given up no secrets. Even the drier patches in the swamp were just mud. So, no bullets, no bullet casings. No discernible or neatly identifiable tracks of brand new hunters' boots.

Nothing to indicate the spot where a clumsy irresponsible hunter might have stumbled in the murky morning to fire off a bad shot.

"You can gather up the barrier tape from the ditch," Pete said. "I'm going to make one more pass around."

Pete slogged once more as far as the *No Hunting, No Trespassing* sign on the Rowan Tree old rail fence. There were shotgun dents in the metal. Rusted dents though, from another winter. He looked out at the darkening woods, his mood almost as numb as his legs. In the distance, the lights of the retirement home were orange pinpoints of warmth in the dusk. This night wasn't going to bring any comfort for Lina Russell's friends and family. Such a cold and lonely ending. He'd seen death before of course, too much of it.

A phrase from his military training crossed his mind. *Peace, that's what we're fighting for. To help make a better world.* But sometimes he wondered whether humans really wanted it.

When he got back to the road, Halstead had arrived, to get the dispiriting report.

From the tire marks on the road they'd been able to determine the direction of the car's skid after the shot. They'd briefly discussed the possibility that the shooter had shot from a moving car but not even the men at Snake Point Lodge seemed that crazy. So, the bullet had come from the north side of the road, smashed through the driver's side window and passed out the other open window.

"Why would she have had the window open?" Pete wondered.

Halstead looked bleakly along the streaked pavement. "Likely to let in some fresh air. Inside windshield probably was fogged up."

It was a miracle that the bullet hadn't killed Lina outright, although the tragic end result had been the same.

"At least then we would have had a bullet," he said grimly.

Pete took off one of his arm-to-elbow rubber gloves and shook out a stream of dirty water.

"Maybe they'll find it when they dry out the car," he offered, with all the optimism of a cop who had just spent the better part of a day on a wild goose chase.

"Yeah maybe. Then maybe we can match the damn thing to a rifle. And that would be a piece of cake if I didn't have g.d. rifles coming out of my ears."

He explained about Guy Russell's gun.

"What do you figure?" Pete asked.

Halstead shook his head. "Russell's jeans were wet but he probably fell into the ditch on his way home. It looks as if he was too drunk to have noticed anything or anyone and certainly too drunk to have remembered it if he did. He was pretty broken up about the news though, that's for sure."

He walked over to the ditch and looked into the rapidly darkening swamp. "You say you found a deer blind back there?"

"Yes, but no human tracks, just some critters."

Evidence of the other life in the swamp. Deer hoofprints. Some predator's tracks, probably a fox, leading to a spatter of blood and what was left of a rabbit pelt. A record of stalking in the mud. Too bad there hadn't been a similarly easily read record of stalking humans.

Halstead sighed. "Well if the turkeys or the deer or the coyotes know anything about this mess, they aren't gonna be much good on the witness stand."

He patted the younger man on the shoulder. "Time to go home, Pete. I'll take Poitras back to town, we've done all we can for this day."

"I just hate to think of those Snake Point guys getting away with this. Going back to the city and telling stories about another fun hunting trip."

"I hate it too but we're never going to find a bullet floating around in this swamp. I'm sending the cracked window off to forensics. Maybe they'll be able to tell us something about the bullet that went through it."

But he didn't sound too hopeful.

Nick had taken off the soaking waders before getting in the car but his clothes still smelled of the swamp.

"How are you doing at the motel?" Halstead asked. "Everything O.K.?"

Young Poitras was residing for the year in the motel behind the Island Grill. The half dozen units were normally empty for all except the summer months and Gus Jones, the owner of both establishments, was glad to get the rent. It wasn't luxury accommodation but Gus also gave his tenant a discount on meals at the Grill, which was handy for the young rookie.

"Yeah, it's O.K. Tonight I'm just gonna have a hot shower and watch the hockey game. I've got a book to study up about turkey hunting too. Say chief, do you think there's any turkeys there in those swamp woods?"

Halstead chuckled. "Oh those birds are in there all right. They've been there all along. They don't migrate or hibernate."

"What do they eat then?"

"This time of year, mostly acorns and seeds, maybe some berries. In the summer, almost anything they can find. Bugs, frogs, even small snakes."

"So they're just roosting up there in the tree branches, right now?" Nick seemed dazzled at the prospect. "Great big birds like that? Sounds as if it would be easy to just pick a few off."

"You mean if it was hunting season," Halstead cautioned. "And even a month from now, it won't be easy. If you do spot a bird, he'll likely have spotted or heard you a whole lot sooner. So you likely won't see him at all, he'll have flown away."

Nick shrugged. "Some of them get shot. Thousands of them my book says. Did you ever get one, chief?"

"I don't hunt any more," Halstead said. "I used to hunt with my dad when I was a kid, but that was a long time ago."

"I bet you eat turkey though, don't you?"

"Oh yeah, I eat turkey."

12

The Bonville Record gave the accident in the swamp a streamer headline.

CARNAGE ON MIDDLE ISLAND ROAD.

Home Care Worker fatally distracted by stray bullet.

Vern was in an awful state. He didn't even sink wearily into his usual chair in front of Halstead's desk.

"Why are you dragging your feet, Bud?" he demanded anxiously. "People want to see those hunters charged and fined at least. Everybody knows it's those city fools staying out at Snake Point who shot at Lina."

"There's a little matter of evidence," Halstead pointed out drily. "And so far all I've got is not much evidence and a whole lot of public opinion. So everybody's just going to have to wait."

Vern sank then and tossed the newspaper discouragedly down on Halstead's desk.

"Yeah, I know," he said soberly. "Sorry, Bud. This one just makes me sick. Lina tended my mother last year, saw her out. You couldn't find a kinder lady. And when I think of them hunters down at the Point, shooting up the woods like a pack of know-nothing kids . . . ."

Halstead nodded sympathetically. "It might not have been them though, Vern. You've got to keep that in mind."

The clerk didn't look convinced. "Those fellers aren't real hunters anyway," he said. "I doubt that they even eat what they shoot. They just want to play with their guns and gadgets. They don't even look like hunters."

Halstead knew what Vern meant. There was a point to the clothes the Island hunters wore, the red flannel jacket and shiny orange cap from the hardware store. That new combat gear might hide the cidiots from the deer and the turkeys but other hunters couldn't see them either. Unfashionable orange made for better odds that your buddy didn't accidentally shoot you instead of the birds.

"It was council who voted to allow the hunting camp zoning in the first place," Halstead reminded him. "Even though the neighbours got up a petition against it."

Vern protested. "The business people said they wanted the chance to make some winter money."

And Byers' gas station was one of those businesses, Halstead thought but forbore to mention.

"The owner of the camp isn't even a local," Halstead said, compounding council's sin. "I've got Jane tracking him down now. He's got to provide better supervision of the place. I'll need a copy of the original zoning terms from the council records."

Vern nodded meekly.

"I want to be able to talk tough to this guy. Tell him that he could be charged too. That you could revoke the zoning and shut down the camp."

The clerk arose, speedily for him. "I'll get right on it."

Halstead glanced again at the newspaper with its lurid headline. Yeah, that's just great Vern, you go and hustle now. A fat lot of good you're going to accomplish though, running around after the dismal fact.

*   *   *

An hour later, he scowled at the forensic report, not bothering to hide his frustration from the white-coated lab technician.

"That's it? That's all you've got to tell me?" He smacked at the paper with the back of his hand. "That a bullet shattered Lina Russell's car window? I knew that already, I didn't think it was a roadside rock or a piece of gravel for chrissake."

Roger Huma was unfazed. After twenty years on the job, he was used to dealing with dissatisfied and disappointed customers. Smaller than Halstead by several inches and forty pounds, he was not intimidated one bit.

"You get me a bullet," he said. "Then I might be able to tell you something."

Halstead tossed down the report. "I'd need a magic trick to find that hunk of lead in that swamp. Damn me though, I've heard of cases like this happening during deer hunting season down in the States."

"Yep, it happens," Huma said. "Bullets are known to have caused human injury up to a half mile away. In one case, a woman in Pennsylvania was shot while she was sitting in her car in her own driveway. The courts call it reckless gunfire. But during hunting season there are usually dozens, if not hundreds of hunters out shooting in the woods and the cops seldom make an actual arrest."

He picked up a photo from his desk, Lina Russell's shattered car window. It looked like a spider's web with a big hole in it. On the car seat below, chunks of safety glass lay scattered like the jewels of a cheap dollar store necklace.

"Can't you at least tell me what calibre bullet smashed that glass?" Hasltead asked.

Huma shook his head. "A .30 could do it, so could a .22"

"And there wouldn't be any difference in the result?"

"It depends on the distance. A bullet shot up into the air can travel a mile but would lose any accuracy and effectiveness."

"So how far away was this shooter? Close enough to see the road? To see cars on the road?"

Huma shrugged. "As I said, could be as much as half a mile away. But of course any experienced hunter would want to get much closer to his target." He took a pencil and made a quick sketch of a stick-figure holding a stick rifle.

"A typical trajectory is like so . . . Your hunter is holding his rifle about three feet off the ground and he's aiming at the deer's flank at about the same level. So the bullet is travelling approximately level with the earth's surface and is reasonably likely to hit the intended target."

He used his pencil again and altered the angle of the stick rifle. "But if our hunter trips or jerks his arm up suddenly for some other reason, he fires off what we call an error or errant shot. The steeper the angle, the wilder the shot. I've got a video here of an errant bullet smashing through a corrugated metal wall. "

"Terrific. Now folks aren't even safe in buildings."

Huma looked up from his sketch. "This type of data has been used in court, where residents are objecting to the presence of a gun club in their area. These errant shots fired at even a five or ten degree angle can overshoot a club's protective baffles on their firing range. And these are the ones that can injure neighbouring residents."

He shrugged, "But we don't have a convenient gun club to blame in this case."

"We've got hunters, though," Halstead said grimly. "But you're saying it would be no help to check out the individual rifles?"

"Not without a bullet, sometimes not even then." Huma grinned wolfishly. "Contrary to the wisdom of sexy television forensics babes, it's not always that easy to match even if you have the bullet."

"What about firing the rifles and keeping the casings in case we do find a bullet?"

Huma's look was eloquent. "The .22 cartridge is one of the few cartridges that are accepted by a large variety of rifles. What are you proposing to do, commandeer every rifle on the Island?"

Halstead scowled. "No, I'm grasping at straws. I've got rifles all over the place, the goddamned dogs have got rifles on the Island." He added not too hopefully, "What if we could find the casing?"

Huma took pity. "I've got an eager beaver student here. He's researching various studies for me. If we find anything useful, I'll let you know."

*   *   *

"I hate to say it," Halstead said to Jakes as they got in the cruiser. "But we'll have to let Davy Crockett and his mountain boys go back to the city. For now anyway."

"You're just going to let them go?"

"We've got their home addresses," Halstead said. "We know where they live, where they work – Hawrie and Walsh have got families. They've all got firearms licenses valid for this year."

Which meant the men had each taken the Canadian Firearms Safety Course at some point in their hunting lives. The one-day course demanded an eighty-percent mark in safety practises and firing techniques.

Pete swore. "There's no live-fire testing in the course, just a mechanical run-through. Doesn't prove that an applicant can shoot straight or that he won't get careless."

"It's the best control we've got," Halstead said. "Better than our neighbours to the south, that's for sure."

Jakes gunned the car in frustration and Halstead settled resignedly against the seat back. He was thinking what Vern would say, what the Bonville Record would print and how dumb the police chief was going to look when it became known that he had to let his three chief suspects just waltz off the Island.

"I don't know that we'll ever be able to link any of them to the shooting without a bullet, some hard evidence."

"I know," Pete said. "And the same goes for the husband. It's a real bummer."

They'd questioned Russell's buddy, Gary Johnson the day before.

Halstead went over it again, "So, according to good buddy Johnson, when he gets up at ten a.m., Guy has already left. But in buddy's expert drinker's opinion, he figures the condition Guy was in, that he would need a few hours to sleep it off before he could manage walking home. So he wouldn't have got home before nine or so. Several hours after the shooting happened."

"Johnson's not the most reliable witness," Jakes pointed out. "Russell could have staggered home earlier in the dark."

Halstead nodded. "He certainly knew the road well."

"And then maybe he decided to do some bunny hunting in the woods. Though you'd think someone might have seen him, or heard the shots anyway."

Halstead shrugged. "They wouldn't think it was out of the ordinary, or suspicious. He was out there every day chopping wood. He pretty well made his own hours."

"I'm surprised he hasn't chopped his own hand off, a boozer like him."

"And we can't ask the dog."

So, not much of an alibi. Just more doubt and uncertainty and murk. Like the dank waters that had muddied Lina's broken car.

Re-entering the Island, they drove silently past the curve at the swamp. The sawhorses and yellow plastic police tape were gone and the pavement was bare of skid marks but Pete thought he would never again view that stretch of road in the same way. He realized that if a person stayed in an area as long as Halstead, soon every patch of it might bear some significance, though hopefully not all so tragic as this spot. Something to think about.

"How is Ali taking all this?" Halstead asked. He had been delighted to hear that the Island was going to be welcoming a new baby resident, who should be an interesting combination of blond, stalwart Jakes and exuberant, exotic Ali.

Jakes looked worried. "Not so well. It's been a terrible shock and she doesn't need shocks right now. Doctor Baird won't even let her go to Lina Russell's funeral. I'm worried that she's getting depressed."

"That's hard, lad, but you've only a couple of months to go. Then all will be right as rain again."

He remembered going through that last stretch of waiting time both with his wife and later his daughter. Now he had a teenage grandson who hopefully wouldn't be rushing into marriage just yet. At least not if grandpa had anything to say about it.

Jakes still looked worried.

13

What dark days seen! . . . the very birds are mute.

There were two churches on the Island, Presbyterian and Catholic. Neither manse was occupied any more but the minister and priest shared services with several rural churches outside Bonville and travelled between them.

Lina Russell's soul would be journeying to a Catholic heaven.

Outside the church, crocus shoots were poking up out of the lawn. In mid-March, Halstead marvelled. But for once, the crazy weather was appropriate, the bright green a sign of life on a sad day.

He had attended a number of funerals in his time, the hardest his wife's. He wasn't a deeply religious person himself, but he appreciated the comfort generated by the church ceremony and the sympathetic presence of neighbours and friends. The press of shoulders together in the old wooden pews, the voices raised in song. Accompanied on an erratically tuned piano and led by the choir, whose quality might vary according to the available singers at any one time, but whose enthusiasm never flagged. The current choir was actually pretty good. Eleda Norton was a good clear soprano and there were a couple of strong male voices for bass.

The victim's family and close friends occupied several pews at the front of the church. There were Lina's grieving parents, old

Hanna and Gerald Berman, Lina's sister and spouse and most sadly, her twenty year old daughter, Alison. The girl was slightly built and had inherited Guy's dark hair and olive complexion, rather than the red hair and colouring of her mother. Beside Alison, at the outer edge of the group, sat Guy himself, rigidly sober this afternoon, his back straight, his face pale.

This was not a cheerful celebration of life event. The family would hopefully feel that way some time in the future. For today, though, there was only shock and grief.

The pianist struck up the opening chords of the hymn and the congregation rose to their feet.

Abide with me: fast falls the eventide, Lord with me abide.

Stephanie Bind had brought lots of Kleenex, she knew she'd be needing them. She'd gone through school with Lina Russell's older sister. The news had been shocking and frightening too. For days after the accident, she had found herself actually wincing at times, imagining the crack of a shot, a stray, murderous bullet smashing through the car window.

My god, if Livy had been at home this winter, it could have been her.

Had it been like this in the past? Of course there were lots of violent happenings then, but of a different kind. Dreadful accidents with old farm machinery, runaway horses, lumbering disasters of falling trees and in the days of sailing, the ever-present shipwrecks. But nowadays you heard of such irresponsible recklessness, lunatic speeding on the highway for instance. As if people no longer felt concern for their neighbours or even knew them.

Things were so different now, the whole world was changing, even the weather. Yes daily weather had always been changeable, but not entire seasons, not like this. Every day, you heard of strange occurrences in the natural world. Starving owls falling from the daylight skies, fish drowning because there was no winter ice, apple crops lost because the trees bloomed too early. What to make of it all, what strange portents were these?

A person might even wonder whether the strange weather was also influencing the human psyche. The big city papers reported several shootings a day and people had become inured to the news. Not Island folk thank goodness, not yet anyway. But now it seemed that the violence was overflowing the city's borders and tainting country life as well. Time was when she knew every car and pickup truck in the neighbourhood. Not any longer. At least the December deer hunt was over, you could thank the Council for that lovely treat. Let's invite a bunch of strangers here to kill a bunch of deer just before Christmas. And now one of these strangers might have caused Lina's death.

Get a grip, she told herself, and look around you at a church full of relations and friends. Besides, there were nice strangers too, new folks like Pete and Ali Jakes who had become friends. And not that it was any comfort, but Bud said the city hunters might not even be the ones who shot at Lina. That it might have been Guy Russell on one of his benders. What a horrible idea.

She'd hate to think like a cop, she told Bud.

He said sometimes he hated it too.

Again, the choir rose in song. *All Things bright and beautiful. All Creatures great and small.*

Stephanie dove for her kleenex.

Confined to home, Ali Jakes found one of Lina's oatmeal chocolate chip cookies forgotten in the cookie jar. And wept.

* * *

After the funeral, Pete drove away, under the solace of the crisp, blue-skied day. He opened the car window, needing the bracing cold air to clear his thoughts. He thought his driving was aimless but found himself once again nearing the Snake Point camp. He had driven past several times in the last few days.

He was seeing green SUVs in his sleep. Ali thought he was having the bomb nightmare again, till he explained.

"I just have a feeling that guy Boone was out there that morning," he said. "The others could be covering up for him."

"There's nothing you can do until the forensics office reports again," she said soothingly. "You have to stop beating yourself up over this."

But he felt bad, it wasn't right. He felt he was letting Lina Russell and her family down. There was no way he could make up for their loss but it was his job to see that they at least knew the truth about what had happened.

This time Boone's SUV was actually there, the Cherokee too. Back for the weekend, he guessed. He could hear shots from the shooting range out back. He got out and walked around the SUV, looking in the windows. There was a rifle rack, properly installed behind the seat. No infraction there, couldn't even chew out the cidiots on that score. Then Boone came out from behind the cabin, a rifle trailing from his hand, the other two men behind him.

"Good morning," Pete said easily. "Just checking that you're staying on the land."

Boone scowled. "Yeah right."

Hawrie pretended no friendliness today either. The three of them watched stonily as he turned the cruiser around.

At Little Swamp, he stopped again. He had been back there a few times too. Stopping to look into the dim reaches of the drowned cedars. Somewhere in there, impossibly concealed, was a bullet, maybe several.

Perversely, on this sad day, the sun lit up even the depths of the swamp. His eyes registered a flash of red and he automatically reached for his binoculars. A rose-breasted grosbeak. He scanned the nearest cedars for another glimpse. He now kept Ali's rejected bird watching guide in the car and consulted it regularly. He had already identified many of the winter birds in the area and even some early migrants who had returned off schedule because of the erratic weather.

He jotted down the details of the grosbeak sighting in his notebook. You could buy proper record keeping books he knew, but he still felt a bit silly about getting one. Instead, he kept this unofficial record in a small notebook that he kept in his jacket pocket. Now he wished he had been more interested in the subject when he was stationed in Afghanistan. He had missed an opportunity to see storks for instance. Also flamingoes, and the exotically named Tibetan snowcock.

His buddies might have ribbed him but it would have been worth it. The opportunity to see any of those birds might become much rarer. He had heard that the war had destroyed habitat and disrupted migratory pathways, causing bird numbers to drop by eighty-five percent. Yet another casualty of war.

He left the car, still holding his binoculars. The sun warmed the skinny swamp trees and made small pools of melt at their bases. He bet there'd be lots of frogs here in the springtime and made a mental note to check it out. He was already chalking up spots to bring his new daughter, not this spring of course, but maybe next year.

She might like to look for birds too. Like the grosbeak, which he now spotted high up in a big cedar, a beauty with his red breast and handsome black cap. He stood still while the bird munched on pine seeds, its soft movements hardly ruffling the air. He liked to listen to the silence of the woods that wasn't really silence. He felt as if he was in a fragile glass bubble of blue sky, and gold shivering light. A moment of sheer peace in a turbulent universe.

Then a shattering, mighty roar erupted beside him. His soldier's reflexes leapt like flames in his limbs and he dove for the ground. He felt squelching mud beneath his splayed hands and a cold splattering on his face.

What the hell?

In three quick body rolls, he reached some nearby tree roots. When he looked cautiously up, he laughed aloud at the sight of the big old tom turkey that looked down at him from a tree branch. He'd been as surprised as the man. A monster bird, nearly three feet tall, feathers up in a great black fan and his red gobbler angrily gobbling. Might be the legendary old warrior himself.

Pete got up and dusted himself off in shared embarrassment.

"Don't worry, fella," he waved. "I won't tell anyone where you hang your hat."

In the car, he looked back over the ditch and sketched a little map to help him find the frog place again. To recapture that sense of peace. Yes, there was no lurking malevolence in this wild, special spot, no sinister intent in the simple arrangements of nature. The wild creatures had borne Lina Russell no ill will. The violence had come from the world outside.

14

*F*unerals were creepy. But it was good to feel safe again.

It would have been better just to scare the dame though, to run her off the road. Who knew she was going to break her freaking neck? Probably wasn't wearing her freaking seat belt, the fool.

But she wouldn't stop snooping around, she had to stick her nose in.

Just like that other woman, the old broad with all the stinking cats.

That was her own fault too. She had to send that old newspaper clipping. Could the past never stay buried? All you could do was to rip it out and kill it all over again.

That was the thing about murder. They drove you to it.

You thought about doing the right thing like when you found the old hag lying there on the cottage floor. You thought about calling 911 but then they'd be asking all their nosey questions. Besides, you wanted to get the hell out of there before some snooping neighbour noticed your car.

And the old hag was most likely to die anyhow. She'd looked like a corpse already that's for sure, like a doll with no stuffing left in it. You probably did her a favour, there couldn't have been any joy living in that dump.

Anyway, she died, which was really a great piece of luck.

"You're a lucky kid," that's what pop used to say. "But what luck you don't get, you have to make."

So when the other one started to ask questions, that was just another problem to fix.

And that should truly be the end of it. Nobody else was ever likely to try to sift through those piles of junk in the old dame's shack. It was a hell of a job and who would want to bother. Soon, it would all be carted to the Island dump. Burned up and forgotten.

*   *   *

"What's all that?" Ali asked, as Pete staggered in the kitchen doorway, arms wrapped around two big cardboard cartons.

He dropped them unceremoniously on the floor. Emily was immediately interested, sniffing round the cracked and battered bottoms. The cartons were definitely exuding a strong smell. Ali hoped of mere mustiness, but feared of cat.

"They're boxes from that old lady's cottage," he gasped. "There are another two in the car."

She waited, without much interest. It had been another dreary day. Rain threatening but never really happening, just an early darkening of evening.

"I'll get the other boxes," he said. Then over his shoulder, he called, "It was Jane's idea."

He stood for a moment out by the car, listening to the owl. Halstead said the bird was a rare visitor for that time of year but he or she had been around for several nights now. The hoot sounded lonely in the damp dark. He turned with a sigh back towards the house. Their house, the lights of the living room lamp glowing warmly in the window. Soon there would be a whole new person living in the house, their baby. It would be a place of happiness and laughter.

If only he'd be able to get the baby's mother through the next few weeks!

Ali was so horribly depressed over the news about Lina. Pete was thinking of contacting Nuran himself, asking her to come earlier but that was risky too of course, considering their complicated relationship. That might just make things worse.

Then Jane at the station had come up with her idea. Apparently matters hadn't yet been resolved at Akantha Samos' cottage. The lawyer had finally discovered a remote connection, a third cousin twice removed who had never known either of the sisters. Even her mother, the original cousin hadn't known them. This person wasn't interested in the contents of the cottage, and had instructed the lawyer only to contact her if there was any money left after the place was sold for taxes.

There wasn't even going to be an auction of contents, they were too pitiful and the lawyer was just going to call the junkman. That's where Jane came in. Her sister was on the Bonville museum archive board which had expressed an interest in the boxes of newspapers and possible photos of the original Samos island home, but the two thinly stretched staff members had no time to go through them right now. They needed a volunteer and maybe Ali would be interested in the job. She could do it from home.

Pete had no idea what Ali would think. Still, nothing ventured . . . .he picked up the box. Inside, Ali was stirring listlessly at a cup of tea.

Daunted, he started to explain, "This stuff was all slated to go to the dump . . . ." his own limited enthusiasm trailing off as he saw her already losing interest. But then she sighed and with a watery smile, reached a hand across the table to grasp his.

"Please thank Jane for the thought. I'm having nightmares about Lina and I do need something to take my mind off all this. Maybe I can immerse myself in somebody else's life for awhile."

But the next day, just the sight of the heavy boxes exhausted her. They sat ignored by the kitchen door.

15

An increase of two degrees in temperature will affect the growth and survival of living things by altering their physiological behaviour.

A new week. People had genuinely cared about Lina Russell but they had paid their respects and now the daily rhythm of Island life resumed. The formal obit would be in the newspaper on Wednesday and the Letters to the Editor page would be filled once more with complaints about the recent tax hike.

Halstead usually enjoyed a trip out to Collier Bluff whatever the time of year. Like the other three Island points, Collier's was a rough, cedar sprinkled, rocky spear that jutted out into the lake. But the Bluff was the highest spot on the Island and gave the best view of the lake and the other two islands of his jurisdiction. Not there was much to police. North or Boulder Island, as the locals called it, was really little more than that, a big boulder with barely enough soil to support a couple of gnarled jack pines. Remnants of an old frame lighthouse stuck up like a battered monument to the days of ship and sail. Nowadays, a series of buoys or the GPS warned marine traffic away from the rocky shallows.

On South Island there were a couple of cottages but no permanent residences. The police did run random patrols out there in the police boat in the summer, mainly to make sure the islands didn t become teenage party destinations.

Beyond that, on a clear day you could even see the smudged outline of the city on the U.S. shore, twenty miles away. The Bluff was a good thinking spot. The view was wide and mind-freeing, any time of year. Winters when he was a kid, you could skate across to Boulder Island, but you'd get a cold soaking this winter for sure. The water was pretty well open, right out past the bay. Still, it would be long months before boating time. And he was not sight-seeing today.

"You see any terrorist activity?" he resignedly asked Jakes, who was scanning the small island with a pair of police issue binoculars.

Jakes grinned, "Just those little bufflehead ducks that stay here all winter. Maybe they're up to something, but it's hard to tell. And how are we going to catch one to interrogate?"

Halstead snorted and started back to the cruiser.

"O.K. we've checked it out. Glad this fool's errand is done."

Old Maudie Anderson who lived in a farmhouse a mile from the Bluff had called the station to report that she'd seen lights on South Island at night. The emergency drills, though important, had whipped up a lot of concern with older folks. And Vern's terrorism rants had only aggravated the problem.

"We'd better stop in and talk to Old Maudie though, before we head back."

Pete laughed. "Do you think she'll take our word for it, that she's safe?"

"I doubt it. Her version is much more fun."

They were half-way to Maudie's place when the radio began to crackle. Halstead was about to reach for the receiver when he stopped, hand in mid-air. It wasn't Jane's voice coming from the black plastic box, but a man's. Not Nick either. An angry yelling voice. Drunk too, and slurring words.

"Where's Halstead, I want to talk to Halstead. He knows those city bastards shot at my wife and the friggin cops won't bring him in."

Halstead recognized the voice. Guy Russell.

Jane's voice came now, muted. A soft soothing murmer of protest. No discernible words.

Halstead looked over at Pete and motioned *silence*. Pete nodded, they had realized at the same time that Jane must have surreptitiously turned on the transmitter at the station.

Russell's loud voice came again, completely overpowering Jane's. He wasn't listening to her. His voice kept rising, till he was shouting out the words.

"I bet he's hiding back there in his office. But he can't hide from me. I'm going in there and drag him out. "

They heard something crash. Halstead could only hope it was Russell and not Jane. Right now he didn't really care whether the fool had broken every bone in his dumb body. Jakes didn't have to be told to step on the gas. But they were still about ten minutes away, the telephone poles now flickering past like flash cards as Jakes gunned the motor.

Halstead thumped the dashboard with his hand. "Damn, I should have expected something like this. I should have kept my eye on the idiot. "

Russell was back on the air, sounding slightly winded, as if he'd fallen and pulled himself up.

"You can tell your boss that I'm going to go do his work for him. I'm going to shoot up those bastards and that hunting camp of theirs myself."

Jane's burst in, she'd grabbed the transmitter. "Bud, he's got a gun, you better get here fast."

Pete sped the cruiser past the beer store and a couple of angrily honking horns.

"I can't keep him here Bud, he's going to get away!"

Another crash. Worse than the first. Then, as Pete skidded into the station parking lot, a shot.

Halstead practically fell out his door but Jakes was way ahead of him. By this time, Halstead had noticed the other cruiser in the lot. As he burst in the door of the station, he saw young Poitras entangled with Guy Russell on the office floor. Poitras had Russell in a hammer lock but he was still having a time keeping the man down as he writhed and struggled towards the rifle now out of his reach. Halstead picked up the gun while Jakes helped haul the others to their feet.

"Jane?" Halstead called anxiously. "Where are you?"

"In here, chief." The dispatcher stepped out from behind the coffee cubicle wall.

She was wiping dust from her trousers but otherwise looked unscathed.

"You O.K?" he asked, keeping one eye on the trio in the centre of the room. Poitras seemed to have knocked the stuffing out of Russell. He sagged now like a sack of peat moss between the two cops, mumbling incoherently.

"I'm O.K.," Jane smiled at Nick. "Thanks to young Tarzan rushing in here to save the day."

Poitras' grin was ear to ear. "Who's Tarzan?"

"Seriously," Halstead asked Jane. "Are you O.K? Why don't you take the afternoon off, you've had quite a shock."

Jane looked at her crowded desk. "Are you sure? I'd probably just go to the mall."

"So, go. And buy yourself a nice dinner, it's on me. "

*   *   *

The holding cell at the station hadn't been used for a couple of months, not since a New Years' fracas at the Island Grill. Halstead had taken the night shift, he wanted to talk to Russell himself. But Russell was in a deep stupor and soon Halstead too, fell asleep. In the morning, he found Russell sitting up on the bunk, rocking his head in his hands.

"You got more bad news for me, Bud? Jeez, I guess you're gonna tell me now my dog's been shot."

"Your dog's probably O.K. unless you took a shot at him before coming down here. You're the bad news, Guy. Drinking and shooting and running around making death threats. That's not just good old boys having some fun. I can't allow that. There's going to be charges this time."

"What about charging those jerks who shot at Lina?"

"We don't know yet that they did it, Guy. This is Canada you know, and in Canada we're all innocent until proven guilty. The same law goes for everybody whether you like them or not."

"Who else would shoot at Lina? And why for chrissake?" At this, Russell gave a helpless wail and rocked back on the bunk.

Halstead eyed him coldly. "Ever think maybe you did, Guy?"

Russell stopped and wiped his nose on his sleeve. "Maybe I did what?"

"Maybe *you* shot at Lina."

"Oh no, Bud, not me. I loved the woman. She was my wife."

"Not any more she wasn't. Maybe you just couldn't stand watching her make a new life for herself. Remember, we had to put you in the clink last fall for a night. You were hollering outside the house and Lina had to call us."

Russell put his hand on his chest, over his heart. The gesture was stagey but in the surroundings, the plain monkishly furnished cell, oddly moving. His faded blue eyes blurry but his gaze straight, he said simply. "I could never shoot the mother of my child."

Halstead leaned back in his chair and crossed his arms. "I'd like to believe you Guy, but when you act the way you did yesterday, it's sure not easy."

Russell dropped his gaze to his palsied hands. "To tell you the God's honest truth Bud, I don't know what I did that night. I have these blackouts lately, it's like looking down a dark, empty tunnel and I can't find the light switch."

"Well, we're going to try to remember, Guy. Try to piece together the night that Lina was killed."

"I told you before," Russell said despairingly. "Like I said, there's nothing in the tunnel."

"Well now I want to hear it all again."

Because if the shooter wasn't one of the trio from the hunting camp, and it wasn't Guy Russell then who did do it? He hoped they weren't dealing with some completely untrackable, off the wall crazy.

16

Henry the old redboned hound dog, raised his head from Gary Johnson's front step and thumped his tail. At this third visit, he regarded a man in a police uniform as a pal.

Pete bent to pat the bony old head as Johnson came out.

"He's doing O.K." Johnson said. "Eatin' and all. He misses Guy though, I think. Wants to go home."

He looked accusingly at Pete. "Any idee when that's gonna be?"

Pete straightened up. "Not for awhile. Guy's got big trouble now, there's going to be jail time."

"Geez." Johnson shook his head disgustedly. "There's no harm in Guy, everybody knows that. He's just been so broke up about Lina, can't you guys cut him some slack?"

"Not this time," Pete said. "He crossed the line. Threatening Jane, shooting up a police station. That's dangerous behaviour." He added, deliberately. "A week ago, Guy may have taken a couple of drunken wild shots and caused his wife's death. That's really dangerous behaviour."

He paused, then asked. "Have you ever thought maybe that's why he's so broken up?"

Johnson grimaced and looked for a long moment out at the road. Then asked, "So how much time we talking about?"

Pete shrugged. "That's up to the judge." He looked assessingly at Johnson. "Just to be sure, you said no way Russell could have been out on the road at 5:30 that morning?"

"That's right."

"How can you be so certain when you said you were passed out yourself?."

Johnson's tone was scathing. "I know my friend. Ain't you never had a friend? Guy and me, we've been drinking buddies since high school. That's a lot of beer under the bridge. But you wouldn't know about that, would you, being new around here."

He turned to his door, obviously considering the interview ended.

Pete looked down at Henry. "Are you going to be able to keep looking after the dog?"

"Yeah, sure. But you better explain it to him."

And Johnson closed the door.

* * *

In a laborious, tearful recap from Russell, Halstead hadn't gleaned anything new.

"So, what do you think?" he asked Jakes.

"I wouldn't trust the guy to remember what he did five minutes ago. I hope the judge throws the book at him," he added fervently. "And takes away his firearms permits."

Halstead nodded. "At least he'll be safely out of the way. And it would do him good to dry out for awhile."

"I doubt if he'll stick to it." Pete sounded pretty disgusted.

"He wasn't always this bad," Halstead said, "but the booze has definitely taken hold. And now he's had this terrible loss."

"So has his daughter," Jakes said tightly. "And he's no help to her."

Halstead had noticed this reaction before. He figured that Guy Russell wasn't the only failed parent in Jakes' experience.

"Coming to the Grill for lunch?" he asked. "Gus's pea soup today."

Pete went home for lunch whenever he could, but Halstead knew that Wednesday Ali had the home help to visit. And the guy looked as if he needed a break.

Jakes' facial muscles relaxed. "Sure," he said. "Sounds good."

The Grill was warm and crowded and smelled of pea soup and fried onions. Even without the summer tourists, Gus Jones did well with the Island road crews, rural mail carriers, the staffs from the bank and the police station, and anyone else who just wanted to get out of the house, have a coffee and get the daily news.

Proprietor Jones, grizzle-haired and bulky-armed in a t-shirt and flannel vest, wore a battered Maple Leafs cap that he never took off not matter how badly his favorite team was playing in the season. This year pretty badly. There had been a Missus Jones once, talk amongst the local oldsters was that she was flighty and had run off with a farm equipment salesman.

"How're things?" Halstead asked.

Normally, this time of year there was a big restaurant-sized pickle jar on the counter for bets. The jar was still there, but empty of folded paper ballots.

"Hell, we got nothing to bet on this year," Gus said. "Couldn't put the plywood turkey out because what ice there was melted in January."

For years Gus had parked an old junker car out on the bay ice in front of the motel and folks had bet on when it would fall through. With the advent of new and stricter environmental regulations, he had grudgingly switched to the turkey alternative, a larger than life sized painted gobbler, screwed to a four by eight piece of plywood on a board platform and anchored into the ice.

He had a further complaint. "We had to cancel the polar bear swim, too. No ice to jump through. And then you went and locked up Guy Russell our chief jumper. Bill Benson says we could bet if there's gonna be any more snow this year but I can't find no takers that there *will* be any."

Pete made his way to the quieter table near the back, away from the television set that hung over the bar. Behind the newscaster's face was the now standard footage of a convoy of Canadian APVs rolling along a dusty Afghanistan road. He fervently hoped the next scene wouldn't be the also standard portrait of yet another Canadian soldier casualty in the war. He didn't want to look, he never did, but he couldn't stop himself. The urge to know if one of his former buddies had been killed, was too strong.

Today, thank Christ, there appeared to be no casualties, just the promise of more to come, as the newscaster spoke in sombre plummy tones:

"The Canadian military is taking extra precautions in Afghanistan following terror attacks and riots in response to a mistaken burning of copies of the Qur'an, the Arab holy book. "There is definitely a climate of heightened risk for our troops," says Canadian defense minister, McKay."

No kidding.

There followed the inevitable analysis of what the defense minister had just said. None of the pundits elaborated on the meaning of 'heightened risk'. Everyone knew too well what that meant, more boys coming home to Canada in flag draped caskets. But here was Pete Jakes survivor, bloodied but unbowed. With a gorgeous wife and a baby on the way. He hoped he could make the most of his luck and pass some of it on.

A raucaus ad for a Bonville used car lot came next. He was waiting for the local sports report. Several of the Island kids played on the regional hockey team and they'd been doing pretty well this season. He hoped some of their success was due to his volunteer coaching. He'd played hockey himself as a teenager and thought the game had helped use up a lot of angry energy and kept him out of trouble. Maybe he could do that for some other kids. He'd seen enough of crime and trouble in the world, now he could see that prevention was as important as policing.

He smiled, watching the chief's slow progress across the room. It seemed there was someone at every table who had a greeting, or some request. One reason why in the summer, they often just went to the burger truck and ate lunch in the cruiser. He tried to picture himself years hence, an old guy like Halstead, known to all on the Island and knowing everyone. There were worse fates, much worse. Such as bleeding to death on a desert road half-way across the world.

Halstead settled his long length carefully into the wooden restaurant chair. His back was probably acting up. He glanced briefly up at the television set, then back at Pete, then did the same again. If it didn't seem kind of crazy, Pete would almost have thought the chief was embarrassed, even nervous.

"Mind if I ask you something, lad?"

"Sure, I guess." Now Pete was getting nervous. Was the chief going to chew him out about something?

"Why did you and Ali get married? I mean, I can see that times change, that things are different now than when I first got married thirty years ago. I know that lots of people prefer not to get married. I'm not trying to be nosy, I'm just curious."

Pete looked up at the television, where people were eating some kind of yogurt and dancing in hula skirts. He guessed from things he'd heard, that the chief was talking about himself and Stephanie Bind but he hardly knew what to say. Although he worked with the older man every day and they had gone out for a beer at Christmas, they'd never talked of anything so personal.

"I got married because I knew I couldn't let Ali go," he said finally. "I keep trying to figure out why she married me."

Halstead smiled. "But you would have lived with her anyway?"

"Sure, if that's the way she wanted it. We only had a small wedding anyway. Just us in a registry office."

Halstead looked off up the restaurant aisle but not as if he was really seeing anyone. He seemed kind of blue. Maybe things weren't going well with Stephanie Bind.

Pete added hastily, "But just because that's worked for us, doesn't mean marriage is for everybody." Then, because he wanted to comfort, he went on, "All I know is that when you find that special person, the one and only, then you have to go for it with everything you've got."

Halstead smiled weakly. "Thanks, lad. Here comes our soup."

17

IS IT SAFE TO GO ACROSS THE CAUSEWAY?

*MIDDLE ISLAND SHOOTING STILL A MYSTERY –
POLICE HAVE NO LEADS.*

Halstead tossed the copy of the Bonville Record into his wastebasket and dialled a number.

"Bob Denys," he said curtly.

"Thanks a lot," he said, when the Record editor came on the line. "What kind of a headline is that?"

Denys, a long-time acquaintance and captain of the Bonville old-timers curling team, was unrepentant. "Just keeping the public informed, Bud."

"More like keeping the public scared to death."

"Well, *do* you have any leads?"

"You'll be the last to know."

"No come on, you must have *something*," the editor said. "What about those city slicker hunters? The locals are pretty upset I hear. Want to tar and feather them, or whatever the modern equivalent."

"They've got their licenses," Halstead said. "And swear they were all tucked blamelessly in their beds that morning."

"What about forensic evidence?"

"Can be handy if you've got some, I guess. Unfortunately, our evidence is somewhere out there in that swamp."

Undaunted, Denys persisted.

"What about the husband who shot up the station?"

"He fired a shot – why do you news people have to exaggerate everything?"

To sell papers of course. But Denys didn't bother answering.

"The big question is, did he fire the shot in the swamp? I see you've sent him over here to the jail till his hearing."

"That's right. Maybe you can make a story out of that."

"Yeah, well keep in touch," Denys said sarcastically.

Halstead switched off the phone and kicked out at his desk chair. The chair swivelled mockingly back to face him.

Jane was familiar with these signs of the chief's frustration. "Still nothing from Roger Huma?" she asked sympathetically.

"Nada, dammit. We've got hunters, we've got rifles, we've got shots in the night. But we've got no bullet to track, no concrete proof of anything. "

He gave the chair another shove and glared at the stack of paperwork on the desk, mostly to do with the emergency preparedness report. Desperately, he grabbed up his jacket.

"Hold the fort will you, I've got to get out of here. I'll go on the cottage run, might as well do something useful."

He drove quickly past the town offices, fighting a ridiculous urge to hunch down in his seat to avoid being seen. Pictured Vern charging out the front doorway, "Where is that report?"

Twenty minutes later he pulled up in front of Lakeside Marina. The Petersons' two lab dogs came barking up to the cruiser, tails wagging, to take the threat out of it. He usually enjoyed the weekly swing around the south shore of the island to check out the winter's empty cottage properties and often dropped into the Marina for coffee, half way along the road. Ralph and his wife Edna were always glad of the company. Though they only lived fifteen kilometers from Middle Village, they holed up in winter as if they were in a cabin in the far north.

"It's busy enough in summer," Edna would say. "We get enough of company then. And we've got you to keep us up on the news."

She liked to quilt and Ralph mostly slept. Hibernating he called it. The man must be over seventy by now and Edna was getting up there too.

"It's been a sad winter on the Island," Ralph said. "We felt real bad about Lina Russell. I'm right glad that hunting camp full of cidiots is clear across the Island from us." He patted his dogs, "They'd probably think these fellers were a couple of bears. We wouldn't dare let them out the door."

Edna looked up from her quilt. "That camp should be closed down."

"You should take that up with Vern Byers," Halstead said with satisfying venom. "You could drop in at the council offices next time you go to town for groceries."

Though that would likely be another couple of months off. The Marina freezers were no doubt stocked with enough supplies to last the Petersons through a nuclear meltdown. They probably wouldn't even know about it.

When he left, Halstead waved out the car window to Ralph. "Take care, don't do anything I wouldn t do."

"Shoot, that don't leave me much."

At times Halstead had thought seriously about making an offer to buy the Marina. His own boat, the *Lone Loon* was already stored there on pylons at the the back, along with about a dozen others. Then there was the bait shop, the gas pumps for the boats and a small shop selling fishermen's lures and in the summer, chips and pop.

From the sale of his house, he would have enough money to buy the place and he could manage fine on his policeman's pension. That was how he used to think anyway. Before Steph had come into his life and changed his ideas about everything. He shook the thought out of his head and tried to concentrate on his task. Or surveillance check, as Vern would call it.

There were more and more residences along the shore. Though city folks called them cottages, many of the structures were bigger than the neighbouring original farm houses. There was even a cottagers' association, whatever that meant. What it meant for Halstead was more friction with Vern and the Council. The association had the bright idea of setting up an electronic surveillance system, to be monitored from the police station. Wouldn't Jane love that, a real headache in the making. Halstead's opinion was that the cost of setting up and maintaining the system would probably be more than any small losses from theft.

"How are we going to attract new residents if the police won't provide security for their properties?" Vern asked.

Some security, Halstead had pointed out. What good was it to set up an alarm system in a cottage that was across the island from the police station and only accessible by an unplowed road? The thieves would be long gone before a cruiser turned up.

But as he drove past bare branched fruit trees and empty vegetable stands, he had the feeling the issue wasn't closed yet. Security was the issue of the age. Household security, mall security, and now this major headache of border security. Still, there wasn't much he could do on that front till spring. To everything there is a season, or there used to be anyway. In the Grill yesterday he'd heard that the farmers were already concerned that since there was no snow, there wouldn t be enough moisture on the land in the spring. But then farmers were always concerned about something. At least they weren't worried about security, the family dog took care of that.

At Round Bay he stopped to see the swams. It wasn't uncommon now for Canada geese to overwinter on the Bay but this year there were also about fifty elegant tundra swans. The birds' sleek heads now turned as one to view some activity coming up the deserted stony beach. Not Vern Byers' tormenting vision of a horde of balaclaved terrorists, just the Peterson's friendly labs snuffling along and splashing through the water. They came up to the car, wagging their tails, real tough guys.

He patted the big bony heads, wondering idly how the U.S. military proposed to protect the five thousand mile border between Canada and the United States. Or even his own small bailiwick, two hundred miles of the Lake Ontario north shore. Anti-terrorist nets in the water? A dome over the Island?

And who was he to laugh, he thought ruefully, thinking of that damning headline. *IS IT SAFE TO CROSS THE CAUSEWAY? POLICE HAVE NO LEADS.*

The safety of Middle Island residents was his responsibility and he'd better come up soon with some answers.

Out on the open water, a pair of swans entwined their long necks. A prelude to mating? "Too soon for that," he wanted to warn them.

The birds couldn't read the weather either. Everything was off-kilter in this weird winter. The critters were off their natural game and he was too.

"Off you go fellers," he waved the dogs away. The afternoon felt suddenly colder.

18

There's a certain slant of light on winter afternoons
That oppresses like the heft of cathedral tunes

Ali glared at the mini blood pressure testing kit, now always to hand on the bedside table. On her side, of course. Mr. Cool's blood pressure was just fine. No doubt his cool, calm blood flow had contributed to his success as a soldier under fire. She fidgeted angrily and uselessly with her blameless pillow. She couldn't even give it a good, satisfying punch, it might raise her darn blood pressure!

And it was frightening too. She hated the feeling, always acutely aware of the pumping of her own heart. She felt as if there was a thermometer in her head, the kind you saw in cartoons with a big red bubble at the top about to burst.

One o'clock in the afternoon. On a normal weekday, a teaching day, the children would just be coming back in from lunch recess. She might even be conducting a gym class. Stretching exercises before a run around the gym. *Head and shoulders, knees and toes. My fair lady.*

She looked past the mound of her middle area, searching for her toes. They were down there somewhere. But where was the fair lady? There was no sound from downstairs other than the soft click of clothes in the dryer. Anita, the new homemaker, from a Bonville service had left for the day. A nice enough woman but not a cheerful chatterbox, nor was she as involved in Island life as Lina had been.

Careful, she'd better not think of Lina and add gloom to her already overloaded emotional barometer. It wasn't good for the baby. She scowled at the gray screen of the television. No joy there, if she watched one more episode of that afternoon women's talk show, she'd burst the blood pressure monitor with her readings.

She looked for something, anything to divert her pressure-rising thoughts.

Akantha's boxes! Overcome by lethargy this past week, she'd forgotten all about them. If nothing else, the task might send her to sleep again. Which would be good for the baby anyway.

She moved awkwardly down the stairs, holding tightly to the handrail so as not to trip over Emily. The poor dog was so excited just to see her up and moving. Pete or the homemaker had moved the boxes into the living room and shoved them under the window. The boxes were all taped up, she had to get the scissors to open them.

The first carton, crammed to the top with a stack of yellowing newsprint, seemed too daunting. She sank awkwardly to the carpet and pried open the second box. Under the cardboard flaps, she found a book with a cover of cracked brown leather. A photo album. Inscribed inside the cover in spidery sepia ink was an autograph.

Akantha Samos.

She stopped then, feeling like an intruder, her palms resting on the album.

"What do you think, Emily, are we just a couple of snoops?"

Emily rolled on her back, tail wagging.

"On the other hand, is it right that the woman should be forgotten? That her memories be destroyed and sent to the dump?"

Justification enough. Besides, her curiosity had taken over.

Inside, small black and white pictures were mounted by sharp little corners on the velvety black pages of the book.

Mother and Father was written in the same sepia ink below the first picture. A slim man with a neatly trimmed beard stood behind a woman seated in a chair. She wore her hair piled up high on her head in the style of the times. Neither was smiling, also the style of the times, when having a photo taken was a a fairly rare and important event.

In the second picture, the same unsmiling woman was holding a baby, the froth of a long white christening gown pouring over her arm.

Akantha Samos. June 2nd, 1922. So Akantha was in her eighties when she died in her Island cottage.

The gown had been made use of again, three years later.

Adelpha Samos, December 10, 1925. The sister she had mentioned to Lina.

There were more photos taken through the years, each with a short caption written underneath, such as:

Christmas outfits. The two little girls, at about seven and four, in matching fur coats and bunny trimmed fur hats.

At the beach. The girls, maybe twelve and nine, in cumbersome bathing suits and snug-fitting caps. Ali thought she recognized the spot as one of the Island's more well-known beaches.

High School graduation. Our trip to New York. Nana and Grandfather.

Interspersed between the family pictures were various newspaper clippings.

Ali wedged herself against the baseboard and began to read.

*   *   *

That night when Pete came home, Ali was setting the table.

She met him with a beer and a wide smile. "Come and sit with me," she patted the couch. "I've had an interesting afternoon with the Samos family and I'll tell you all about it."

He would have listened to her read the back of a cereal box. He was just so pleased to see the return of a sparkle to her eyes.

"I've made a bit of a mess," she laughed. "The homemaker will have a fit." The contents of the box were spread about the couch and coffee table.

He wouldn't have cared if the stuff was piled up to the ceiling, if the house had looked like the old lady's cottage. That sparkle was worth it.

"None of it is in any particular order," she explained. "I'm having to work my way down through the layers. But I think I've come up with a sort of basic overview of the early years."

She moved to a small stack of papers, and chose a clipping. "Apparently Akantha's father, Pitr Samos – was an ambitious fellow. Listen to this article from MacLean's Magazine in 1960.

From Busboy to Theatre Owner
Pitr Samos sells independent theatres to Megaplex Cinemas.
A Classic Rags to Riches Story.

Samos came to Canada as a poor Greek youth in 1920, with little more than the clothes he stood up in. He worked as a busboy in his uncle's diner and within a year was able to bring his young wife Ariadne to join him. When his uncle was invalided by a heart attack, Pitr took over managing the diner. Ariadne helped too, as well as looking after their growing family, two young daughters – Akantha and Adelpha. The couple made a living for themselves and Uncle and Aunt which would have satisfied some, but not Pitr Samos.

He listened to the working class patrons of the diner and heard the yearning in their voices when they spoke of not being able to afford to go to the big uptown movie theatres. They also felt they had no clothes to wear to these 'fancy' places.

Pitr rented some upstairs space in a nearby warehouse and a second hand projector and began to show movies on a curtain to his fellow expatriates. He charged a nickle to get in and another nickle for popcorn which Ariadne made at the diner. Just like the fancy uptown theatres.

At first he made no profit. But his patrons told others and the audience grew. He ordered Greek movies from Greece and showed them once a week as well.

When the opportunity came to purchase a bankrupt theatre, Pitr knew the move he had to make. He invited the bank manager to attend the packed Saturday night showing at his warehouse theatre and convinced the man to lend him the mortgage money.

Eventually Pitr Samos owned and operated an independent chain of three movie theatres in Southern Ontario. Turning seventy, he decided to accept the Megaplex Cinema offer for his theatres and retire. But he still eats his breakfast every morning at the diner where he began his ascent to success.

"And the family owned a place on the Island?" Pete asked.

Ali picked out the picture of the sisters at the beach. "They had a summer place here for a few years when the girls were very young in the 1930s. It was probably that memory that drew Akantha back here."

"There were just the two girls?"

She frowned. "I think there might have been a miscarriage of a son in between. But look at some of these framed pictures, they're marvellous. Here's one of Adelpha's wedding in 1950. Very fancy. The cake is six tiers high. "

She put the picture carefully down on the table.

"I haven't found any pictures of an Akantha wedding though, and when she died she still had her maiden name, though of course she could have reverted to it. But I did find out that through her twenties, Akantha was a champion swimmer. Here's a picture of her with her team in Toronto. She's the one holding up the award cup."

The old photo showed a dozen young women in the plain serge bathing suits of the times and white caps. Akantha Samos was tall, lean and shyly smiling.

"She was supposed to be on the Olympic women's swim team in 1943," Ali said, "but the Olympics were cancelled because of the war. She didn't try again later, maybe she felt she had missed her peak."

Pete turned from the stove, balancing two plates loaded with microwaved chicken lasagne and the salad bowls.

"So the old man was a success. Quite a story."

"I found his obituary printed in Canadian Business Week. It was estimated that Pitr left an estate to his wife and daughters of close to a million dollars."

Pete whistled, "That's a nice piece of change." He sneaked Emily a piece of chicken when Ali looked back at the clipping. "How did our Island Samos lady end up so broke then. Did her sister do her out of her share?"

"I doubt it, they seemed very close all their lives. I guess they just gradually used the money up over the years."

"But a million dollars," he said sceptically. "And back then, it was worth even more. If they'd had proper investment advice, they could have managed comfortably if they lived to be a hundred." He ignored Emily's beseeching gaze. *Not now girl, Ali's watching.*

"Maybe they didn't have Pop Samos' business sense. The sister's story was even worse. Adelpha died about fifteen years ago. She hadn't been out of her house in ages, but one day a neighbour got worried and called the police. Apparently she was pretty well out of it. The authorities eventually found her a place in a nursing home but she died after only a few months,"

Pete shook his head sympathetically and raised his glass. "Never fear, my love. When we get to that stage, we'll get a double room at the Rowan Tree Retirement Home and spend happy days playing pingpong and bingo."

She smiled. "And that will suit me just fine."

At bed time, Ali placed one of the framed pictures of the two young Samos women on the dresser.

"You don't mind, do you?" she asked Pete. "I've been thinking of them all day and it's such a lovely picture. They look about twenty here, two young women on the threshold of life. They feel like my aunts."

A substitute for her own. She knew that there must be aunts and uncles and cousins somewhere in the world but she had never met them. Ali was the sole issue of a mismatched marriage between an ardent Turkish feminist and a bookish American professor, and had spent most of her childhood at boarding schools.

Her mother Nuran refused to use the term 'broken home'. "A fixed home is more apt," she said. "We had a problem and we fixed it."

Ali guessed that was one way to look at it.

Pete looked up from his copy of the emergency preparedness manual he was diligently studying. "Look at that car behind them, that's an early Lincoln. Pop Samos must have spent a good buck on that beauty."

He turned out the light on his side and leaned back against the pillows.

Ali was still looking at the picture. "So what's your guess, mister policeman," she asked. "As a student of human vices?"

"What's my guess about what?"

She punched his arm. "About how the old ladies lost all their money, of course. Gambling? Booze? Ill-advised investments? Wastrel husbands?"

He yawned. "Maybe our old lady gave it all to the humane society. She was obviously fond of her kitties."

Ali settled back against the pillows. "They didn't spend it on wastrel children anyway. Akantha never married and I haven't come upon any record of Adelpha and her husband having kids. Maybe Akantha was a secret miser," she said. "And she'd hidden some of her fortune away."

"You mean in these boxes? I doubt it. She was cashing her government old age cheques every month. Presumably she needed them."

"No mysterious secret bulging bank accounts? No stacks of bills in the mattress?

He grimaced. "You don't want to know what was in that mattress." He kissed her shoulder. "Nighty night my love. I'm pooped."

But Ali was still puzzling as she fell asleep. She would tackle another box tomorrow. Who knew what treasures she might find in her search? Perhaps a packet of yellowing stock certificates from a defunct gold mine. Or a musty stack of Canadian government bonds. Improbable, but you never knew.

It was good to feel a sense of anticipation again.

19

Pete drove past Turkey Woods, his spirits high. He'd left Ali ensconced on the couch, sifting happily through a pile of newspaper clippings. Beside him in the cruiser, Nick blew into his latest hunting gadget, a turkey locator. *Bluart, bluart.*

"Do you think that sounds like a girl turkey? It's supposed to attract the Toms."

"Yeah, you sound just like a love-starved hen," Pete said drily. "I'm sure the fellows will come running – or gobbling, or whatever."

"It's Old Tom I'm after," Nick said. "I've been studying up and I've ordered all the best gear from the Net. Should be here at the post office soon."

Pete thought of the big, strong gobbler he'd met in the woods. Said drily, "I'm sure the old guy is shaking in his feathers."

Nick ignored this and blew the gadget again, then showed Pete a loaf-shaped, plastic-wrapped parcel. "This is for you and your wife. It's a banana bread."

Pete's brows raised. "You've been baking?"

Nick scowled. "Yeah sure. No, it's from Jane. She thinks I'm starving or something. Ever since I took down Russell at the station, she's been bringing me food."

Pete looked at the parcel. "I bet it's good."

"You've got to help me," Nick pleaded. "I've got another one in my room. Plus about six dozen cookies. Last week she made me a whole pie."

Pete laughed. "So, enjoy."

"It gets worse," Nick said. "I had to stop her from sending a thank you letter to the newspaper. Then she wanted the chief to send in my name for a citation for bravery or something, even though I explained to her I was just doing my job."

"Well you are brave, tackling a drunk with a rifle. If I were you, I'd take all of the banana bread and glory you can get. Except for this one of course. Unwrap it and give me a piece."

Nick slouched down in the seat. "Oh thanks, you're a big help. This is going to be a great day all around. The chief was grouchy as hell this morning, too."

"He's got a lot on his mind," Pete said. "He knew the woman who died, and her whole family. It's not like investigating just another shooting of a Jane Doe in the city. He feels personally responsible for looking after the folks on the Island."

Nick shrugged. "The chief has to look at things more practically. We're never going to find a bullet in that swamp, so it looks like a case closed to me. Cops shouldn't have to be magicians."

Or have to carry out boring emergency exercises, apparently. Nick was openly scornful about the coming drill at the Rowan Tree home. Like Pete and any other police officer in training, he had taken the all-day course at the police college. Tabletop drills, they were called. Eight hours of a mock incident scenario that wasn't revealed until the morning of the drill. A flood, a hurricane, an earthquake were some of the possible scenarios. Nick had been happy to get a bioterrorism incident.

"Training which I will never get to use here," he bemoaned. "We've got no trains, so we won't get a derailment. And we're unlikely to get a chemical spill on the Island."

Unless one of Black's septic tank removal trucks has a rollover, Pete thought. Now there would be a disaster!

But he doubted Nick would appreciate the joke. Not with the morning he had to face, wheeling some feeble old folks out of a nursing home dining room. At least at yesterday's evacuation drill at the primary school, the kids had been lively, keen and interested in getting out of class for a few minutes. And they liked the handouts of the emergency kits stocked with bottles of water and granola bars.

"What are we guarding against here," Nick asked plaintively. "A diaper accident?"

Actually, Pete wasn't fond of the emergency training drills either. They reminded him too much of his army postings such as Afghanistan where danger was always on the horizon. And a tragedy such as Lina Russell's death seemed to make a mockery of any kind of preparedness. No amount of bottled water or first aid kits would have helped her. How could anyone prepare against the random recklessness of fate?

He acknowledged too, that the language might seem ridiculous when applied to peace-time conditions. Terms such as *command post, incident command system, emergency response consultant, communications headquarters, evacuation co-ordinator,* hardly seemed to apply to this morning's drill for instance.

But there were millions of people in the world who could tell Nick Poitras a thing or two about how fast peace-time could change to war-time. Before you knew it, before you knew what was happening. And these internationally recognized terms were often crucial to the survival of thousands of people.

At the Rowan Tree, Pete parked the cruiser and he and Nick mounted the steps of the porch. The door opened into a square hallway with a black and white tile floor. On a polished side table sat a tall glass vase full of pink silk flowers. From a side door that seemed to open into a common room, came the booming sound of a television set. From another door, a restaurant-type clatter of cutlery and chinaware.

There was no information desk or greeter. *Where to?* Nick asked with his eyebrows. Pete poked his head round the door of the common room. The couches and chairs seemed empty except for a tiny white-haired woman standing beside a large bird cage in one of the corners of the room. On closer look, he could see that she seemed to be struggling with the cage door catch. He could see that she carried a lettuce leaf in one hand and was swearing steadily as she struggled. Far back in the cage, two little yellow birds huddled nervously against the bars.

Nick suppressed a laugh as Pete asked, "Good morning ma'am. Can I help?"

The woman turned a round little face, pink as a candy apple, up at him. "I sure wish somebody would. This damn door always sticks!"

"I'll open it," he said. "Then you can put in the lettuce."

He unhooked the door while she reached in with palsied hand to deposit the leaf. If the birds were grateful, they didn't show it. He wondered if they had to suffer the excruciating ritual daily.

The woman tottered off towards the couch with no word of thanks. "Ma'am," he called, following her. "Can you tell me where we can find Mr. Guardian? We're policemen," he added, as she eyed him dubiously. He wondered if she suffered from Alzeimer's, she seemed to have already forgotten him.

Instead, she answered him with brisk and avid curiosity. "Why do you want Doug? What's he done?" She screwed up her face knowledgeably and said with juicy emphasis. "*Men.* I was married to one of them. You never know what they're going to get up to. Drinking, marrying women half their age."

The policemen shifted their feet, guilty by association. She tired suddenly, slipped down into the couch and closed her eyes. Slipping back into that weird world the very aged inhabit. Literally a twilight zone, with only brief forays back out.

They found Doug Guardian in the dining room. He rose immediately from a table where he was breakfasting with some of the older residents. Tanned and buff, he looked like a virtual superman in these surroundings. Or superman's dad at any rate.

"Come on down to the staff room," Guardian said. "Dawn's there, briefing the employees. She pretty well oversees every detail of running this place. She's a wonder, could have captained the Queen Mary."

He led them down a corridor, proudly pointing out the amenities of the home.

"You've seen the cafeteria. There's also a more private room where residents can invite guests to dinner or a birthday celebration. The exercise equipment is in here, next to the staff room."

Guardian' s big toothy face lit up at sight of his wife. Today Dawn Guardian was dressed in well-fitting jeans and a white blouse, but she was hardly the stereotypical bimbo the old lady had implied. The Guardians seemed to cultivate a healthy, casual look, with clothes appropriate to hop into a Maserati car or a yacht. But there was no doubt that Dawn was the boss of the workers in the room. She had a natural, if rather tense, air of authority. Now she turned from conversation with a woman pushing a cleaning cart, reluctantly shifting her attention to the policemen.

She couldn't conceal her impatience. "How long is this going to take?"

"Now darling," her husband soothed. "The officers are just doing their job. The emergency drill is important."

"You'll have to forgive Dawn," he explained to Pete later in the corridor. "She's such a perfectionist and ever since she was nominated for that Businesswoman of the Year award, she's been trying to make this place absolutely perfect for the committee's visit. Plus of course, we're all upset about Lina Russell's death. Lina came once a week to do foot massages and was very popular with our residents. We took several of them to the funeral."

The next two hours were busy. There were fire alarms and smoke detectors to check in the individual residents' rooms, which Pete noticed were comfortably carpeted, well lit and cheerful with flowers and framed family photos. He was glad to see that Nick was polite and respectful to the old folks. And most of the elderly ladies seemed quite aflutter at the attentions of two young stalwart officers.

Next they reviewed staff knowledge of entrances and exits, locations of fire extinguishers and smoke alarms, cell phones and emergency connections to call police, fire and ambulances. All the permanent staff members had up-to-date first aid certificates.

But the evacuation drill loomed. Even though the staff had been explaining the procedure to the residents for the past week, there was still much confusion. Pete saw that several residents were using walkers and there was at least one wheelchair. Most were wearing some kind of jersey sweatsuit. They shuffled down the hallway towards him like a pack of ancient zombies.

Doug Guardian approached Pete and said in a low voice, "I hope you're not expecting us to put these old folks out into the cold of the front porch. Unless you and your partner want to help us wrestle them into overcoats and scarves."

"Just get them down to the front lobby," Pete agreed. "I have to time how long it takes."

He checked his watch, then noticed the pink faced lady scuttling back into the common room. "We can't leave the birdies behind," she called in a quavering voice.

Pete nodded at Nick who came back a minute later, birdcage grabbed up in one hand, old lady in the other. They finally managed to herd everybody into the lobby. The old folks were like a bunch of dazed, bewildered birds themselves, Pete thought, like a flock of sparrows that had crashed into a plate glass window. The evacuation had taken forty-five minutes. He hoped they never had to put a real one into play.

"I'll write this up," he told Nick, when Dawn Guardian and her staff had left to guide their twittering flock back to the safety of their rooms." "You can go out back and check the generator, and see that there's extra gas for the vehicles. There's the residence van and the Guardian's two snowmobiles."

He was just about finished with the report when Nick returned, his face flushed as if he'd been hurrying. "Look what I found out there," he said, breathing heavily and holding up his arm.

A rifle.

Pete grabbed it. The gun was wet and the barrel packed with mud.

"Where did that come from?" demanded Guardian.

"The handyman was showing me the generator," Nick gasped. "Then he noticed that the cover on the old well behind the garage, wasn't tight. When we checked it out, we found the gun."

Pete turned to Guardian, "Do you recognize this gun, do you have any idea who it belongs to?"

Guardian nodded solemnly. "I think it belongs to me."

Guardian led them to a storage area in the basement. The big man was moving quickly, talking as he went.

"I haven't used that gun in years. I don't hunt anymore, so I just unloaded it and put it away down here."

"Locked up?" Pete asked.

In answer, Guardian pushed open the door of a small storeroom and led the way to a shallow wooden cupboard attached to the wall. He brought out a key ring and began shuffling through it.

"Look," Pete pointed to some scratch marks in the wood, next to the metal hinges. "Somebody took the hinges off this door, then replaced them."

Guardian had found the key. He opened the cupboard door to reveal an empty slot in a two gun rack and a couple of boxes of .22 ammunition.

"That's my father's old .12 gauge shotgun," he said. He nodded at the gun that Pete held. "The rifle belonged to my dad too. Like I said, I haven't used either gun since I came back here, I only kept them out of sentiment. They were moved in here about two years ago, when we did some renovations."

"Who had access to this storeroom?" Pete asked. "Is it always open?"

Guardian shrugged helplessly. "I think so." He looked around. "There's nothing much in here. The cleaning staff keep all their equipment in another room down the hall. And of course none of our residents would ever have any reason to come down here."

"Do you have any idea who might have stolen the rifle?"

"I can't imagine. If one of my employees wanted it for her husband or her kid, I would have probably given it to them."

Pete hefted the gun in his hand. "We'll have to question your staff and I'll need the shift schedules for the past three weeks."

"Do you really have to do all that?" Guardian asked. "The emergency drill has upset our residents enough for this week. I didn't even know the gun was gone and now it's back. I won't press any charges."

"No but we might want to," Pete said. "As you know, somebody with a rifle took a shot at Lina Russell recently and caused a fatal accident."

The manager looked horrified. "You're saying this rifle might have been used to shoot at Lina Russell? I sincerely doubt that. The gun could have been taken at any time in the last two years."

"I'm sorry Mr. Guardian. I'm not implying anything, I'm just saying we have to check it out."

Guardian seemed utterly bewildered. He backed away a step and looked with distaste at the gun. "Of course, Officer Jakes, take the rifle with you. It hasn't been here, anyway. Apparently it's been down in the well."

*   *   *

Halstead had asked Doug Guardian to come in to the station and make a report of the gun theft.

"Less interruption, here," he said.

The manager of the Rowan Tree Home didn't seem his usual healthy self this morning. Overnight, his tan seemed to have faded, and his sporty blazer to hang more loosely from his shoulders. Without the brimming glow of his bonhomie, he seemed strangely shrunken. He looked seventy instead of sixty.

Halstead was surprised and wondered if the man was ill.

"Sit, Doug," he said, not unsympathetically. "Let's just go over this form. I gather from Officer Jakes that you're not sure when the gun might have been taken."

Guardian shook his head. "As I told your officer, it could have been any time within the past two years."

Halstead looked over the work shedules Guardian had brought with him. "Have all of these employees been with you at least two years?"

"All the full-time staff, and most of them much longer. Then there are a couple of co-op students from the high school who come in one morning a week. Jenny Pape the hairdresser, and poor Lina of course who ran the foot clinic . . . ." he stopped.

Halstead nodded, as he flipped through the pages. He recognized most of the names. If not the actual person, he knew the family. "Who are the people on this sheet?" he asked. "They don't seem to be staff."

Guardian passed a hand wearily across his forehead. Was it shaking?

"Regular delivery people, handymen, the plumber, etc." He managed a weak smile of pride. "My wife is very thorough in everything she does. She thought you might need that information."

Halstead wrote for a moment on the report form, then passed it over to Doug for signing.

Guardian hesitated. "Are you sure I have to do this, Bud? The gun's back. I'll get rid of it and the shotgun, donate them to a gun club or something. I'll pay the fine for improperly securing them. I'll pay it right now."

Halstead shook his head. "Sorry Doug. Besides, it's not just me. Two of my officers are aware of the situation."

Guardian looked bleak. "It's not for me. I'm just concerned about how this kind of mess might affect Dawn's chances to win the Business Woman of the Year award. She's such a perfectionist and she's worked so hard for this. She lost both parents a couple of years ago and she's poured her grief into Rowan Tree Homes."

Halstead patted him on the shoulder. "A theft at the premises shouldn't affect the committee's decision, Doug. Problems happen in business all the time. It's not as if you've lost one of the patients."

But Guardian didn't even notice the joke.

He got heavily to his feet. "I guess your officers will be out at the Rowan Tree again."

"Likely," Halstead agreed.

*   *   *

An hour later, Halstead yawned widely and looked across his desk at Jakes. The space between them was littered with the staff work sheet schedules from the Rowan Tree.

Halstead re-stated the obvious. "It would be a big help if Doug had some idea when the gun was taken."

Without that handy little piece of information, they were just basically searching for another needle in a haystack, he thought. Chasing that wild goose, or fishing for a bullet in a swamp, pick your cliché. Jakes studied another worksheet, though they'd already looked over the whole kit and kaboodle twice.

Halstead sighed, "Well there's one charge at least. Those guns weren't properly secured. Anybody who worked at the place in the last two years would probably have had a chance to get at that cupboard. And we'll be able to find out whether the gun was fired recently. Roger Huma should be able to tell us that at least."

Jakes dropped the sheet and scraped back his chair. He looked frustrated and no wonder. "There's got to be more to this," he said. "It's just too much of a coincidence. We're looking at rifles and now we've found one hidden in a well."

"There's rifles all over the Island. Too many of them." Halstead scowled. "Too many guns in the whole damn country."

Pete added nothing to this rhetorical rant. He agreed with it, most policemen agreed with it.

Halstead went on, "Some workman or handyman must have lifted it. There's always people working out at the Home."

"And then tossed it in the well, a perfectly valuable gun? Why would they bother stealing it in the first place?"

Halstead spun his chair, looked gloomily at the wall, at the picture of *The Lone Loon*. The peace of a lazy day fishing on the bay was still months away.

"So what are you saying? That the gun wasn't stolen, that Doug is lying? He admitted right away that it was his gun."

"Maybe he was just being smart," Jakes said. "He knew we'd find out soon enough."

"And just why would he be lying? Why would he throw away his own gun?"

Jakes got up and paced over to the window. He turned and said excitedly,

"Because it might *incriminate* him. He was pretty mad about how those hunter guys upset his wife."

Halstead sat up so suddenly in his chair that it creaked in protest. "So, what are you saying here, that maybe *Doug* used the gun himself. That he got so fed up, he turned vigilante and went out after the cidiots?"

"Yes," Jakes said eagerly. "It could have happened that way. Maybe he thought he saw them by the road. Maybe he *did* see them, or that Boone guy at least. He's pretty hard to miss, he could have been out prowling around."

Halstead shook his head. "And when Doug realized that he'd shot at Lina Russell, he ran home and tossed the gun in the well? I don't know, that's a pretty terrible thing to think."

"What else do we have?" Jakes asked. "We're not getting anywhere with the Snake Point crew. And not even Guy Russell knows what Guy Russell was doing that morning."

"I don't know," Halstead said again. "Jeezus."

Jakes just kept on looking at him.

Halstead drew in a breath. "O.K," he conceded. "Keep that possibility in mind when you're out at the Rowan Tree. But for god's sake, keep it to yourself."

He watched Jakes leave on his task, his own thoughts reluctant. Homicide detection wasn't his strength, he probably hadn't handled more than a half dozen cases over the past twenty years. And most of those were manslaughter, the result of erupting tempers and alcohol. Pretty much open and shut cases.

Maybe he'd been on the Island too long though, when his first instinct was to push away any thought that Doug Guardian had caused Lina's accident. Maybe it was a mistake for any cop to stay in his own community, where he would likely know either victim or suspects and quite likely both. That made it difficult to maintain an objective distance from tragic events.

He hoped he never reached a time when his protective instincts threatened to overcome his judgement. Because there was a good side too, to being a local cop, a familiar and trusted symbol of authority and safety. A vital part of the community. Still, you could get burnt out eventually. He wondered whether young Jakes would be affected by the same circumstances down the road if he too, became an Island local, a fixture.

His gaze rested again on the photo of his boat.

Is that what *he* was, a fixture?

At least a fixture was an identity of some sort. Better than being retired and off the radar altogether. Once, he had idly googled the word and scared himself.

Retirement: withdrawal, retreat, regression, abandonment, solitude, resignation.

Not much joy there.

Was that it? To chug along for the few remaining years, till he became a black-edged card on the post office notice board.

William (Bud) Halstead. Widower, Owner of Marina Bait Shop, formerly Middle Island chief of police.

No point in rushing it. He rose to his feet. To hell with the dictionary.

21

P op would have made a good teacher, he said.
But he never got his degree.

Not like a temperature degree, he said. It's a paper that says you've passed the test to be a teacher.

At least I can teach you to be smart, smarter than the rest of them out there.

That's one thing I can do for you.

That's the only thing I can do for you.

Because after I go, and it won't be much longer with this AIDS thing I've got, you won't have anybody but yourself to count on.

So remember this, rule no 1. You don't have enough money, other people have too much. Who's the crook here? If you have to take some of their money, you're just doing what you gotta do to survive.

After pop died, life was just different stops in a long tunnel of hell.

The agency called the stops 'placements'. In one, there was a deer head mounted on the wall of the living room. Not just the antlers, the entire head. The hide was chafed and bare in spots and the eyes were a dreadful sort of purplish glass. Dull and lifeless. Dead. There were other horrors too. A fox with a skinned back, tortured mouth. A hawk caught and stuffed, wing outstretched in a in a horrible imitation of flight.

That place was the worst of all the placements. But they were all bad and after enough of them, you lost count. You just stood at the new door with your suitcase, quivering. Like a rabbit, hesitating on the edge of a thorny thicket. It looked safe, but how to be sure?

Sometimes there were books. The best books were the ones about other kids who had horrible lives but in the end got their revenge. Kids with powers to beat the adults. Now, there was something to dream about.

But the dreams never lasted. For it was never safe. The pursuers would get you eventually and change you into a dead, stuffed thing with blank glass eyes.

You were the hunter or the hunted. It was always the same.

Only money could buy you freedom, could make you safe.

22

The seniors' scamming plague had reached even Middle Island. Yesterday, the bank had received five complaints about fraudulent telephone calls. The caller would claim to be a bank employee trying to correct an error involving an unauthorized withdrawal from the person's account. They just needed the person's permission and pin number to go into the account and correct the mistake.

"Oh sure," Jane said. "Then the scammer makes a quick trip to the ATM machine and makes a withdrawal. How do these crooks even know where the person banks?"

Halstead smiled sourly. "They probably get the info from the Net. Criminals should pay a special users fee. The Net's been a godsend to crime."

He shuffled through the week's bulletins. "Here's one to make you lose any faith in humanity. The sleaziest one yet. The con artist even sold the old guy's house out from him."

"Did they catch the rat?"

"Not yet, but the old man's family have taken the bank that held the mortgage to court. They say that the bank's at fault, that bank staff should red flag seniors who are making sudden and major changes in their assets."

"Maybe they should."

"You'd think. But if the person is adamant, right now they can't do much. There's talk of calling for a review of the policy, requiring that the bank call a relative, or send them home for a 24 hour cooling off period. But for now, it's perfectly legal to steal an elderly person's money, even their home."

"Legal maybe," Jane said. "But morally just downright rotten."

Nick, passing through to rinse out his cup, snorted in disgust. "I can't believe the old guy fell for a con job like that."

"You don't know what it's like to be old," Jane said. "These victims are generally widowed, lonely, living on their own. They don't see many other people, if any. That's why the crooks single them out. And the crooks are smart and know what they're doing. They worm their way into the old person's confidence. It's one of the meanest crimes, if you ask me."

Halstead dropped the sheet back on the pile. "Statistics estimate that only one in a thousand victims of fraud report it."

"You mean they just let the bad guys get away with it?" Nick asked. "That's even dumber."

"They're ashamed," Halstead said. "Old people especially are afraid they'll be thought incompetent and have to be put in a home. And some of them are so gaga they barely know what's happened. They never knew what they were signing."

Jane rolled her eyes. "Ah, humanity, aren't we wonderful. Makes me think at times that I wouldn't mind joining another species."

Halstead was sceptical. "Who would take us?"

"Seen this?" Jane asked, after Nick left. "Might be of interest," she added slyly. "There's a nice picture of Stephanie Bind."

Then she sashayed out of the office. So much for his efforts at discretion. It was the *Bonville Record's* special weekend supplement profiling the candidates for the Eastern Ontario Business Woman of the Year. The article Steph had been talking about.

There were twelve nominations in all, with two nominees from Middle Island. Stephanie Bind, whose YourPlace Retreat had just been awarded four stars in *Medea, Ontario Professional Womens Magazine*. And Dawn Guardian, whose Rowan Tree Seniors Homes had attracted the notice of a chain of American seniors' residences.

Other nominees from the eastern end of the province included several real estate representatives, the owner of a health food store, and a woman who had successfully used the internet to promote her line of desserts for diabetics. Apparently the products had gone viral. There was also a clothing designer, whose dress had recently been purchased and worn by one of the English princesses at a royal benefit.

He skipped to the individual profiles.

Stephanie Bind, 48. Steph's photo was from last fall and showed her standing in her garden looking out over the lake. She wore black pants and a red sweater that looked terrific with her chicly cut hair, all black save for that lightning streak of white.

"Born and bred on Middle Island, Ms. Bind is divorced, and the mother of a teenaged daughter. She and her former husband operated a motel on the outskirts of Bonville, for twenty years."

This was followed by a description of the Retreat, mostly cribbed from Steph's own brochure. *Beautifully appointed rooms overlooking picturesque bay, populated with overwintering swans. Poetry appreciation weekends, yoga classes, masseuse available by appointment, sessions with local women's drumming group.*

The piece concluded with, 'One of the charms of the Retreat is the pleasure of making the acquaintance of the ebullient Ms. Bind.'

You got that right, reporter.

Dawn Guardian, 42. Dawn had chosen a professional studio shot, as opposed to Steph's more casual look. She was also an attractive woman, like a skiier he thought, or some other type of winter athlete. Short, blonde hair, the smile a bit marred for his taste by the terse jawline.

"Rowan Tree Homes has become a front-runner choice for retirement living in Eastern Ontario. Chiefly due to the efforts of Ms. Guardian who co-owns the homes with her husband Doug (he's her biggest fan!)

"I haven't done much but play golf these past years," Doug says. "Dawn has overseen everything to do with the business."

Dawn hails from British Columbia where her parents ran a fishing camp on the coast. "We never had much money," she says, "just a whole lot of fun. We had nature on our doorstep and our home wasn't much bigger than any of the fishing cabins we rented out." She laughs, "I think I got my organizational skills from my mother. She was one fantastic short-order cook and she did it all in a very small space." Both parents are now deceased and she has one brother.

The Guardians were recently approached by the American Royale Retirement organization who are interested in buying the two Rowan Tree homes but keeping them under the Guardian management. With an aging population, the retirement home business is fast growing.

"We're not selling at this time though," Dawn Guardian says, "We like the smaller, more intimate atmosphere that we can provide for our residents."

Jane sniffed. "That's not quite what I heard from my sister. She runs the cafeteria out at the Rowan Tree, you know."

Halstead knew. Jane's family network infiltrated the entire island. He sometimes wondered whether Jane's husband Barry Carrell, a long distance truck driver, actually welcomed the four-day breaks from his own home where Jane's sisters, nieces and nephews were constantly popping in and out.

"Marie says that Doug isn't interested in expanding, that he wants to retire. She says that Dawn is the one who'd like to move up."

"No doubt the Guardians will work it out," Halstead said mildly. As a general policy, he found it best not to fan the flames of gossip. Not that he was above using it of course in his job. He thought of Jakes' recent nutty theory of the rifle in the well and if true, how Doug would work that out with his wife. But there must be another rational explanation.

"Have you seen the Royale Retirement brochure, chief?" Jane asked. "Listen to this."

Library, laundry. Heated swimming pool, movie theatre, guest speakers, in-house financial services. Supervised bus trips to the city, games lounge, screened outdoor courtyard, state of the art security.

"Wow! I'm ready to move in there now." She tossed the brochure in her waste basket. "But I guess I've got another few years of working for Halstead the slave driver before I can think of retiring."

Halstead looked again at Steph's picture. He should ask her for a copy to frame. Some company for when he came home alone at night.

* * *

"So what have you got?" he asked when Jakes came in, welcoming the diversion.

Pete dumped the Rowan Tree worksheets unceremoniously on the desk.

"We've questioned everyone currently working at the home. Most of the staff have been there longer than two years and are all well known to each other. Several of them mentioned this Curt guy, a handyman who worked there last summer but has supposedly gone out west. We visited his mother and she says she hasn't heard from him for a couple of months. So, even if he did steal the gun, I can't find any evidence that he was around here at the time Lina was shot at."

"Then it wasn't him," Halstead said. "Have a look at this. Roger Huma faxed it over to me a half hour ago." He pushed the sheet of paper across the desk.

Pete read and made a low whistle of appreciation.

Howdy chief:
I can't tell you when the gun was last fired, but I can tell you that someone has cleaned the barrel sometime in the last few months.

He glanced at Halstead. "Huma can't get it any closer than that?"

"No, it just means there's cleaning oil in the barrel. Could be from anytime in the last while."

"But it does mean that rifle hasn't been in that well for two years or anything like it."

"So we go over these work sheets again," Halstead said unhappily. "Who has legitimate access to the basement room where Doug kept the guns?"

Pete pointed to the top sheet of the report. "There are four cleaning staff who go back and forth in the hallway to get equipment. It would be odd for other staff to go down there but not totally out of the question, say if they wanted to find a cleaner for an emergency spill. Then there are various maintenance men, furnace inspection, things like that."

"Sounds like a busy hallway."

"Yep. It would be pretty difficult for a thief to find a quiet moment to duck into that storeroom. And even harder to find the time to dismantle the hinges of the gun cupboard. Then there would be the problem of sneaking the gun out."

"What about at night? – presumably it's quieter then."

Pete nodded. "Less opportunity though for a workman or stranger. There are the Guardians themselves, whose private quarters are on the second floor in the original part of the house. But of course they can go anywhere they want to. And then one staff member stays overnight in a spare bedroom, in case any of the residents rings for assistance. The overnight shift is on a rotation basis, it's all there in the schedule."

"But a staff member could have stolen the gun then. It's possible anyway."

Pete looked unconvinced. "You have to ask why anyone would go to all that trouble with the hinges, when you can buy a rifle over in Bonville at the Canadian Tire store any day of the week."

"Save $300 bucks," Halstead pointed out. "Or more."

"But you'd get a new one. This gun was thirty years old."

"It was still a gun, still worked."

Pete pushed his chair back and indicated the schedule sheets. "You know these people much better than I do. Can you pick a thief out of them?"

Halstead turned a page or two. He did know them, or at least their families. A couple of them had teenaged boys.

"It could be another robbery prank. Some kids fooling around."

Pete shook his head. "Staff would have noticed them. Anyone under ninety would stick out like a sore thumb in that place."

Halstead smiled briefly. "O.K., I'm pretty sure I know where you're going with this. But, spell it out for me."

Jakes hesitated, then leaned forward. "I think I was right, that Doug Guardian unscrewed those cupboard hinges himself and made up the story about the gun being stolen because he caused the accident that killed Lina Russell."

Halstead let out a tense breath, even though he'd known what was coming.

"The man looks like hell," Jakes continued. "Several of the staff members mentioned it when I was talking to them. They say he hasn't been the same man since the incident."

There flashed before Halstead's eyes a picture of Guardian in the chair where Jakes sat now. Begging Halstead not to go ahead with investigating the theft of the gun. Frantic about how an investigation would affect his wife's chances at the Business Women's award.

"I don't like it," he stalled. "That's not a lot to go on."

"If you don't mind my asking," Jakes said. "How well do you know the guy?"

Halstead considered, thinking and not for the first time, that the past was getting a bit fainter every year. Like a fading photograph.

"We were both on the high school football team but he was a senior and I was a junior."

"So you both went to public school on the Island?"

"No, actually. You know I haven't thought of this for years but Doug was adopted by the Guardians. I'm not sure at what age, but I remember my mother talking about how they were good folks to

take him in. I don't really remember him though, till high school."
Halstead shook his head, as if clearing cobwebs.

"Funny, I've known him so long, I always think of him as an
Islander born and bred. He married an Island girl though, Maryanne
Hitchens. Her parents operated the nursing home. Then he and
Maryanne went away – a common story." He smiled ruefully, "Most
everybody with any get up and go, gets up and leaves the Island at
some point. "

He rubbed his forehead, as if physically scouring his memory.
"Let's see then, he used to come home occasionally to see the folks.
He and Maryanne were doing well, she was a teacher and Doug
sold cars I think. And I saw both of them at the twenty year high
school reunion. Soon after that, I heard that Maryanne had died of
an embolism and that Doug was really broken up about it."

He stopped, thinking back. "Then I was away from the Island
for a few years myself. When I came back, he had come back too,
with Dawn."

"So, what do you think?" Pete prodded.

"Do you mean whether I think he's nutty enough to do this
vigilante stunt?" Halstead shook his head. "Not on the surface
anyway. You've met him. That hearty, have another drink type. You
know what men are like. We never really talk much, it's all about the
beer and the football. Or hockey or baseball."

Jakes knew. Men without women never talked about anything
very deep, they kept things to themselves. He'd been like that, till
he met Ali.

Halstead looked glumly at the worksheets. "O.K. I guess we'd
better have the fool in tomorrow for another interview," he said.
"Before he makes any more dumb mistakes."

"Hey chief," Jane called excitedly from the other room. "Look
out the window. It's snowing! "

23

Frosty mornings, tingling thumbs

The white stuff lent a Rockwellian charm to Main Street. Halstead drove slowly and carefully, it was a wet sloppy snow. Already a couple of inches had piled up and the road was slippery. Kids were running around crazily in the schoolyard, faces raised up to the big, soft flakes that splattered over their cheeks. At the traffic light, he called out to Vern Byers, bootless and picking his way awkwardly across the intersection.

"Hey there. Better get those snowplows out of drydock tonight."

Vern returned an expression that was his equivalent of giving the finger.

Halstead laughed. He thought he'd have supper at the Island Grill and chew the fat with Gus, get the day's gossip. Steph was busy and he didn't feel like eating leftover spaghetti at his place. Though it was three years since Kathleen was gone, he'd never got used to returning to the empty house. He should have sold it long ago but inertia and depression had slowed the process. Now that he felt alive again, he felt able to make the decision. Certainly he could never imagine Steph living in the modest bungalow. It wasn't her style at all. But what then? He tried to imagine himself living at the Retreat but that had kind of a funny feeling to it. He'd be like a bull in a china shop. And there was Steph's daughter Livy to consider too. What would she think? Questions, questions.

With relief he ducked into the simpler, homey atmosphere of the packed diner, steaming with wet coats and stamping boots and conversation.

Here's the white stuff finally – sure took it's time though.

Ah it don't look like much, just sap snow this time of year, probably won't stay the night.

By the jeez it's coming down pretty thick right now though.

Halstead took a seat at the counter.

"The regular?" Gus asked.

Halstead nodded. "A brew first."

Five minutes later, Gus brought his chicken in a basket with fries and a checkered red napkin.

"Don't see too much of you for supper anymore," Gus said, with a grin. "I spotted your truck out on the Point Road though the other day. I see it out there quite a lot."

"Fire inspection," Halstead said, crunching into a fry.

But he didn't mind the ribbing too much. The Grill and a beer served up with Jonesy's friendly grin had been a lifesaver for him at one time. A haven. Might be again some day, if he couldn't navigate the waters of Modern Love.

* * *

Steph stood looking out the big picture window at the Retreat as the thick snowflakes floated softly onto the branches of her blue spruce. Down at the shore, the lake was a pointillist blurry grey. A pretty scene to be sure, but being a country-bred Canadian, she almost immediately started to assess how long the snow was going to last. She had the winter's first full weekend booked and two representatives of the Award committee were coming by on the Saturday to view the Retreat in action. It would be ironic to say the least if after weeks of dry fields and clear roads, her guests were going to be balked by a March blizzard. A reminder once again that Nature was the most temperamental of decorators and worked entirely on her own whim.

Restlessly she prowled the kitchen and great room, checking her list of to do's for the twentieth time. Were the dried flowers in the right place? She moved the vase again, chuckling at what Bud would have to say. He was such a good man, an easy going big solid man. It was fun to tease him. Though actually she wasn't really teasing, she meant to challenge him. She was into challenges herself, these days.

It seemed as if all her life she had just followed the mainstream, fit herself into the pattern. She hadn't always felt the chains, indeed there had been many highlights. She'd had good looks, some said she still did! She'd been a cheerleader in high school, married a good-looking local fella. Neither of them had gone on to college but her in-laws had staked them to an investment in the motel. With lots of hard work and enthusiasm, they'd done really well, capping their efforts with the birth of their beautiful daughter, Livy.

Then one crisp January day Rick went to the city on a motel management course and met Rosemary and everything changed. Steph hadn't seen it coming but she sure saw Rick going. She took her half of the divorce settlement and poured all her raw hurt energy into her plans for the Retreat. And now four hectic years later, she wasn't sure that she was ready to share her life with a man again.

Did she really want to set up house—and what house?—with a man again?

Why did it have to be marriage. Why must it be all or nothing? When she was just learning to enjoy the freedom to make all her own decisions.

Why was love so complicated, teen-aged Livy had asked her once.

And who had the answer to that one?

*   *   *

Penny Loo stood in rapt contemplation of snow-covered boughs framing a view of the lake. Snow at last! Behind her in the new-white field, her bootprints had pricked out a design like the markings on a bedquilt. With deft movements and a sense of delicious anticipation, she set up her portable easel and fetched the paintbox from her backpack. Wet snowflakes dissolved like sugar on her knitted purple toque, as she opened the box.

Painting time was so precious. For the past three years she had saved enough money from her work as a layout designer on a magazine, to rent the house on the Island and invest several months in her art. Ironically, this year she had chosen the winter season as her theme. But here was some winter at last. Of course she'd have to stop if the snow got too thick and she could only make a preliminary sketch in these conditions but that could be exhilerating too. Standing like a lightning rod in the swirling white, and transferring the beauty to her canvas.

If only there would be no rude interruption of the magic. She looked warily towards the abutting woods of the hunting camp and cocked an ear. Often the peace of the Point was shattered with the unwelcome volleys of their target shooting. that scared away her avian subjects. But the woods remained blissfully silent. It seemed her loutish neighbours were away this week, thank goodness.

Painting time was so precious.

She poised her brush and gently stroked the canvas with a thin line of cobalt blue.

*   *   *

Nick lay on his bed at the Island Motel, took a swig of his cola and turned the page of his book.

Tracking a Tom in the Snow

Look for fresh tracks after a snowfall and turned up forest litter where turkeys have scratched the ground in search for food. As you follow the tracks, keep a sharp look around you, stopping every few steps and scanning the area with your binoculars. It has been said that if a turkey could smell as well as a deer it would become an un-huntable animal. Their eyesight is remarkable.

Fortunately for the hunter, turkeys are noisy birds. When the flock is gathered together and scratching for food, you can hear them from quite a distance.

Once you've found the birds, how can you keep them from finding you?

Camouflage clothing is essential. Avoid stepping on twigs and other debris. If you do make a noise inadvertently, immediately use your lost hen turkey caller and hope that the other turkeys will be fooled.

So now you've got a chance to take your shot. A normal deer hunting rifle will kill a turkey but also make it inedible.

Ugh! that was kind of crude. But yeah, no point in blowing the suckers apart, no Thanksgiving dinner then.

For minimum meat damage, use a smaller calibre. He looked towards the case in the closet. Yeah that was the gun he'd got.

He put down his glass and started to open the packages on the bed. They were all from the Outdoorsman Gear on-line store, sent to Nick Poitras, General Delivery, Middle Island. He'd picked them up at the post office on his way home.

Here we are, here we go. Look at this terrific camo stuff!

There were trousers, a jacket and cap, all made out of tough army-type brown and green patterned, camouflage cotton. He donned the complete outfit, saving the best for last, the turkey hunter's vest.

The vest was in the camo pattern too, and crammed with pockets. He'd watched a video on his phone and had already bought supplies. There was a pocket for binoculars, one for a map and compass. A pocket for shotgun shells, others for various turkey callers. And a larger pocket for gloves and a mask. Now he dropped the mesh mask down over his face and stood before the closet door mirror.

Yeah, he looked like a hunter. Like the real thing.

Almost like someone in a James Bond movie, trying to stop a nuclear missile from blowing up New York.

All this against one ol' Tom turkey. One old crazy bird.

For a moment he felt kind of *silly*.

Here he was though, eating a turkey sandwich, a crappy one sure, soggy slices from a package, the fridge in the motel room wasn't that great. But it was turkey and the damn bird was killed, cooked and chopped up somewhere wasn't it? Anybody who didn't like hunting and wasn't a vegetarian was a hypocrite really. If you thought about it.

A picture flashed across his mind. Of a little red car broken in a ditch. Of a smashed windshield. But he wouldn't be an irresponsible hunter. He would be one of the good ones. That's why he was responsibly studying up on it.

*   *   *

"It's the first snow in ages," Ali insisted. "I'm going out. At least to stand on the porch."

Pete grabbed up her coat and wrapped her in it. Or tried to, the buttons no longer reached. But oh, the frosty fresh air was delicious!

"Isn't it pretty!"

She leaned far over the porch railing and put her tongue out to taste a flake, feeling as excited as her little first grade students.

Emily barked and bounded down the steps after Pete. He made soft snowballs to toss, that broke apart as she leaped up for them. Ali laughed at the dog's puzzlement.

She looked gorgeously alight, Pete thought. Like a fairy princess, as the snow formed a tiara in her dark hair. He half expected her to lean down from her porch to touch him with a silver sword and call him Sir Knight. He grinnned, that was one of the many special things about Ali, she could make a dumb soldier think poetic thoughts.

"Come up here," she beckoned provocatively.

He bounded up and they stood, a warm unit in the snowy night.

Things were going to be all right, he knew. They were going to be O.K. And little Nevra too, the Jakes girl, their daughter. A year from now, he'd be building a snowman for her. He could hardly wait.

Somewhere out in the fields, a snowmobile revved up, disturbing the owl in his suppertime hunt.

You wouldn't think they'd be out already, Pete thought. With only a couple of inches of snow on the ground.

Go Islanders Go!

The score was Bonville Bulldogs 3, Middle Islanders 2, bottom of the third period.

The shouts rang out in the chilly air of the Bonville community arena, all eyes on the puck as it richocheted across centre ice towards the Bulldogs goalie.

Pete, along with the other Middle Island supporters who had come across the causeway to cheer on the highschool team, kept his eye on Brent Patrick, centre man, and best hope to score a tie goal. And here the miracle kid came, darting in and expertly wielding the puck back across the line Pursued by three Bulldogs, racing down the ice. The crowd roared as Brent easily won the race and neatly popped the puck in past the dazed Bonville goalie.

"Yeah Brent!" the elated Island cheering crew roared. "Only one goal to go!"

As Pete sat back down on the bench, Patrick's mother Elaine, principal of Middle Island elementary school, turned to him with a beaming smile. Tonight she was all proud mom.

"Good going to you too, coach!" she said.

At first Pete had his doubts that the teenagers would want to come to a practice being coached by a cop.

"Worried they'd be caught smoking joints between periods," Nick said cynically.

But after a couple of practices, Pete had won the kids over. He just concentrated on the skating and the game, which he was pretty good at. He'd played through his own high school years and also for the two years he'd been posted in Bosnia. So he coached the Island players at the Bonville arena a couple of mornings a week and drove them to the games. In other years, there had been shinny skating on the Bay, but with this contrary winter, that was no longer an option.

The Island team's euphoria was short-lived as one of the forwards got a penalty for icing, followed by a face-off which the Bulldog kid won. He passed the puck off to a sideman who headed down towards the Islanders net. Eileen anxiously grabbed her husband's arm, as Brent sped in quick pursuit. The action became fast and furious, that action which made the game famous as the Canadian national sport.

The Middle Island contingent rose to their feet and hollered encouragement, rising to a crescendo as the Bulldog player's shot glanced harmlessly off the goalpost. Brent scooped the puck out from behind the net and headed off down the ice to the other net.

Fifty seconds left to go and Pete felt the vibration of his pager in his pocket. He fished it out, wondering how long it had been ringing. The sounds in the arena faded, became only a hollow humming in his ears. Was the baby coming? Was Ali alright? He should never have gone out for the evening.

He took the bench steps three at a time. In the quieter outer hall, he switched the phone on. It was the chief.

"Jakes. We've got one hell of a mess over here. Doug Guardian's taken a bad spill off his snowmobile."

"Where are you?"

"In one of the fields out back of the Rowan Tree. He must have hit a stump or a rock or something. I'm there now."

Pete glanced at the black oblongs of the arena plate glass doors. "He was out on the snowmobile in the dark?"

"They've got some kind of a trail out here but somehow he got off it."

"Sounds bad."

"The ambulance and paramedics are here. Apparently Dawn came riding back on her machine, screaming for help. The staff called the ambulance. They had a hell of a job going out there in the dark and hauling Doug back, though luckily the spot was along the fenceline, not too far off the road. Still, they had to carry the stretcher quite a distance. A dangerous slippery trip, especially with an unconscious man and not knowing his injuries. "

"I'll come right back."

"No, I want you to meet me at the hospital. We'll have to talk to Dawn Guardian, calm her down and make some kind of report."

Pete pulled into the well-lit hospital parking lot. Bonville General's emergency department was always lit up, a beacon of hope and caring in the large, sprawling complex. He saw the chief right away when he entered the waiting room, sitting on a bench with Dawn Guardian.

Dawn was still wearing her blue and silver snowmobile suit — the colour of the matching machines in the Rowan Tree garage. She looked weirdly out of place in the bland, austere room. Like a circus performer or trapeze artist who had wandered into the hospital waiting room by mistake. Her face, though, was ashen above the bright collar.

She was speaking distractedly to the chief, her hands moving restlessly in her lap. She seemed hardly to notice Pete's arrival.

"Doug wanted to go for a moonlight spin. It was just his romantic whim,"she said with a desperate, brief smile. "I should never have agreed — and God I wish I hadn't — but he just swept me up in his enthusiasm. He said the snow and the moonlight made him feel like a kid again."

For a moment she seemed about to lose it but she got control and shakily continued.

"I hated to leave him but I had no choice. I just got on the snowmobile and drove back to the Rowan Tree as fast as I dared. I think I hit some branches and got a couple of cuts myself." She felt tentatively at her forehead where a bruise was coming up on her fair skin.

"We've just got a few questions, Dawn." Halstead said gently. "We got some of the story from your staff at the home but it would help if you could just tell us in your own words what happened out there. Or what you think happened."

She nodded.

"We went out right after supper. The snow had pretty well stopped and the moon lit up the fields. We could see the trail markers fine. The same regular, marked-out route that we've used all the other winters." She stopped.

"But Doug went off the trail . . ." Halstead prompted.

She took a breath. "We were coming up to the fenceline near the swamp, there's a big curve there. I saw Doug stand up on his machine and wave at me. I got closer and he shouted out something. It was hard to hear over the roar of the snowmobiles but I think he said something about seeing a light near the swamp. That it could be the hunters again. Before I could say anything, he wheeled his machine around and headed for the fence. As if he was going to take a look."

"Did you see any light?" Halstead asked.

She shook her head. "At least I don't think so. It's hard to remember. There was the noise and it all happened so fast. I was watching his light move toward the fence and then the machine suddenly reared up and flipped over. I turned my machine off and ran towards it and there was Doug lying on the snow. Thank God he'd been thrown clear and the machine hadn't landed on top of him. I dropped to my knees, screaming his name but he didn't answer. I didn't see any blood but I didn't dare move him. And the snowmobile was still roaring like some kind of monster. For a moment I just panicked."

Pete could picture the scene. The stark white field edged with the dark fringe of the swamp. The loudly moaning machines, their twin lights stabbing like light sabers into the night. And the two human figures, one bent sobbing over the other. Like the eerie setting for a stage tragedy.

It was almost a shock to hear the actual woman continue.

"I think it was anger that got me going," she said. "I got up, ran over to that damned snowmobile and pulled the key out of the ignition. I threw it in the snow and jumped up and down on it till it was buried. Then, though I doubted he could hear me, I told Doug I was going for help."

She stopped, exhaustion catching up with her. "And now we're here. Waiting, just waiting."

The doctor came out forty minutes and two rounds of weak styrofoam-tasting coffees later. He reported that they were keeping Doug Guardian in the intensive care unit. He had suffered severe trauma to his head. In layman's language, his skull had hit something hard, such as a boulder under the snow. Because of potential swelling of the brain, they had to induce a coma for the time being. His vital signs would have to be carefully monitored.

"How long will Mr. Guardian be out?" Halstead asked.

The doctor raised his shoulders under the white coat. "Depends when that swelling goes down. Could be a week, could be longer."

Dawn sagged. She was so exhausted, she hardly seemed to take in the news, to realize the import.

"I'll take you home," Halstead said. "Do you have a friend you want to call, or maybe someone on the staff at the Rowan Tree?"

"I'm staying here for the night." she said tiredly.

*　　*　　*

The two cops stood out in the chilly parking lot, their breath puffs visible in the cold air. An ambulance was leaving, siren wailing.

"Damnation!" Halstead whacked the hood of the cruiser. "What the hell's going on in Middle Island this winter? Crazy weather and all this crazy stuff happening. We get our first snow in weeks and now this. Of course the fool was nuts to get the snowmobile out with nothing but a dusting on the ground."

"Do you think he actually did see a light in the swamp?" Pete asked. "That some hunter was out there?"

Halstead growled and opened the cruiser door. "Who knows, but you'd better check it out. That cursed swamp. I'd like to drain the damned place dry."

25

Koma : (from the Greek) a state of deep unconsciousness that lasts for a prolonged or indefinite period.

Three days later, Halstead walked down Main Street towards the Middle Island Municipal Office, his shoes hitting dry pavement. Old Man Winter had played fickle again. The snow had been fool's snow, as taunting as fool's gold. For the Guardians, it was an especially cruel joke. The light dusting had only brought bad luck. Now the sun shone mockingly in a callous blue sky, and Doug Guardian was still comatose in Bonville Hospital.

Reluctantly, Halstead mounted the steps of the building. The regular Monday morning chat with Vern was unavoidable but at least this way, he could leave when he felt like it, whereas if the gabby clerk came to the station, it was tough to get rid of him. So in he went.

"This is a nasty turn-up," Vern said in greeting. "Usually when you say a rough March, you're talking about the weather. Now we've had two bad incidents in a month. Seems it always gets you one way or another." He sighed, at this additional confirmation of the miserable way of things.

"How is Doug doing anyway? Any change?"

"I'm going to check in at the hospital this afternoon," Halstead said. "But apparently it's never good when a comatose state lasts like this. The longer the time out, the more severe the damage. And even if he does come out of it, progress could be slow. It's not like the movies where there's an instant return to normal life. He could have memory loss, trouble with speech, with movement."

Vern clucked his tongue in sympathy. "A good man. Like they say it's hard when bad things happen to good folks."

Halstead wasn't about to mention that before the accident, he had decided to question that same good man about a small matter of criminal negligence. Guardian certainly seemed to have had hunters on the brain, even to the point of obsession. The first time he went out on a vigilante hunt, he might have been responsible for Lina Russell's death. And the other night, he'd come to the point of hallucinating that he saw lights in the swamp. Almost killing himself, or as bad as.

"Unless he *did* actually see a light out there," Halstead had said to Pete.

But Jakes had driven out to the Snake Point hunting lodge and found no sign of recent occupancy. The woodstove was cold, the beds stripped of sheets and the kitchen clean and tidy. The morose deer head presided over an empty camp. Penny Loo also reported no shooting on the property, much to her joy.

* * *

The intensive care unit was an eerily quiet oasis in busy Bonville General. Halstead supposed that nobody liked hospitals but now he found the experience particularly difficult, remembering his last visits to Kathleen. The antiseptic smell, the nurse's almost ghostly gliding walk on her crepe-soled shoes. The *whiteness* of the place, broken only by the brave splash of flowers.

But here he was, and thank Christ, in a lot better shape than Doug Guardian. The Rowan Tree owner lay on his back, loosely covered with a light hospital sheet, his grey-haired chest bare and taped with various tubes. Most of his head above the eyebrows was swathed in a bandage. The big man looked shrunken and vulnerable.

It was impossible not to feel shock and sympathy to see him so changed.

A nurse, one of Jane's many nieces, came in to check the tubes and monitors. She replaced the saline bag on the intravenous drip and when Halstead raised his eyebrows in a question, she put her finger to her lips and beckoned towards the door.

"Any change?" Halstead asked.

She moved even farther away from the door. "You never know if they can hear you," she explained. "But no, there's no change."

So no answers from that quarter yet. If ever.

He was about to leave when he saw Dawn Guardian coming along the corridor, carrying a paper cone of flowers. She looked in better control of herself today, dressed in jeans and her silver striped parka and moving with some of her former athletic grace. Her expression became anxious though, when she saw Halstead.

"Is Doug . . . ."

He quickly reassured her, if that was the right word, that there was no change. She glanced into the room where her husband was lying, as if to confirm this.

"I try to get in a couple of times a day," she said. "But I've been so busy with Rowan Tree matters." She looked almost defensive. "I have a duty to the residents and the staff to keep the two homes functioning responsibly. And now there are all the tasks that Doug did as well—it's almost overwhelming."

"I can easily imagine," Halstead said. "But can't your staff manage things, at least in the short run?"

She smiled ruefully, "Doug would say that's one of the flaws of my A-type personality, I'm afraid. I've always liked to know every aspect of the businesss. I hate to delegate and now I'm paying for it."

"Well fortunately you seem to be more than competent to handle things," Halstead said. "At least according to the article in the weekend supplement."

"You read that!," she said, her cool skin pinkening slightly. "Oh but it was a nice article on Stephanie Bind too."

She waved the flowers in a little movement. "Such an honour," she echoed Steph.

But the moment passed quickly and her face became shadowed again.

"Would you like a cup of coffee?" Halstead asked. "I could use one before heading back to the Island."

"No, but thank you," she looked towards the room. "I'd better get these daffodils in some water. I try to put fresh flowers in there every few days. I have to think that Doug is somehow aware of them. I simply have to."

He left her arranging the flowers. He wondered if she had any doubts of Doug's story of the stolen rifle. If that was part of her stress, fearing that her husband was facing a negligence charge. It would be difficult to hide much from a spouse. Ah well, no need to add to her distress at the moment, she had enough on her plate. And unfortunately it would all be water under the bridge anyway, if Doug failed to wake up.

*   *   *

First the accident, then followed the vultures.

Halstead was scowling over the roofing repair bill when Jakes looked in.

"There's a fellow here from the Guardians' insurance company, wants to talk to us."

Name of Bunt, Halstead had glanced at the card. Bunt was on the heavy side, packed tightly into a suit. His flushed face and loose tie hinted at a liquid lunch at the Grill. Halstead indicated the chair across from his desk.

"How can we help you?"

Bunt hiked his briefcase clumsily up onto the desk and opened it. "We received your written report of the accident, thanks."

Halstead waited.

Bunt sat back in the chair which complained with a squeak. He played with a pen, moving it through his meaty fingers. "So now I just had a couple more questions."

"What more is there to say?" Halstead asked. "The victim is in hospital possibly in an irreversible coma. The witness, his wife, has described the circumstances. Seems pretty clear to me."

"You want a free pen?" Bunt asked, reaching into the briefcase. "I got lots of them."

Halstead shook his head. "No thanks."

"O.K." Bunt said, stopping the nonsense and tossing the pen on the desk. "I was wondering about the state of Guardian's mind. It seems a pretty crazy thing to do, number one, going out snowmobiling at night and number two, then leaving the marked trail even though he knows it's dangerous."

Halstead affected a casualness he didn't feel. "His wife said he felt like a kid again, maybe he was trying to recapture his youth. We old guys sometimes do crazy things."

Bunt had the restraint not to state Guardian's obvious loss of that youth forever.

"So then why does the guy go off the trail? His wife says he might have seen some lights or some bull like that. But your report says there were no tracks, no sign of anyone there."

Bunt had that right. Jakes and Poitras had thoroughly covered the ground area of the accident the next morning in full sunlight. The snowmobile was still there, someone had righted it. The vehicle seemed undamaged, the silver stripes glinting evilly in the light, like a mocking grin. The area where Doug had flipped was badly roiled up by the bucking runners and the subsequent traffic of the paramedics. But the severely gouged mound of rock and grass tussocks he'd hit was obvious. Why he'd gone off the trail wasn't. The cops had walked right back to Turkey Woods but saw no other tracks.

"Was the guy hallucinating?" Bunt asked incredulously.

Halstead winced, aware of his own similar thought.

But he merely said, "There had been some hunters in his woods a few weeks ago. Maybe he thought they were back."

"So you're saying that Guardian was as happy and sane as the rest of us, that everything was hunky dory." Bunt shifted in his chair. "I heard there'd been some trouble at the Rowan Tree lately, something about a stolen rifle. That Guardian was upset, snapping at the staff."

"He might have been under some strain," Halstead allowed. "We did have him in here for questioning.".

Bunt's gaze quickened. "Questioning about what?"

"Confidential," Halstead said. In other words, none of your damn business.

"You can at least tell me if it might have caused enough of a strain to unbalance Guardian's mind."

Halstead shrugged, "It's not my call. Maybe his doctor would know something."

Bunt packed up his briefcase. "Thanks for helping a guy do his job," he said sarcastically.

Yeah sure. Like all the other vultures.

"What's that look?" Halstead asked Pete, when Bunt had grumpily departed. He knew that Jakes frown.

"What do you make of that, chief? That unbalanced bit. It sounded as if he might be talking suicide."

Halstead looked as if he'd tasted something bad. "He's a typical insurance investigator. They're paid for getting out of paying."

"Maybe they're right sometimes. You said that Guardian was a basket case when you interviewed him after we found the rifle. And we were practically on our way out there to charge him with reckless endangerment or manslaughter. That could have set him off."

"You think he'd commit suicide with his wife right there? Doug Guardian wouldn't put her through that. He was crazy about the woman."

Jakes was unconvinced. "Maybe the kind of strain he's been under, he wasn't thinking too clearly. You said he was already blaming himself for screwing up. First he kills Lina Russell in a horrible accident and then he's going to get sent to jail, wreck his business reputation and his wife's career. That's a lot of strain."

Halstead nodded judiciously. "If it's true." He was beginning to think it might be. He looked out at the last of the thin snow mantle on Henderson's field. *Covering a multitude of sins.* Apparently not. This snow was pretty well gone, it wasn't going to last the day.

"It could be true," Jakes said. "And it would wrap up Lina Russell's case at least."

"Unfortunately we can't interview the perp," Halstead reminded him. "He might not wake up for a real long time."

Stalemate. Again.

Jakes flopped frustratedly down in his chair.

"Maybe his wife could help us out here," he said, after a moment.

Halstead frowned. "Her husband's in a coma. And you want to ask her whether he put himself there on purpose?"

"Our insurance pal Bunt has probably already done that."

Halstead mimicked spitting. "Even if Doug was suicidal, I'd hate to help that vulture do the Guardians out of their insurance."

"She must have noticed his state of mind," Pete said doggedly. "The Rowan Tree staff did."

"If she did suspect anything, she probably didn't want to know. And she certainly wouldn't want to know now. Or tell us about it." He sighed. "Anyway you look at it, it's a downright tragedy."

"You said they've been married about ten years?" Pete asked.

Halstead nodded. "Yes, they met on a cruise I think, that corny old story. Anyway they came back to the Island and renovated the Hitchens' old place into the marvel you see today. His parents were actually their first residents, till they passed on. But you'll have to ask Jane for any scuttlebut on their life since, I'm sure she'll give you chapter and verse."

Pete grinned. "Gossip, you mean."

Halstead reached for the phone. "Don't knock it, kid. Cops would be lost without gossip. Though we prefer to call them informed sources."

In fact he would be checking with his favourite source that night. Dawn Guardian might have talked to another woman if she had some concerns about Doug.

26

Stephanie pulled the *frittata* out of the oven. That's what she called the dish anyway, though it looked an awful lot like the Island Grill bacon omelet to Halstead. But hey, Steph in her apron was a lot prettier than Gus's grill cook. He had no complaints. Especially as she was pouring out a long draft of his favorite brew to accompany the eggs.

"Enjoy the pampering now," Steph said. "I'll be so busy next weekend, you'll be lucky to score a left over bran muffin."

"Don't worry," Halstead shuddered. "A weekend of ten women spouting bad poetry — you won't see hide nor hair of me."

"How do you know they'll be bad? You're such a judge of fine poetry"

He shook out his napkin, thick red linen. "I know poetry, you bet your pretty shirt." And he quoted

There was a young man from Madras

Who . . . .

"Never mind," she said. "Unfortunately, I already know it."

The eggs were good, so was the beer.

"So, how well do you know the Guardians?" he asked, with about half his plate cleared.

She looked surprised. "What brought that up?" she asked.

He shrugged. "Just curious."

"Just curious, I bet," she rapped his fingers with her fork. "If you're going to pump me about people Bud, you might as well be open about it. You can't fool me anyway."

"O.K.," he said. "What do you know about the Guardians? Think of this as just a routine police inquiry, looking for background regarding the accident."

"I know Dawn's about to lose her husband. That Doug might not survive. That's not very routine."

He waited.

She considered, then began. "We've both served on the Beautify Main Street Committee, the last three years," she said. "Is that the type of thing you want to know?"

"Did Dawn ever talk to you about more personal things? Was she worried about Doug at all. His state of mind?"

She looked doubtfully at him "Just where are we going here?"

He sighed. "There's a possibility that Doug was trying to commit suicide."

"Because of the stolen rifle thing?" She looked bewildered. "I can see he might have felt that he'd been negligent but surely . . . ."

"He asked me not to go ahead with theft charges because he didn't want to jeopardize Dawn's chance at winning the Business Women's award. Now it looks as if he may even have fired the actual shot that hit Lina's car."

"Oh my god," she said in horrified awe, "why would Doug ever do a thing like that?"

"He thought he was firing at jacklighting hunters."

"That's terrible!" she clapped a hand to her mouth. "Poor Lina."

They took coffee to the great room, to his favourite couch. The chairs were nice too, in some striped yellow and cream coloured fabric. Pretty, like everything else in the place. He may have had no fancy taste himself but he could recognize it when he saw it.

"So, tell me about the Guardians. What was Doug doing the years I was away? What do you know about his wife?"

"Dawn has been good for him," Steph said. "She got him out of his depression after Maryanne died and she's been a real whiz on the business side. You know they run the other home in Bonville too. Between both homes, I think they employ about twenty people either full or part time. And they do a wonderful job. My aunt lives at the Rowan Tree and she's very happy there."

"Jane says that Doug wanted to retire."

She frowned, "I doubt that Dawn would want to give up the business just yet. Of course everything could be different now. God knows what she'll do. And how bittersweet for her if she wins the Business Women's award, while her husband is lying in the intensive care unit at Bonville General."

He stroked her arm. "You'd still get all the awards if I was the judge."

She smiled, "For my frittatta?"

"Yeah sure, for your frittata."

Later, he let himself out into the chilly night.

"Same time, next year?" he joked.

But she wouldn't rise to the bait. "See you on Tuesday," she said. She was already back at her computer, poring over her website. Obviously not bothered by their open 'relationship.'

Lord, how he loathed that word. One of these days, maybe sometime soon, Old Man Halstead was going to get a fistful of posies from the flower shop and propose to his woman. Damn the danger, full speed ahead.

*   *   **

Next morning, Pete didn't glean a heck of a lot more from Jane.

In fact, Jane was a fan.

"Doug's a great guy," she said. "My sister Pam works at the Rowan Tree House. She says that the reason Doug doesn't want to merge with the Royal Retirement chain is because he's worried they'll make the homes too expensive and that some of the current residents might have to move out."

Her expression sobered. "Pam says it was a happy place to work."

That was the popular opinion, Pete had found. Guardian was a hard-working, blameless businessman with a soft spot for old people. Not exactly the reckless vigilante of his theory. Still, *somebody* had shot at Lina Russell, had sent her into that water-clogged ditch. If he was wrong, he was wrong, but if you didn't stick your neck out sometimes you'd never know whether you might have been right.

His thoughts churning, he drove away from the station, pulled as always these days towards the swamp. But the bleak scene seemed discouragingly impenetrable today and he didn't feel up to another unproductive search. He continued on out past the Rowan Tree, not wanting to think about that mess just now either.

Spotting a redtail hawk circling over the fields behind, he turned into a dirt road and idly followed it. A few days ago, he'd sighted a redtail on the side of the road, tearing apart a rabbit and wondered if this could be the bird's mate. He'd found his new binoculars were a great aid for sightings. And there the bird was again, moving in wide circles above Turkey Woods. He stopped by the rail fence and pulled out his notebook to jot down the date and time of day of the sighting.

He also marked the location on a map he'd got from the municipal office, showing the gore roads and property lines. As he added the red dot for today's sighting, he noticed that he wasn't far from Akantha Samos' house. He hadn't been back there since the break-in, was that only a month ago?

So much had happened since then. The visit to the boarded-up house now seemed to have launched a series of sad events. Lina's accident in the ditch, and now the Guardian's tragedy, all happening on the edges of Turkey Woods. A tough month. A real season of doom, as a mystery writer might put it. Though that was perhaps a bit strong. The old woman's death had nothing to do with the other accidents.

Still, his pencil seemed to have a life of its own. He watched as his fingers guided the piece of yellow wood to sketch a triangle in three neat lines, joining up Akantha's cottage, the Rowan Tree, and the ditch where Lina had died.

But that was just the way his mind worked. He'd always liked math at school, he liked tidiness, to connect things up. He was always seeking connections, even if they weren't there.

27

A nother setback! Was there no end to this?
    Now it turned out that the old dame's boxes hadn't gone to the dump at all but to some museum, of all things. So someone else would be squirreling away at the stuff. Nosing through it. Sifting, sorting, finding.

But who? And where?

Should have burned that junky shoebox of a house down when you had the chance.

It was so unfair. You did what Pop said. You kept the dream through all those hellish years. Finally got enough money to get out, go clean, start back at the beginning.

But what happens to the dream now?
Instead, there's the awful wakening again
To another day of running from the relentless pursuers.
Who would never go away
Who would never leave you alone.

It isn't your fault if you have to fix it.
Whatever it takes.

28

Ali stood at the top of an elegant staircase, men and women in elaborate party dress, looking up at her in admiration. Her own floor-length gown was an elegant confection of cream satin and meringue lace, the waist a smooth dip in her hourglass figure. Up the stairs came a handsome blonde man in faultless evening dress. It was Pete. "You are the most comely woman here," he said, his eyes ablaze with passion. But then she turned sideways and the crowd gasped as he turned away in horror.

She's a whale, she has no waist at all.

Ali struggled awake. If you could call it waking, this semi-torpor in which she spent her days. Akantha's photo album slid from the blanket to the floor but she couldn't rouse the effort to retrieve it. She had been looking through the book once again before she fell asleep. Or passed out, that was what it actually felt like.

Her mind was so woolly now, she spent her days in a lethargic haze. Some vague foggy area betweeen waking and sleeping.

"Why am I so tired? she demanded of Doctor Baird. "I'm not even doing anything."

"You're busy creating an entire, brand new human being, cell by cell," Baird soothed. "What could be more important than that?"

"My brain is a vegetable," she moaned to Pete. A squash, a pumpkin."

She was now officially merely a protective cocoon for the baby. Sans thought, sans memory, sans movement. She had only vestiges of concentration. Summoning up a great effort, she would check her e-mail. Miranda had returned from the rainforest and was back at the central school.

Our trip was wonderful. A once-in-a-lifetime experience. Like being in the Garden of Eden. A very hot and humid garden, but not to quibble. Gloriously coloured parrots and toucans. And the plants – orchids in all colours. Here is a picture of me standing by a Bird of Paradise bloom.

And there she was, seventy-five year old Miranda Paris in shorts and sturdy hiking shoes, grinning under her Tilley safari hat. It was a wonderful picture. She sounded so excited, so inspired, so involved.

Ali smiled back at the photo on the screen. That made at least one good thing she had managed to do this year, convincing Miranda to go on the trip. She hadn't wanted to leave the Island with Ali expecting but Ali had urged her to take advantage of the opportunity to visit Costa Rica while her former student was working on the teaching project. Finally, Miranda had agreed to go, but cautioned,

"Now don't you be having that baby before I get back."

Judging by the size of her bump, Ali wondered if she could last another week, let alone five. And whether she'd be sane by the end of it.

Sometimes for amusement, she looked up baby names on the Net. About the only kind of research project she was up to these days.

Hundreds of sites offered the *Top Ten Female Names. Brandi, Tiffany, Amber, Crystal, etc.*

She preferred reading of more historic names and their definitions.

Her own name meant 'exalted' or 'lofty' which made her laugh. And Nuran meant 'taking or receiving light'. Interpret that any way you wanted.

She typed in 'Peter'. *A rock.* Well that was apt for a strong, dependable type like her husband. The type that the exalted need for balance.

"For our daughter's name, I want to combine our languages, our heritages," she'd told Pete.

"I don't know what heritage I've got to add to the mix," he'd said in the caustic tone he used on the rare occasions when he even mentioned his background. "I think my mother's folks were from Holland originally. My father never talked about her though, after she died. He never talked much about anything."

It made Ali sad to think of this man who had shut down all emotion years ago. So sad for Pete too, no wonder he'd left home as soon as he could to join the army.

"But our daughter will have *us*," she said. "That's a good starting point."

So far they had chosen Nevra Alice Jakes. *Nevra for new.*

She tried it out several times a day, liking the sound of the syllables on her tongue.

When she clicked on Greek names, she found:

Akantha – thorn

Adrasteia – courageous.

Adelpha – dear sister

She looked guiltily towards the corner of the living room where the Samos cartons sat ignored and forgotten. Today was the first time she'd resumed her so-called archival work in nearly two weeks.

And so far she'd only gotten as far as the photo album and this musty-smelling copy of a book called Etiquette in Society by Emily Post. She wondered what the independent-thinking, athletic Akantha had thought of Mrs. Post's suggestions regarding the proper deportment of young ladies. As she flipped through the pages, a slim packet of letters fell out into her lap. Several browning envelopes, bound with an elastic band that dissolved when Ali touched it. The letters were addressed to Akantha Samos at an address in Hamilton and the first was dated about ten years earlier.

Dear Sister:

I have been so lonely since Steven died. Some days I have hardly wished to get out of my bed. And I have such terrible pain from my legs. If it wasn't for the weekly homecare visitor, I wouldn't see anyone for days on end.

I have been looking through the old photo albums recently. It makes me melancholy of course but there are happy memories there too.

There you are in your swimsuit. The beginning of your triumphs. Even Poppa was proud I think, though he would never say so aloud. He was of an earlier generation and a different culture, where women stayed at home. Of course I always knew that you were a wonderful swimmer, you could always swim the farthest out into the lake.

And here are the pictures of my wedding!

I find it so hard to believe that Steven is gone. Perhaps if we had had children, I would not be so lonely. There would be a part of my dear husband still here.

Isn't it strange the way our lives turned out? We have no issue, either of us. Poppa would have mourned.

Although I have been blissfully happy with Steven, I would have so liked to have given him a son or a daughter.

Ali turned the abum pages until she found the wedding picture. There was also a picture of Adelpha and Steven at about age sixty. She studied it closely. Adelpha's husband didn't look like a wastrel and Adelpha mentioned no financial concerns in her letter. The two looked happy.

Though she searched through the box, Ali could find no answering letters from Akantha. But even through the one-sided conversation, she could see that the sisters were very close, Adelpha wrote again,

Dear Sister:

It is sweet of you to ask me to come and live with you but I have my allergies and would never ask you to give up your beloved cats.

And I don't think I could bear to leave this house where Steven and I spent so many happy years together. A lifetime really.

Perhaps I will take your advice, though, and apply at an employment agency for some help with the house.

At least that would give me some company.

The timer on Ali's watch buzzed, time to take her medicine. She put the letter down, also noticing on her laptop screen that she had a new e-mail.

From Nuran? She could hardly believe what she was reading.

Arriving next Tuesday by train to Bonville, six p.m.

The message could hardly be more brief. As if it was a telegram from another century and she was paying by the word.

But Mr. Cool was going to get a lot more words at suppertime! What had he done?

In her frustration, she tossed the letters and album back into the carton.

29

5:00 p.m. The streetlight outside the station came on, casting an acidic orange glow on the parking lot. Jane looked up from her weekly bookkeeping, yawned and stretched. She called into Halstead's office,

"Say chief, what do we want to do about Sammy Pinder? He's had the nerve to submit a bill charging *us* for late payment, when the ceiling is still leaking in the lunchroom."

"I'm sure you can think of something to tell him," Halstead said drily.

Unfortunately he could find no humour in his own afternoon's work. He'd been engaged in writing much grimmer reports. It had been nearly a month since they'd found Lina's car in the ditch. Doug Guardian was still in intensive care, totally unresponsive. They might never have any proof that Guardian had caused Lina to run off the road. He might soon be left with that most dispiriting of a policeman's options, to write up Lina's death as an accident caused by circumstances or persons unknown.

Jane's warning broke into his thoughts. "Here's Vern coming now, likely bringing in the pay cheques."

Probably going to tell me I haven't earned mine yet this month,
Halstead thought. And he may be right.

"Want to hide?" Jane hissed.

"No it's too late."

But in fact, the clerk seemed in a rush and handed over the envelopes with only a quick query about Doug Guardian. On hearing that there was no change, he tssked gloomily.

"The man could be there for years. His wife might have a vegetable for a husband."

"Could you be a bit more cheerful, man," Halstead protested.

Jane smiled determinedly. "People wake up from comas all the time, don't they chief? Just wake up one day and ask what time is dinner."

"Sure they do," Halstead agreed. He didn't want to remind her that the longer the comatose state lasted, the more deterioration of the victim's brain tissue. At least Vern couldn't claim that Doug's snowmobile spill was the result of a terrorist plot.

For a moment he found himself wishing there really were some terrorists, some kind of bogeyman anyway who was destroying the lives of Island residents. Better that, than someone he knew. Guy Russell, a murderer? Doug Guardian, a ruthless scam artist? Even to think these thoughts was some kind of nightmare.

"April will be better," Jane said soothingly.

She smiled at young Jakes who had come in to sign off for the day.

"What's Pete doing tonight?" she asked chirpily.

He answered with reluctance. "Picking up my mother-in-law at the train station in Bonville."

Jane smiled. "Is she staying for awhile, till the baby comes? That will be nice for Ali, a woman wants to have her mother near at a time like this."

Pete managed a weak smile. That hadn't exactly been Ali's reaction to the news.

"How *could* you! I'm *well!* I may have been depressed for awhile but that's over."

"I didn't write her," Pete protested. His first lie to his wife but it was in a good cause. He supposed that was what all liars said.

"Then why is she coming?"

"Maybe she's worried about you. Maternal ESP or something clicking in."

"Ha. She's probably coming to tell me she's setting off on another trip to Africa or India. Then she can escape before there's an actual grandchild to view."

Ah well, into the breach.

It was a chilly night but the Bonville train station was stuffy and overwarm. Nuran's train was running a half hour late. Frustrated travellers who were going on to Montreal, paced by the door looking out into the dark night. As if their own restless movements would make the train arrive more quickly.

Pete wouldn't mind a longer wait. Part of him even wanted to run back out to the car. He hoped he was doing the right thing. On their last visit to the doctor, Baird had taken Pete aside and said he would be happier now if there was someone with Ali virtually full-time.

"We don't want your daughter arriving any sooner than necessary."

There was a stir in the station as a wailing whistle announced the approaching train. Students gathered up backpacks, seniors looked around anxiously for their things. Soon the thunder of the train's arrival filled the station.

He stood on the platform watching the attendants put out yellow plastic steps for the passengers to disembark. More students, an elderly man with a cane and yep, there was his mother-in-law. A woman of Ali's height and carriage, she looked nearer forty than sixty. She wore a black wool belted coat and long black boots, a turquoise patterned silk scarf round her shoulders and held the handle of a wheeled suitcase.

Nuran Sezer. Thank goodness she had insisted early, on using only first names. No Ma or Mum Sezer for her. They'd only met four times in all in the two years that he and Ali had been married. That introductory supper, and a couple of other times when she had been in the city. They always went out for dinner, it gave them something to do. One reason why Ali couldn't cook much, she had been eating meals at school or in restaurants for most of her life.

He waved to catch Nuran's eye, then moved to help her with the suitcase. About the same time that they'd decided on first names, it was acknowledged that neither one of them was a hugger, so that awkwardness was out of the way as well. Still, it was a train station, there were greetings in the air around them, and he was about to become the father of her grandchild. He felt the occasion required some small ceremony. He put out his hand.

"How was your trip?" he asked.

They managed the half hour car ride fairly smoothly. Nuran was an accomplished speaker, used to addressing the public and she liked to talk about her work. She brought with her a faint and pleasant scent, more like cardoman, a spice than a perfume. Her black hair was streaked with grey, but still vibrant and thick. Cut short and under control though, unlike her daughter's free-flowing mane.

"You have little snow," she noted, "even here in the country."

He nodded. "It's been a strange winter."

"Global warning," she said. "Humans being fools again."

He let that one pass, in fact he agreed with her.

He said that he had enjoyed reading her recent book, a study of community in an African village and how the people were being affected by the gift of a computer learning centre.

"And how are you liking *your* work?" she asked. "It must be very different from your army life."

"Yes, it's much quieter."

"Still, there is so much grief in the world, so much to be done. I wonder how you can bear living in this smug North American society."

Well, Ali had warned him. "When you're thinking of bringing a child into the world, you think of her safety," he said "You want your child to live in a peaceful place."

She looked somberly out at the dark night. "It is peaceful here on this side of the world," she acknowledged. "On the surface. But other, less fortunate people are left to pay the price."

"We're lucky," he said, "We can raise our child away from bombs and war. I'm well aware that many people in the world don't have that choice. But I'd be a fool to throw away the opportunity for my wife and daughter when I have it. And I feel my work here is valuable too."

"And what is your work here currently?"

He could have mentioned the other tasks, the community service work, the emergency preparedness drills, the drug and alcohol prevention programs, but he answered honestly.

"I'm investigating a possible murder."

She smiled, "So there is violence even here in your little piece of Paradise?

He agreed. "Unfortunately, there's violence pretty much everywhere where there are humans." They both had seen enough evidence of that.

Nuran was silent for the rest of the trip.

"Here we are," he said. Emily was in the house, barking at the car's approach.

He was nervous about the meeting. More of a reunion really. Though mother and daughter had conversed through e-mails and telephone conversations at holidays and birthdays, they hadn't actually seen each other for nearly a year. And that was just a quick meal in the city. Nuran hadn't visited the Island yet.

But they hugged. A bit awkwardly but that could be explained by Ali's baby bump.

"Oh, your cheek is cold!" Ali exclaimed, drawing back. "But you look wonderful, Nuran. I love that coat."

"You look . . . . big." Nuran said.

Ali rolled her eyes. "Yes, well this is what eight months pregnant looks like. Basically an elephant."

Pete hastily stepped forward.

"Let me take your coat, Nuran."

"The kettle's on for tea," Ali said, none too warmly.

"Did you get what you wanted from Sears?" Nuran asked. She had told them to order something for the baby.

"Yes, the crib arrived thanks. Pete has already set it up in the nursery. Would you like to see what we've done?"

In the cheerfully painted nursery, Nuran looked very elegant and ungrandma like, standing ill at ease and turning over a stuffed zebra toy in her hands. And yet Nuran had gone through this experience once herself, Ali thought resentfully. She must have found a crib, bought soft blankets and sets of tiny clothes. Ali couldn't remember that first room of course and her room as a teenager had been at the boarding school.

"What is this?" Nuran asked, looking at a plastic unit.

"The baby intercom," Ali explained. "There's a speaker in our bedroom and another speaker downstairs so that we can hear her when she wakes up."

Nuran dropped the zebra toy into the crib. "Millions of women in India, Africa and around the world sleep with their children in the same bed. At least in the same room."

Pete felt Ali stiffen beside him. "The baby clinic at the hospital recommended we get the intercom," he said. "And of course she'll be in our room at first."

Nuran left to freshen up. She was to stay in the sunroom off the kitchen, where there was a comfortable day bed and a desk for her laptop. She was working on the draft for her next project.

Pete squeezed Ali's hand. "Think of your blood pressure, honey. I'm sure your mother will be thrilled to meet her granddaughter."

"I don't see why. She never seems thrilled to see me."

They had tea in the living room, Ali stretched out on the couch, Emily with her nose on Pete's feet. Nuran talked about her latest book tour. Usually Ali was keen to hear her mother's always intelligent and interesting observations but tonight her mind was so dopy, that she drifted off. It was strange to hear Nuran's richly modulated voice rising and falling in the room. She resented the fact that she liked it, then gave up the fight and fell asleep.

Even sunlight was made chilly in the cavernous main chamber of the old Bonville courthouse. There were plans to build a newer, more energy efficient building in the next few years but for now, the accused and the accusers shivered together. Pete was glad of his uniform jacket, as the usual Tuesday morning parade of traffic violators, shoplifters and this morning, a burglary suspect, took their turn before the judge.

Then the bailiff called Guy Russell to answer the charges related to the disturbance at the station. Two weeks of enforced sobriety had left the man pale and shaken. Pete spotted Alison Russell sitting in one of the sparsely populated benches. Dressed in jeans and a parka, she clutched her backpack tensely as she watched the proceedings.

Russell was fortunate that he lived in the Middle Island community, Pete thought. He could have been facing charges of kidnapping or forcible confinement but neither Jane nor Halstead would have it. As it was, the charges of uttering threats and reckless use of a firearm were serious enough and could bring a large fine and possibly jail time.

The lawyer played the sympathy card – the man had recently lost his wife in a tragic accident, was temporarily unbalanced with grief. The judge ordered a thousand dollar fine and two months in a rehab facility.

Alison hugged her father briefly before they led him away.

"Do you think it will do him any good?" Pete asked, when he reported back to the station.

"You never know," Halstead said. "He might surprise everyone and shape up for his daughter's sake."

"Let's hope so." Pete looked unconvinced. "Now we know about Guardian and his rifle stunt, at least it seems unlikely that Rusell drunkenly took a shot at his former wife."

Halstead sighed. "Yes, I guess we're going to have to close the book on that sad event. Lina's gone and Guardian's pretty close to it. A sad story all round. "

Jakes sat silently for a moment. Long enough to raise Halstead's suspicions.

"Yes?" he asked in an ominous tone.

"I've been thinking some more about our Doug Guardian theory."

"Why? And by the way, it was your theory, remember."

"I still think he was the one who took the shots. We've never found any evidence that those city guys were there that morning."

"And no proof except their own word that they were blamelessly in bed that morning either." Halstead pointed out.

"Then they'd all three have to be lying," Pete said. "Of course it's possible but they're a pretty lazy bunch. I can't see them crawling around the Little Swamp at six in the morning. Besides, I've been out at that swamp several times since and found nothing. No casings, no broken branches in the ditch. It's not even a.particularly popular deer crossing. So the question is, why would Guardian be out there?"

Halstead shrugged impatiently. "We've been over that. Doug had hunters on the brain, maybe he was waiting on the chance that they'd show up. He was pretty upset, he was reckless, nobody's arguing that now. Not even Doug." He scowled. "Nobody except you, I guess."

Pete shifted in his chair, said apologetically. "I don't like loose ends, I can't help it, it's a habit of mine. I have to tie things up, make things neat. It drives Ali nuts sometimes."

"I hate to tell you lad, but police cases aren't always neat. In fact they're rarely neat. We may have arrived at the only solution possible."

Jakes leaned forward, his voice intense. "I've got this wild idea. Maybe it wasn't an accident at all. Maybe Doug Guardian *meant* to kill Lina."

Halstead took in a big breath. "Jeez son, do you dream this stuff up in your sleep? You're the one who sat right there in that chair and figured out that it *was* an accident, remember? That Doug was so mad at those hunters upsetting his wife that he went out that morning to scare them off."

He shook his head. "Isn't it enough that he acted like a reckless vigilante? That he's likely put himself in a coma out of guilt. Now you're saying that the man was a deliberate murderer?"

Jakes looked uncomfortable but determined. "Just hear me out, O.K."

Halstead subsided. "Sure. Go ahead and tell me why, aside from Guy Russell who we're pretty sure is innocent, would anyone want to kill a sweetheart like Lina. A pillar of the community, loved by all, as her obit quite rightly put it."

"To start off with, at least there's a connection," Jakes said earnestly. "Lina worked at the Rowan Tree a couple of days a week."

Halstead threw up his hands. "So, she was connected to the Rowan Tree. She was also connected to her husband and her Granny and to half the people on the Island."

"So she was there a lot, at the Rowan Tree," Jakes persisted. "Maybe she found out something about Guardian."

"Like what? From what everybody says about the way Doug adored his wife, he certainly wasn't fooling around with other women."

Jakes lifted up the pile of scam sheets, as if he was weighing them in his hand. "Maybe she found out he was scamming his residents."

Halstead gave a short laugh. "Not on Middle Island, he wasn't. All the folks around here have got nosy relatives. He'd never get away with it." He leaned back in his chair. "Is that all you've got? Boy, you've got one busy imagination."

And persistence. "Jane told me he's put a whole lot of money into the Rowan Tree," Jakes continued doggedly. "And then there's that other seniors residence in Bonville. I was just wondering how he made his start up money."

Halstead shrugged. "How does anyone get money? Inheritance, married into it, smart thinking, sometimes just plain hard work."

"Or maybe scams," Pete said mildly. "Cheating old folks."

Halstead nodded reluctantly. "Or maybe scams. Truth is I don't know how Doug made his money all those years he was away. How anyone makes money. I certainly never learned the secret."

Jakes tossed the scam sheets back on the desk. "I'm just asking if it's possible. He's right there in the retirement home business, you might say he's had a captive audience. And maybe he couldn't resist another scam. Lina Russell knew a lot of the residents, maybe someone told her something. Maybe her Granny, maybe he was even trying a scam on the old lady."

He looked at Halstead with that disconcerting straight-up gaze. Like a kid who was asking a perfectly reasonable but unanswerable question, such as why are some people mean. There was no way to wriggle out of it.

Halstead sighed. "I guess anything's possible. But if Guardian never wakes up, what he did in the past may not make much difference. I'll get Jane to run it through the computer though, see if there's any old charges on record."

"I've been doing that."

"And?"

Pete shrugged. "Nothing's shown up so far. Doug Guardian has no record of fraud. There are no suits against any of the retirement homes he's operated."

Halstead spread his hands. "So, no dirt. Maybe there is none to find." That would be nice. Rare, but nice.

Jakes looked down at the weekly scam bulletins on the desk. Papers that represented a sea of troubles, misery and loss. "You said yourself, chief, that thousands of these frauds are never reported.

That the victims are ashamed or worried that their relatives will call them senile and unable to look after themselves."

"Doesn't seem much point in going on with it then," Halstead said.

"Lina Russell might want us to," Jakes said. He stood up, pushing back the chair. "Like you say, none of this has seemed straight, right from the beginning. And it doesn't feel sorted out yet."

Halstead watched him go. Yes, he'd made the right decision last year when he signed the kid on permanent staff. Jakes cared and he had the courage to float crazy ideas. And, oh yeah, he was pretty smart too.

31

Stephanie Bind had called and said that she was bringing all the fixings of a baby shower to the Jakes' house.

"You can't come out, Ali. So we're coming there next Saturday. All you have to do is sit on your couch throne and receive presents and attention."

Stephanie was under Doctor Baird's orders to keep the occasion small and had invited Eileen O'Brien, Ali's principal from the Island school, several other teachers and Jane from the station.

"We'll be on your doorstep on Saturday afternoon," she promised. "You'll be able to recognize us by our funny hats."

"A baby shower?" Nuran looked pained.

"It's a weird North American custom," Ali teased. "Other women in the community bring gifts for the new baby. Africa isn't the only country to have social rituals."

"I know what a baby shower is," Nuran said. "I've been exposed to the silly games and hats. Do I have to attend?"

"Of course you do. My friends want to meet my famous mother. Some of them have even read your books."

Nuran looked reluctantly at the kitchen. "Saturday, you say. We'll have to organize some food. Is there a local caterer? Maybe your home help woman knows of someone."

Ali laughed. "Stephanie says she's bringing everything, Nuran. We're off the hook."

Nuran shrugged, "I suppose if I look on the event as a sociological exercise, I might find it interesting."

A rare joke.

Despite her disinterest in the domestic arts, Nuran put out a decent lunch of sandwiches and soup every day for the two of them. Ali found that she ate better with some company, she had been getting too lazy even to bother with anything more than crackers and tea. And, caustic comments aside, things were going a lot better than Ali had ever imagined. Nuran had been with them for nearly two weeks now and they had figured out a workable routine.

Mother and daughter breakfasted together and mapped out any chores for Anita the home worker to do. Then Nuran worked most of the morning on her laptop at the desk in her pleasant bedroom/sunroom, answering letters regarding her book and doing research for her next project. Her publisher had even mentioned possibly arranging a bookstore event in Bonville while she was in the area. At noontime, Nuran would stop her work to have lunch and chat.

Chatting with Nuran! Ali could scarcely believe it.

"Not that there are any great break-throughs," she said to Pete at night. "We're hardly confiding, girly pals. The last time I asked her about my father was ten years ago and she said the subject was closed. But we can talk about teaching and education. Or any of her books of course. And she's decent about putting Emily in and out on her leash. "

So the days were passing a little more pleasantly, a little more quickly. Ali felt tremendously big now, she was carrying the baby low. Doctor Blair had emphasized the need for even extra caution, ensuring that she could carry the baby as long as possible. So it was a bit scary, she admitted and it was easier to sleep in the afternoons, knowing that there was someone else in the house.

The evenings passed painlessly enough too, as they all liked Scrabble. They either ate what Anita had prepared or Pete cooked them something.

Nuran even complimented Pete on his lasagne.

Once Nuran had asked curiously about the picture of the Samos sisters. Ali explained the facts briefly but didn't mention how she had come to feel almost a family connection for Akantha and Adelpha, as if they were her aunts.

Nuran picked up the photo. "It seems both the sisters had lonely deaths. But I'm not surprised, I know that happens far too often in the North American culture. There is no respect, only neglect for the elderly."

Ali felt the old rebellious rankling.

"There was lots of help available to Akantha," she protested. "Care for seniors, home nursing help, seniors' homes. Akantha Samos refused it all."

"All institutional facilities," Nuran said.

"The neighbours would have been friendly but she didn't want their attention."

Nuran made a moue of distaste. "There is no family support in these disjointed modern communities," she said in her lecturer's, brooking no argument voice. "It is a broken culture."

"Not everyone wants family connections," Ali said pointedly, remembering her own wedding that was notably absent of parents. Nuran had been travelling and sent a gift card for an expensive china shop. Pete's father was a no show altogether, he hadn't even answered Ali's invitation. None of which thank goodness, had ruined the small ceremony, the exquisitely happy occasion.

Nuran shrugged, the barb apparently didn't register. They never did.

She put the picture back on the dresser, beside the small snapshot of herself with five-year old Ali and the posed studio photo she used on her book jackets. Musingly, she briefly held the snapshot.

"Look at my hair," she said raising a hand to her stylish cropped cut. "I can't believe how silly I looked. And that red caftan thing."

"I think you look cute," Ali said, knowing full well how Nuran would loathe the description. "And I haven't a lot of pictures to choose from."

Nuran tsked. "We didn't snap, snap, snap photos every minute. Not like people do today. The most photographed peoples in history," she said scornfully. "Everyone's a movie star."

But she put the small picture down gently. "The school photographer took pictures every year," she said. "I gave them to you years ago."

Group shots of Ali with all the other lonely girls. For a woman interested in social and cultural history, her mother didn't seem to carry around much of her own.

"Our Nevra is going to have a photo album," Ali told Pete that night. "I'm going to start it right now with our wedding pictures. "

*   *   *

On baby shower day, Pete had brushed Emily before leaving and now Ali clipped a bow of pink plastic rosettes to the dog's collar.

"Show Nuran how pretty you look, Emily."

"She looks embarrassed," Nuran said sympathetically. Ali took a picture to e-mail to Miranda. Nuran was elegant as always, in a soft grey patterned silk shirt and slim black trousers. Ali and daughter-to-be wore stretch slacks and a capacious red sweater.

"It's hopeless," Ali had laughed while dressing. "You might as well just drape a curtain or sheet over me."

But Nuran had offered a pretty scarf that she'd bought in India. She'd even helped adjust it through Ali's hair. Ali was touched.

The guests arrived in a swirl of cold air, color, scent, and gay greetings, augmented by Emily's excited barks. Two hours later, the Jakes' living room was a cheerful clutter of pink and white wrapping paper, boxed diapers, sundry stuffed toy animals and what looked like clothes for a tiny doll, never a new human being.

Ali basked on the couch, enjoying the thrill of company. Her teacher colleagues had filled her in on the doings at Middle Island Elementary and how her students were managing with the temporary teacher. They had also brought a giant card signed by all the children in the class.

"It's lovely," Ali exclaimed as she read over the crayoned signatures. "Please tell the children that I miss them a lot."

In the kitchen by the coffee maker, Ali could see Stephanie and Jane deep in conversation with Nuran. They had already talked of arranging for Nuran to speak to the library book club. A bit later, Pete and Chief Halstead arrived, the chief carrying in a two foot tall plush Babar elephant in crown and bright red jacket.

"Kids love Babar right? I know my daughter did."

When introduced to Nuran, he said appreciatively, "I see where Ali gets her good looks." Then when she asked if he wanted coffee, he followed her into the kitchen like a big puppy.

Steph watched in amusement. "Your mother's book may advise against marriage," she said wryly to Ali. "But that hardly means she isn't interested in men. Does she have one at the moment by the way?"

Ali had to admit she didn't know. "Nuran isn't exactly the confiding type, at least not to her daughter."

Steph's smile became thoughtful. Bud certainly seemed to be enjoying himself. Maybe she had been taking his devotion a little too much for granted.

After the guests had left, Ali was amazed at how exhausted she felt. But happy too. She had braced herself for Nuran's comments about the local women but instead Nuran merely commented that she and Pete had made some nice friends. Ali found herself dozing off to the light clatter of plates and cutlery as Pete and Nuran did the kitchen clean-up. Nevra moved lazily in her womb, she liked to hear the voices too.

With sleepy guilt, Ali recalled Jane Carrell asking her how she was coming along with the museum project. In fact, she had neglected Akantha Samos' boxes for days now, ever since Nuran's arrival actually. She would get back to the project after the baby arrived, she promised herself. *Things to do after the baby comes*, an ever-growing list.

At ten Pete took Emily out for her night-time pee. He felt great relief. The house had looked warm and welcoming, their new friends were terrific, Ali looked well.

Everything was going to be alright.

32

In many situations, your turkey calling expertise will mean the difference between failure and success.

Nick stopped the car. This looked like a good spot. A piece of old rail fence snaked along the ditch and there was still some snow lying in drifts under a line of cedars. Not much, but enough to make it a good place to look for tracks. Apparently deer liked to munch on the cedar branches and turkeys could scrabble around in the turned up debris beneath. He knew all this from his *Tracking Ontario Wildlife* book. If his I-phone worked, he could have just used the Net but the reception in parts of the Island wasn't reliable. Out here in the boonies, sometimes you still had to use a book.

Man, it was quiet here in the woods, away from the road. Kind of neat really, if you just stopped and listened. Just the snow and the scrubby cedar trees and himself. And the animals of course. It wasn't the way he usually spent a Saturday morning, usually he wouldn't even be up yet, but today he was eager to get out and practice some turkey tracking.

He saw the rabbit tracks first, just like the picture in the book. The regular pattern of the two big back feet spread out and the small indentations of the front paws in between. And man, what a leaper! Old Bugs Bunny was really moving, there must be three feet between the tracks. Then he saw why. Old Bugs was being chased, looked like might have been a coyote after him. Yep look at those neat padded tracks, telling the story. What a kick.

He wondered where Old Coyote was now? Whether he'd got his breakfast.

He walked carefully, looking for tracks before taking his steps. Maybe those trees over there were the kind that the turkeys liked to roost in. The birds could be up there now, sitting on their eggs. Raising his Thanksgiving dinner.

Oh man, what was that flash of orange moving like a piece of fire over the snow ahead. A fox.

And the gun is back in the car.

He followed anyway, his clumsy progress easily outdistanced by the animal. It even looked back at the human once, as if taunting him. Soon the fox disappeared altogether, like a teasing thought. Leaving him alone in a small clearing. The dark cedars of the perimeter seemed to press in on him, shading the weak March sun. He had to remind himself it wasn't even noon yet. Quickening his steps, he headed for what he thought of as the exit, an opening in the trees.

"What are *you* doing here?" came a high, accusing voice behind him. He nearly jumped out of his skin and turned around to see the small, angry person of Penny Loo, carrying a paintbox and fold-up easel. With wildlife images fresh in his mind, he thought she looked like a furious chattering squirrel.

She sounded like one too, spitting out questions. "I hope you're not here hunting. Don't you know this is a no-hunting area? It's bad enough that I have to put up with those monsters from the camp tramping around and shooting off pot-shots but I don't expect it from the police. Do you think that's a good example to set? I should report you to the Humane Society."

She was so tiny, he felt an absurd impulse to just pick her up and set her back in whatever tree she'd fallen out of. Then he realized she'd stopped talking and was looking up at him, her head tilted aggressively back in her purple knit hat.

"Well?"

"What are *you* doing here?" he returned, childishly.

"This clearing is one of my painting places," she said, with a proprietary sweep of her parka sleeve. "There are purple finches here this week. Pretty sparrow type birds with purple head feathers," she added insultingly.

"I know what finches are," he lied. Christ, she was annoying.

"But you're not looking for finches. "

"Nope. I'm tracking wild turkeys."

She looked shocked at the actual confirmation of her ranting.

Live with it lady, some of us are painters and some of us are hunters.

"It's not turkey hunting season for another month."

"I'm not shooting, I'm just tracking."

Her mouth tightened. "Not in my cedars. You must go somewhere else."

And she started to set up her easel, with quick efficient movements. She seemed to be done with him altogether. He stood there, feeling vaguely foolish. What was he to do now, stomp off like an idiot through the trees? Especially when she was so calmly absorbed. In seconds she seemed to have become a part of the clearing, shutting him out.

Curious, he looked over her shoulder. Loomed over it, more like. She seemed to be working on a painting that she had already begun, perhaps the day before. Just a clump of cedars, but they looked more interesting in the picture, as if they were decorated with something. He moved closer and could see that the tree ornaments were birds, probably those red-headed birds she had mentioned. The birds were bigger than they should be, like kids' toys but somehow it looked right.

"What do you think?" she asked, without looking round.

He shrugged. "It looks pretty, I guess. I don't know much about painting."

"You must know *something*. Weren't there any paintings in your house when you were growing up? Didn't your school class ever go to visit a gallery?"

"Yeah, sure, we had some pictures." His mother bought a calendar every year with kids' drawings of puppies and kittens and there were a couple of dark old paintings of trees over the living room sofa. They didn't look anything like the bright work on her easel.

"And your school trips?" she asked.

"We always chose the baseball game. Never an art gallery."

She widened her interestingly shaped eyes.

"Then you'd better go practise killing birds. You want to get good at it, don't you?"

He scowled and stood there stubbornly, watching her paint.

Finally she stamped her little boot in the snow and turned around.

"Go on, then," she said, waving her brush at his chest. "I've got work to do. I have to paint these birds before they all disappear. So, shoo, shoo, shoo."

He was glad to leave. What a nutbar! He doubted there was a turkey anywhere in the vicinity, after all her chattering. Unfortunately when he got out of the clearing, he wasn't sure of the way back. Shouldn't be hard though, soon enough he'd get back to the road. And wasn't that one of The Rowan Tree *No Trespassing, No Hunting* signs? Easy to find his way from here, just follow the fence. He was pretty near the spot where that Mr. Guardian had flipped his snowmobile.

He swung along, his frustration gradually easing, the farther he got from Ms. Loo. There were some trees ahead, maybe he'd spot a turkey after all. He looked keenly upwards into the thick branches. Instead, something on the ground caught his eye, something that glinted in the morning sunlight. A piece of jewellry? Curious as a big crow, he bent and picked it up, turning it over in his hands.

Oddly, it was just a piece of bright wire, about four inches long. All the fence wire he'd been following was older and rusted. No brightness there. Also both ends of this piece of wire had been neatly cut by something much sharper than anything in nature. Puzzled, he looked around, aware once again of the incredible stillness of the woods once his own crashing and crunching footsteps ceased.

He was standing near a single cedar, a bit apart from the neighbouring clump. About four feet up, at his chest level, he saw a broken mark in the bark. The mark encircled the tough, wiry tree trunk. His hand seeming to take on a life of its own, he held the piece of wire out towards the tree. It fit perfectly into the bite in the bark, though it didn't go more than a quarter of the way round. This piece was just a discarded scrap, originally there would have been more.

He was a bright enough lad under his absent manner and it didn't take more than a couple of seconds for the light bulb to click. Like a man in a trance, he started to walk towards a slightly bigger cedar about ten feet away. And found a similar bite in the bark, about four feet up. He and Pete Jakes hadn't seen the tree grooves before because they were combing the *ground* for evidence. And this piece of wire must have been under the snow.

He reached for his phone, remembered it didn't work in the woods, and set off on a run for the Rowan Tree outbuildings a quarter mile away.

*   *   *

"Well I'll be damned," Halstead swore. "Is there a jinx haunting the Island this winter or what?" He hit the bark of the offending tree so hard, he winced. "And what the heck does it all *mean*? That's what I want to know. If these are all pranks, the jokester has a pretty warped sense of humour."

"Somebody wanted to hurt somebody," Jakes said. "I think we know that much. Anybody who met that wire while driving a snowmobile was going to go down hard. Guardian would have taken a hit right across his upper chest."

"And he was wearing a thick winter jacket, so nothing showed up."

"Not to mention, the doctors were concentrating on his head bump."

An intensive scouring of the area had turned up no more hunks of wire. It was pure luck that Nick had come upon any remnant at all.

"This is real sick stuff," Pete said. "Dawn Guardian could have run into it too."

"Damn!" Halstead swore again. "She could still be in danger. We'd better go talk to her. As if the woman needs this, on top of everything else."

33

Stephanie Bind sang along happily to the song on the car radio. The music wasn't from her time, but she got a kick out of the cheerful goofiness of the song about surfing, sunshine and teenage summer love, especially in this blah, non-winter they were experiencing in the province.

She was on her way to Bonville to pick up some linen pillowcases for the Retreat. Her mind raced with a zillion thoughts which was O.K. She had always liked being charged up and busy. Two more bookings for July had come in the morning's e-mail, both bookings for groups of eight. The Retreat was succeeding beyond her wildest hopes. She could tell the members of the awards committee had been impressed on their visit. Of course you couldn't know how people would vote, until the results were actually announced but on the whole, she thought the Retreat had shown well. And the frittata (tested on Bud previously) and salad had made a pleasant lunch.

Let's all ride the wild surf. . . .

A cheerful counterpoint to the roadside bare-boughed trees and murky, streaked sky. She drove carefully, Lina's tragic end now always in the back of her mind. And the Guardians' terrible misfortune as well. She felt herself stiffen as she approached a strange car ahead on the road. She hated this this new feeling of wariness, that was no way to live. Besides, familiarity was no guarantee of security. Witness her own case — she married a man she d known her whole life and look how that had turned out! She passed the other car, and the driver honked hello. It was Patty Burke, the mail lady, driving her son's car this morning, not a stranger at all. Time to stop these silly panicky thoughts. Besides, the winter's rash of misery didn't seem to be deterring bookings, she reminded herself.

She smiled, thinking how much fun it had been to arrange Ali Jakes' baby shower. And meeting the oh so elegant, accomplished Nuran. Bud had certainly been charmed, she'd teased him about it. Which reminded her, while she was at the Mall, she would look for something special to wear to the awards luncheon next month. Whether she won or not, she might as well look great. For a moment though, she played with the pleasant fantasy of accepting the winner's award.

I'm so excited! I never dreamed I would receive such an honour!
I'd like to thank everyone who voted for me . . . .

But first a quick dart into the village post office, where she ran into Jane Carrell picking up the police station mail.

"Hi Jane, I'm glad to have caught you. I've got your gloves that you left at the baby shower. Come out to the car with me and I'll get them."

She chatted breezily on, "Wasn't the shower fun? And Nuran is so impressive – as gorgeous as her daughter too."

Jane took the gloves, but she seemed abstracted. "Sorry," she said, "I'm kind of in a rush, can't leave the station empty for long."

"Another time then," Steph said. She was about to close the car door, then asked, "Is there any news on Doug Guardian? I ran into Dawn yesterday and she didn't look so great. I hope he hasn't taken a turn for the worse."

Jane looked up from her armful of mail, "No, I don't think so. In fact my niece says there are positive signs that Doug may be coming out of his coma sometime soon. You haven't seen Dawn today have you?" she asked.

"No, this was yesterday afternoon."

"Enjoy your shopping, then," Jane asked. "Though better keep an eye on the weather." She looked up at the sky, "Could be snow coming."

"Oh it's probably nothing," Steph said. "Like last time."

"You never know," said Jane with the pessimism of a true Islander. "You never know what's going to blow in off the lake." And she hurried off across the street.

That's odd about Dawn, Steph thought as she turned onto the causeway. You'd think she'd be looking relieved now that there was hope of Doug improving. The poor woman probably just didn't dare to get her hopes up. She'd heard that Dawn was continuing with her busy schedule of overseeing the Rowan Tree homes. Maybe it kept her mind off her husband's terrible plight, although the awards committee would surely have made allowances. Not that they would have to, the Rowan Tree could easily stand on its merits.

Steph knew from staff accounts that Dawn was a hands-on perfectionist. Steph's own great-aunt, a Rowan Tree resident, had only praise for the place. The rooms were comfortable and clean, the food tasty and in summer, the gardens were a local showpiece.

Almost as nice as my own at the Retreat, the thought sneaked in. Steph had to blush. Women can be just as competitive as men, Bud had said. *Guess he might have a point.*

She laughed, thinking of those highschool cheerleader tryouts. They could get pretty competitive at times. Not downright nasty of course, like that movie she'd seen on television once, where a mother had actually killed another girl who was likely to win the top spot over her daughter. But it had been tough the year that Steph won lead cheerleader over her best friend Julie North. There was a strain for awhile, which Steph understood. She would have felt just as badly if she'd lost. Surely though, two adult women like herself and Dawn Guardian could handle it.

*   *   *

Jane dumped the bundle of mail on the front counter. The station was empty this time of day, which was good. She would have a chance to get caught up on the emergency preparedness reports.

First though, she'd get a cup of coffee and warm her hands. As she was passing her desk, she glanced idly at her computer.

And stopped, sinking into her chair as she stared with disbelief at the screen.

Now, that was interesting.

Dawn Guardian wasn't at the Rowan Tree and the housekeeper didn't know where she'd gone.

"She's usually very precise about saying where she's going to be – she's very precise about everything. But today she must have slipped out somehow. She's probably just gone to Bonville to visit Doug, she goes there at some time every day."

They told the housekeeper to call as soon as she heard anything and set off in the cruiser. They were barely on their way when the radio crackled.

"That you, chief?" Jane sounded oddly hesitant.

"What's up – no trouble?" asked Halstead.

"No, nothing like that," she said. "I've just received some information from an RCMP researcher that you might find interesting."

"I m all ears," Halstead said, "shoot. What do they say about Doug Guardian?"

"No, there's nothing new on Doug's record or fingerprints," Jane said. "This is actually information about Dawn Guardian."

Halstead hunched forward in the passenger seat. "What's happened? Is she O.K.?" he asked anxiously. Christ, he was a nervous Nelly this morning.

"I don t know about now," Jane said. "This info is from the Guardians' marriage certificate. Her name then was Patricia Dawn Smith and her place of birth is given as Callandar, Ontario."

"I thought she came from B.C." Halstead said. "The newspaper article mentioned that her parents ran a fishing camp in B.C."

"That sounded better I guess "

"Sounded better than what?"

"A string of foster homes. According to this report, that's how she was brought up."

Halstead whistled surprise. "How did all this come up?"

"When you make a records request, I guess they automatically do a check on any spouses as well. Dawn or Patricia I guess, ran up some minor arrest charges,when she ran away a couple of times."

"So, no parents, no fishing camp in beautiful British Columbia? No mother the legendary short-order cook?"

"It seems not."

Halstead shrugged. "So the woman changed her name and made up some background for herself. Lots of people have lousy backgrounds and lousy parents they'd rather forget."

"Oh and there's one more thing," Jane added more tartly, "Somewhere along the line, our Dawn or Patricia or whatever you want to call her, has picked up a a certificate in rifle sharp-shooting."

Halstead looked at Pete.

"O.K. thanks Jane, and keep on it. We're headed over to Bonville General to talk to her."

He leaned back in his seat. "It seems that Mrs. Guardian has something to hide. That she's told a few stories."

Pete nodded. "Interesting. The question is, how many?"

"What are you thinking?"

"This wire business is pretty strange stuff. Maybe she lied about Doug's accident too. When you think of it, how could she not know what happened? She was right there."

"Maybe she didn't see it in the dark," Halstead said reasonably. "She was confused, understandably. The snowmobile was roaring, her husband was lying injured on the ground. She had other priorities. And then she headed back to the Rowan Tree for help."

"Then who cut the wire down?" Pete asked. "You didn't see it, the paramedics didn't see it." He turned to look at Halstead. "Because it wasn't there."

A heavy silence descended like a weight in the car, as they considered the implications. The roadside sped past unheeded.

"She could have done it," Pete said at last.

Halstead groaned. "This case has got more twists and turns than a ride at Canada's Wonderland. What are we saying here, that Dawn Guardian planned to kill Doug? Why the hell would she do a thing like that?"

"She must have learned that he'd messed up and killed Lina. She told you herself that she made a point of knowing everything that went on at the Rowan Tree. He couldn't have hidden the truth from her for long."

"So she tried to kill her husband because he'd screwed up her chance to win an *award!* I can't buy that."

But Pete was launched on his line of thought, like a bird dog on a scent. "All the details we got of the accident came from her. She could tell you whatever she wanted to there in the woods."

Halstead nodded reluctantly, remembering the weird moonlit scene in the cedars. "So we're saying maybe it was Dawn who had the crazy 'whim' to go out on the nighttime snowmobile ride?"

"Only maybe it wasn't a whim at all," Pete said carefully. "Maybe it was all part of a careful plan. She could have put the wire up earlier in the day. And of course Doug never saw any light near the woods but she may have told him she did. Then he hit the wire and pitched off his machine."

"This is nuts," Halstead objected. "She was trying to kill Doug? I say again, why for God's sake? They'd been married for ten years, they were successful. He seemed to worship her."

Pete swerved to avoid a pair of crows on the road. "He must have become a threat to her somehow."

"How? Because he didn't want to sell the Rowan Tree? Jane says Dawn was going along with that."

"Maybe he found out about some of her stories – we did. Or because *he* was starting to suspect *her*," Jakes said slowly.

"What do you mean?"

"Maybe it was *Dawn* who took the rifle out after the hunters and accidently caused Lina's accident. Doug said she was pretty upset about the hunters being on their land and we know now that she could use a rifle." Jakes turned excitedly to face Halstead. "Maybe Doug has been covering for her all along. That's why he was so anxious that there be no charges."

"Even if that were true," Halstead protested again, "it doesn't make any sense. Why would she want to kill him, when he was protecting her?"

"I guess she didn't trust him not to blurt it out to someone. Even we could see signs that he was beginning to crack under the strain."

"And you honestly think that's a good enough reason for a woman to kill her husband?"

Pete steered tightly round the curve at Little Swamp, his expression sombre.

"It depends on the woman I guess. Some people wouldn't have covered up the shooting in the beginning but we've been willing to believe that Doug did that. Some people would have taken the responsibility and paid the penalty for making a tragic mistake."

And not very many people, Halstead thought. Not when you put it like that.

"Still, trying to duck a mistake is a long distance from murdering your husband."

Pete shrugged. "Police procedure, not to mention episodes of every television cop show ever written, says first, look to the spouse. We didn't do that."

"We didn't figure we were looking at an attempted murder."

Jakes didn't answer.

Halstead sighed heavily. "It could have happened that way," he said. "Or we could just be making all this up."

"Somebody's made something up," Pete reminded him. "And Doug Guardian is in no shape to tell us his version."

Halstead looked grimly at the road ahead. "Better step on the gas lad. If what you're thinking is possible, we'd best get to the hospital and make sure she doesn't finish the job on Doug."

"Should we use the siren?"

"No. We don't want to alert her."

Pete gunned the cruiser along the causeway. Halstead looked out at the cold, lapping water. How ironic to think of Vern Byers' fears of terrorists invading the Island.

While all along the terror might have been within.

*   *   *

Pete parked the cruiser in the hospital tow-away zone and the two policemen hurried through the emergency entrance.

"This is nuts," Halstead said, "we've talked ourselves into a bunch of nonsense." But he didn't slacken his pace. He punched the elevator button for the sixth floor. Once there, the two officers sped past the startled nurse at the intensive care station.

She chased after them, demanding, "What are you doing!"

Halstead turned to hold her back, waving Pete on. He and the nurse arrived together, just as Jakes had completed a quick search of the room and bathroom.

Guardian lay somnulent and unmoving on his cot, oblivious to the brief drama.

Also alone. There was obviously no one else in the room. A mouse couldn't have hidden in that sterile whiteness.

"What are you doing?" the nurse asked again, rather breathlessly. A different nurse, not Jane's niece. Steely-eyed and quickly regaining her nurse control, not to be intimidated by a mere pair of cops.

Halstead brushed past this. "Has Mrs. Guardian been in here yet today?"

She looked about to sputter.

"Yes or no? This is an emergency." he said. He could be steely-eyed too.

"I don't think so," she said meekly. "I'll check the book."

There was no entry of a visitor yet that day.

"What now?" Pete asked. "She could be anywhere on the Island."

Or off the Island — flown the coop entirely. The unspoken thought.

"Best bet is to split up," Halstead said. "I'll stay here, you go back and wait at the Rowan Tree. She might just be out on an errand and not know that we've found out about the wire. I'll also send out an APB to the provincial police. But remember if you're the first to find her, we only want to talk to her. We don't know yet that any of this is true."

"Right," Jakes said wrily. But he wasted no time, his quick footsteps echoing as he headed down the corridor.

"Got any magazines?" Halstead asked the nurse, when he'd made his call to Jane at the station. "I might be here awhile."

She found him a couple of battered copies of *Readers Digest*. In the hospital room, Guardian was still deep in his seemingly endless sleep. And why would the poor guy want to wake up, Halstead thought. There's a helluva lot of bad news waiting for him.

* * *

Pete passed Turkey Woods for the third time that day, his thoughts racing. What was he going to say to Dawn Guardian if she did turn up at the Rowan Tree? He had to detain her of course, and take her to the station for questioning. But what would she do—was she going to bolt when she saw him or the cruiser? She might have the nerve to brazen it out. So she had told a few lies about her background, she might say. Big deal. She didn't know that the police had found the wire.

He tried to put himself into her thoughts that morning of the tragedy. Say she'd done it, shot the rifle and sent Lina Russell off the road. Bad move number one – she hadn't called for help, but maybe she panicked. Doug must have seen her and wondered why she looked so rough. Or she told him straight away what had happened. She needed his help with the rifle.

So that was bad move number two—neither of the Guardians had called for help. But give them the benefit of the doubt, maybe they'd gone back to the site, seen the other motorist already there and figured he would make the 911 call.

What then? Adoring Doug helps his wife cover up her involvement in the accident. He tosses the rifle down the old well, then takes the hinges off the gun cupboard and concocts the story of the stolen rifle.

But the police discover the cover-up and blame Doug for the shooting.

What are Dawn's thoughts then? Will she let her husband take the rap for the accident? It seemed that she will. But even that isn't enough for her. She begins to worry that Doug will crack under the stress and reveal who had actually made that shot.

So how bad would that be? Was she likely to just pack up and run, leave home and husband and business of ten years? All because of a bad decision? A very bad decision, it was true but she could get a lawyer. The charges would be serious, careless use of a firearm and reckless endangerment but the lawyer could emphasize her anxiety, her temporary imbalance of mind and probably get her a suspended sentence with a proviso not to use a firearm for a period of time. Not that this would be any comfort to Lina Russell's family.

And of course it would be noted that Dawn Guardian's behaviour hardly qualified her for the award of business woman of the year. But he doubted that the Rowan Tree homes would lose any clients, there was such a demand for assisted care nursing homes for millions of aging baby boomers. So if she had a thick skin and could survive the blot on her reputation, Dawn Guardian should have been fine. She'd have her loving husband and her successful business and people would soon forget the details, or at least lose interest in them.

Instead, Dawn Guardian decided to kill her husband.

And not in the heat of the moment either. If his suspicions were true, she had carefully planned her husband's 'accident'. He thought of the scene in the woods that the chief had described. The overturned machine, the sprawled man prone on the snow, the ominous shadows of the cedars, all of it lit only by the spotlights of the paramedics. Like the eerie setting for a stage tragedy, he'd thought at the time. And that was it exactly. Dawn Guardian had painted the picture in their minds. Staged the tragedy.

She couldn't have risked the possibility that someone on the rescue team would discover the wire between the trees. So she must have coolly cut the wire down while Doug lay there on the ground. Even before she ran for help and began to play her part of the distraught and panicked wife. Before she spent the long night at the hospital in supposedly loyal vigil by her comatose husband.

Again though, why? Was the woman simply some kind of monster?

There had to be more to it. Something else, some even darker reason.

But what?

And where the hell was she?

A tyrant spell has bound me
And I cannot, cannot go.

Ali struggled up from her nest of couch cushions and poured fragrant ginger tea from the thermos Nuran had left her. There was also a tray holding her favourite cup and some pretty iced biscuits. She was touched and felt a brief guilt at her laziness. Then she remembered oh yes, I'm a sacred vessel busy creating another being. Not lazy at all.

When Nuran's Toronto agent had called unexpectedly from Bonville and invited Nuran for lunch, she had been reluctant to leave. But Ali had pooh-poohed her doubts.

"Go, go, you've hardly been out of this house for the past two weeks. Besides, you'll only be away a couple of hours and Pete has the pager. He can get here from the station in fifteen minutes. Don't worry, I'll be fine."

Now she looked at the various amusements to hand, or specifically in the vicinity of the couch. There was Nuran's book, *Woman Kind,* which Ali had opened a couple of times. On the book jacket, a photo of Nuran in Africa, surrounded by a group of smiling, young women in brightly coloured wraps and head scarves.

Inside, Ali had read as far as the introduction.

"You've come a long way, baby!"
(one-time popular slogan in North American, advertising a new,
slimmer cigarette created especially for women).

In North American culture, women may feel that they enjoy a
freedom not enjoyed by their deprived foreign sisters. However, they
should be aware that their freedom and economic security is founded
on the virtual economic enslavement of those very sisters. Millions
of women around the world live in poverty and work in dangerous,
unhealthy circumstances for little pay, to provide luxuries for their
pampered Western counterparts. I say that we have a sacred duty to
correct this terrible imbalance . . . ."

Good stuff, which was no surprise as most of Nuran's writing
was on a smiliar theme. Ali meant to read this book too, but perhaps
after she'd had the baby. When her mind was clear again and she
could better concentrate. Instead, she'd been re-reading Winnie
the Pooh. The adventures of that most remarkable bear and his
woodland friends were much more her speed these days and she
reasoned she needed the practice for Nevra's bedtime reading.

But even Pooh couldn't snag her attention this afternoon. Perhaps
she'd have a look at Akantha's boxes again. She'd done nothing for
the archival project since Nuran arrived, in truth had hardly thought
about it. Now she recalled the letters she had been reading at the
time. Were there others? She opened the album again and found
the packet of letters where she had left them. They even smelled of
the musty past. Just the thing to pass away a sleepy afternoon. She
settled down in cozy anticipation.

Dear sister: I have taken your advice to advertise for some home
help and today I have met the most wonderful young woman. She is
strong and smart and can help with the housework but also has training
in massage. She tells me she will be able to ease the pain in my legs very
soon with regular treatment. And she will come right to my house.

The next letter enthused even more.

Dear sister: This woman Patricia, is a godsend. There is no end to her talents. Now she is doing my monthly household bookkeeping. She says that she can save me lots of money by taking the car and doing smart shopping. She is one smart young woman. She showed me that she has saved me almost one hundred dollars in expenses this past month.

Another described a happy day.

Dear sister: Today Patricia drove me to Niagara Falls, the first real trip I have taken outside the city since Steven died. It was a lovely spring day and the cherry blossoms were in bloom along the roadsides. Though it is my seventy-fifth birthday, I felt young at heart.

Ali smiled, how nice that Adelpha had found some company and was getting interested in life again.

Ouch! She winced suddenly and shifted uncomfortably on the couch. "That was quite the kick, little Nevra. I'll remind you of this my darling daughter, when you're expecting a baby of your own."

Darn, she'd dropped the packet of letters and now they had spilt onto the floor. She grunted as she tried to bend over to pick them up but instead, rolled back helplessly against the couch cushions.

Shoot! Was it worth the effort?

She looked up at the sound of light pattering against the window pane. It had started to snow. Probably just fool's snow again, tiny dry flakes that probably wouldn't last but there was a hypnotic effect in watching their descent. She had read that it snowed in the mountains in Turkey and thought she had a childhood memory of pleasure at the sight. Next winter she would build a snowman for Nevra.

A pleasant thought to drift off to.

*　　*　　*

A light scattering of snowflakes was blowing over the causeway. By the time Pete arrived at the Rowan Tree, the snow was already forming a thin film on the cruiser windshield. He glanced quickly around for the Guardian SUV. Damn, he couldn't see it, but maybe she'd parked it in the garage. He didn't waste any time looking for it, but bounded up the front steps of the house.

Inside, there was clattering from the cafeteria, the wait staff cleaning up after lunch. The housekeeper was rushed but apologetic.

"No, I'm afraid Dawn hasn't been back yet. I'm surprised she wasn't at the hospital. She hardly goes anywhere else these days."

"No one's heard from her?" Pete asked. "She hasn't called to check in?"

She shook her head and asked anxiously. "Is something wrong officer, has Doug taken a turn for the worse?"

"No he's still O.K." he reassured her. Then improvised quickly, "He's improved a bit actually, that's what I want to tell Mrs. Guardian."

"Oh, I'm so glad. Just give me a few moments then and I'll ask the other staff once again if anybody has heard from her."

She was back in a few moments, looking flustered and apologetic.

"I'm sorry, Officer Jakes, I didn't know this but apparently Dawn did come back briefly around noon."

What the hell? Pete tried to quell his frustration. "Did she say anything about where she was going next?"

"The housemaid told her about you and the other officers being there in the woods this morning and that you wanted to talk to her. Maybe she drove to town and the police station."

Not likely.

Dawn wouldn't have had to wait to hear the details of the wire find. She knew what that would mean, she'd get the point pretty quickly.

"I'm sorry for the mix-up, and all your extra trips," the housekeeper apologized again. "But it should come out alright now," she said with a return to her usual cheeriness. "She'll be at the station or the hospital and you'll catch her at one or the other."

Pete asked to talk to the housemaid but learned little more. The girl said that Dawn had looked concerned but that wasn't surprising with her husband in intensive care. Any message could be important.

There was no point in waiting at the Rowan Tree. He doubted that Dawn Guardian was ever coming back. Not now, too many bridges had burnt behind her. He stood in the lobby, beset with swirling thoughts. What had they learned about Dawn in the past few hours? Was there anything to help illuminate the whole messy picture of the last few weeks. He felt if he could just adjust the picture mentally he could make some sense of it. His brain ached with the effort, as if he were physically spinning the kaleidoscope of information, adjusting it incrementally, degree by degree.

And then his thoughts arced. A hundred and eighty-degree turn in fact.

He had been wondering at one time whether Doug Guardian might have purposely killed Lina Russell. But if it was Dawn shooting the bullets that send Lina off the road that morning, did the same arguments work to incriminate her? For now, instead of mere speculation, they had a definite motive. Had Lina somehow discovered some other lies in Dawn Guardian's background?

What else was there to know?

There must a clue somewhere in the woman's past. He would go to the station and check out that computer background information himself. But first he would radio the chief from the cruiser to warn him that Dawn knew about the discovery of the wire, that she was now probably panicking and potentially extremely dangerous.

He turned, intent on his thoughts and hardly noticing his surroundings. Or the tiny little white-haired woman he'd just about bowled over.

"Sorry, ma'am," he said, grabbing at her arm to steady her. The arm felt like a chicken bone under her sweater. He recognized the shock of woolly white hair.

"How are the budgies today?" he asked.

"The yellow one's a pig," she said disgustedly, "he won't let the blue one at the food. Somedays I could wring his little neck."

He muttered noncomittally and tipped his hat, trying to edge politely around her. But she kept hold of his arm and stared intently up at him with her rheumy blue eyes.

"I saw on the television about those people who trick old folks out of their savings. But you don't have to worry about me being fooled, no sir. My granddaughter told me about those terrible people and their tricks. She said that I should always check with my bank before trusting any stranger with my money. "

Pete smiled, "Your granddaughter is smart and that was good advice that she gave you."

The old lady's eyes teared up. "Yes Lina was smart, she's gone now though."

So this was Lina's Granny.

"I knew her," he said gently. "She was very good to my wife."

"You're Officer Jakes," she said triumphantly. "Lina used to like visiting your wife. She's expecting a baby."

"That's right." Guiltily and feeling rotten about it, he pulled away from her grip and took a step away down the hall. "I'm sorry, but I have to go right now. I'll come back some day though and we'll talk about the birds again."

Darned if she didn't follow him, teetering on her cane and calling after him in her reedy quavering voice.

"Lina used to tell me about all her clients. Like the story about the lady's sister who got tricked out of all her money and killed herself. That snooty family, the Samos girls. But the rich and the mighty shall be smited down, that's what the Bible says and Akantha Samos had no call to be snooty any more. She wasn't any better off than the rest of us at the end."

Pete had barely been listening, he was halfway along the hallway, thinking about what he was going to tell Halstead.

But he stopped in his tracks, and came slowly, deliberately back.

"What did you say?"

Granny's attention had wandered though and she was busy straightening the silk roses in the vases at the lobby door. She plucked one out and waved it at Pete's chest. ""My husband used to like a posy in his lapel. Here's one for you."

He stood like stone while she fussed with a button on his uniform jacket.

Akantha Samos.

In a proper murder investigation, they would have looked into Lina Russell's work situation, interrogated her workmates. And of course checked out her recent clients. Akantha Samos was one of Lina's clients.

Akantha Samos who had supposedly died of a fall in her home.

Akantha and Lina.

Lina and the Rowan Tree.

The Guardians.

There was a link, there *had* to be.

He pulled out his bird notebook to see the three dots he had made on his little sketch of the swamp. He had sensed that connection weeks ago, had remarked on how the discovery of Akantha's body seemed to have launched the events of the past month. But he had dismissed the thought, as mere coincidence, just a trick of his orderly mind.

Now it seemed his instincts had been on the right track. He didn't quite understand it all yet but the connection was there, staring him in the face.

36

Every why has a wherefore

Jane Carrell looked up from her desk at the sound of a car in the station parking lot. It was young Jakes and he seemed to be in a hurry.

"Seems to be something starting up out there," he said, blowing on his hands as he burst through the door. ""Lots of wind. But the weather network didn't mention anything much."

Jane snickered. "The weather station doesn't know beans about what's happening on these points that stick out into the lake."

"Your computer's on," he said. "Mind if I look up something?"

She watched him awkwardly grab the mouse.

"Your hands are cold," she said. "What do you want to look up? I'll do it."

"Anything on Akantha Samos and her family," he said fervently. "Whatever you can pull up."

He rubbed his hands together, pacing anxiously while she started googling. During the whole drive into town, he'd been cudgelling his memory, trying to remember what Ali had told him about the Samos sisters. Cursing the fact that he'd hardly listened, he'd just been so glad that Ali had an interest in something.

"Here we go," Jane said. "Is this what you're looking for?"

He pulled up a chair beside her and quickly scanned the screen. There was the story about Pitr Samos and the sale of his movie theatres. Also the newspaper photo of Akantha and the Olympic swimming team.

"What about the sister?" he asked. "I can't remember her name." He made a mental note to listen more attentively to his wife in future.

"Adelpha," Jane said. "Here's something."

NEIGHBOUR RESCUES EMACIATED FORMER HEIRESS FROM HER OWN HOME

Ralph Mason wasn't sure he was hearing right when he heard the tapping from his neighbour's third story window. There had been no activity or lights in the house for more than a week and the Masons assumed their elderly neighbour was on a vacation trip, which she often took in the spring.

"The car was gone from the garage," Mason said. "And the house seemed locked up tight."

He described seeing a pale wraith-like figure behind the window pane.

"Just about scared me out of my shoes," he said. "I knew something was wrong, anybody would. So I went over to the house and knocked real loud on the door. When nobody came, I tried to open it but it was locked. Then I hollered over to the wife to call 911."

Fifteen minutes later when an emergency team arrived, they found Adelpha Samos, 75, weak and disoriented and unable to give any coherent account of her circumstances. She has been hospitalized to attempt to stabilize her condition.

Patricia Ennis, approximately 28 years old, a former companion to Ms. Samos is being sought as a person of interest in connnection with the tragedy.

Miss Ennis is described as being about five foot nine, of slim build, with shoulder length brown hair.

There was another article, an obituary written several months later.

FORMER MOVIE CHAIN HEIRESS VICTIM OF FRAUD, DIES IN NURSING HOME

Adelpha Samos, 75, discovered three months ago abandoned and starving in her former home, has died. Samos appears to have been the victim of a fraudulent scheme to systematically access her bank account over the past two years. Her car was also taken.

It is thought that Ms. Samos fell into a depression on learning the news from her banker and took to her bed. She had a telephone but didn't call the police, neighbours or her sister for assistance.

"She simply stopped eating," said Edith Parker of the Bathurst Nursing Home. "It's a common refuge of the depressed and the elderly who have lost their interest in life."

Despite medical attention at the nursing home, Ms. Samos never did regain comprehension of the events that had led to her collapse.

Jane scrolled down the screen. "That's it, other than the funeral announcement."

"No more mention of the mysterious Patricia Ennis," Pete noted.

Jane sighed. "Yep, she probably moved on, rustled up some new I.D. and looked for a new victim. Like the chief says, it's a common story and often never even reported. I imagine the only reason Adelpha even rated a couple of newspaper headlines was because of the Samos name."

The phone rang and Jane got up to answer it.

Pete sat on, staring blankly at the Google logo on the screen. Thinking.

Someone had cheated the elderly Adelpha Samos of a large chunk of money. Someone Adelpha trusted as a companion, a helper, a friend even.

The mysterious Patricia Ennis, who had apparently never been found, who had disappeared off the radar completely.

Or metamorphisized into someone else.

The newspaper description, with the minor adjustments of age and hair colour, would fit Dawn Guardian, or as she had been known in Callendar Ontario, Patricia Dawn Smith.

But how find out, how prove it. Look for witnesses at the bank or at an ATM machine where she made the Adelpha withdrawals twelve years ago? Not likely. If the police hadn't found her then, when the trail was fresh, what chance would he have of finding any of that long-ago evidence. Besides, the more pertinent question of the moment was

Where is the woman and what is she up to now?

"I can't find a photo," Pete said when Jane came back.

Jane shook her head. "And the police didn't have a photo obviously, or they would have put it in the newspaper. Lucky for her that not too many people were using digital cameras yet. And as for the video tapes at the bank, easy enough to don sunglasses and a hat."

Photos. Pete had stopped hearing Jane after the word photos. He was thinking of the albums that Ali had been sorting through the past few weeks. All kinds of photos there. Adelpha had sent pictures of her wedding to Akantha. Maybe she had sent other pictures, maybe a picture of the young woman who had become like a daughter to her. A picture of Patricia Ennis.

Through the blinding flash in his head, he now heard Jane's voice, like a searing accompaniment to his own thoughts.

"There's probably something about all this in those boxes of Akantha's that you took to Ali."

Yes there probably was. Some piece of damning evidence, likely a photo. He thought of the attempted break-in at Akantha's house. It seemed a year ago, not just a matter of weeks.

And those boxes were now in his own house.

With Ali.

Now he knew why Dawn Guardian hadn't gone to the hospital. She was pursuing more dangerous prey. She must have tracked down the whereabouts of the boxes. She was on her way to silence Ali.

He picked up the phone and somehow dialled his home number. No answer. While he listened to the rings, he stared out the front window of the station.

"What's that?" he asked Jane dumbly.

"That's snow," she said. "Real serious snow. Could be a blizzard coming in off the lake, it happens that way sometimes. That was the chief on the phone by the way, looks like he might be spending the night in Bonville. You'd better get moving too, if you plan on getting home."

She'd be O.K. herself, she lived in the village.

"Get Nick, first" he said tersely. "Tell him to meet me out at my place."

She looked surprised. "But the snow . . ." she began.

He grabbed up his parka. "Try the motel. Tell him Ali's in danger. Tell him to get there as fast as he can. And keep phoning Ali too, tell her to lock the door and not let anyone in."

Jane was already dialling as he left. Outside in the parking lot, he had to use his sleeve to wipe away the snow that had already collected on the windshield.

37

Ali was at her boarding school swimming pool. The smell of chlorinated water was strong. Today the class was about diving, only the teacher standing on the diving board wasn't Miss Patton the gym teacher, but Akantha Samos.

A young Akantha, as she was in in the picture in the album. About twenty, slim and tall, as she poised for her dive. Athletic and graceful, despite the ugly blue serge bathing suit.

She dove cleanly into the water, creating barely a splash in the turquoise depths, and started with a strong crawl stroke down the length of the pool. The girls in the class watched in admiration. Then something went wrong. Akantha's arms were moving differently, more like flailing. She called out something and then she started to slip down under the water.

Ali seemed the only one in the group to notice. She rushed to the edge of the pool, knelt down and leaned out over the water. Akantha had struggled back up, Ali could see the yellow bathing cap bobbing in the water. She was calling out again.

Ali leaned out as far as she could and extended her arm. Their fingertips touched. Then Akantha turned her face. Her skin was leathery and wrinkled. She was old! Old and frail and slipping under the water again. Calling and calling, but Ali couldn't make out what she was saying.

Desperately, she leapt into the water herself, but Akantha had disappeared and the pool was empty.

Ali woke up shivering and melancholy, still in the grip of the strange, disturbing dream. Dazedly, she reached for the album on her stomach, hoping to regain the mood of cozy, sisterly comfort. Most of the letters were on the floor where they had fallen but there were a couple shoved in between the pages. The old paper crackled in her fingers and she saw saw that one of the letters had been taped together, as if it had previously been torn or ripped apart.

And no wonder. The letter she was reading was far from cozy. Adelpha wrote in an entirely new voice, threaded with anger and hurt.

Dear sister: I don't like what you are suggesting. Of course Patricia has references, a whole file folder of them. Why should I send you photocopies of these papers? I would never insult Patricia in that way. She is the daughter I never had.

I wish you could meet her Akantha, she has such energy and faith in herself. She would like to have enough money to start a shop of her own to sell health and beauty products for seniors. She says that unless she can do this, she will have to move and find work in the United States. I have decided to invest money in her shop. What good is the money doing in a bank when it could bring such joy to a young person who is just starting out in life?

And the last letter in the bunch. Crumpled and jammed into the larger envelope.

Sister: I won't listen to your poisonous thoughts any longer. Please do not write me any more. Please stay out of my life.

How sad to read of this dissension between the sisters at that stage of their lives. Ali wanted to cry. She lay with the letters on her breast, feeling the pain of the long-ago break. She wondered if they had made up before Adelpha died. She hoped so. What if they had never managed it, had never spoken or written again for the rest of their lives?

But there was worse, much worse, in the envelope. She read the yellowed newspaper clippings with shaking hands.

NEIGHBOUR RESCUES EMACIATED FORMER HEIRESS FROM HER OWN HOME

FORMER MOVIE CHAIN HEIRESS VICTIM OF FRAUD, DIES IN NURSING HOME

Ali reached for Emily, patting the silky ears, savoring the contact. She thought of her strange, disturbing dream. Was this what Akantha was trying to tell her? The terrible ending to her sister's story? She sat for long moments on the couch, overwhelmed.

Finally, she moved. She felt cold, her limbs stiff. The tea Nuran had made for her had long cooled. She wondered if she could get up and manage to put on the kettle. How late was it anyway? It seemed quite dark. And my goodness, look at the snow. It seemed to be filling the sky, the air. She couldn't even see Miranda's house across the road. Now the strange cushiony softness, the silence and insulation seemed to eerily emphasize her sense of apartness from the world. It was actually sort of spooky. The silence was palpable now, thick, like a pressure pushing against her ears.

Smothering.

Nevra moved restlessly in her womb and Ali felt an echoing unease. A tightening in her chest, a mild panic that she couldn't breathe. She had an urgent desire for fresh air. It must be almost time to take Emily out anyway.

She lurched to her feet and rocked unsteadily for a moment, her sense of balance badly askew. Like a teetering ten pin in a bowling alley. But she called the dog and made it to the kitchen where her red wool coat had hung unused for weeks now. With awkward jabs she managed to get her arms into the coat, then drew the rest loosely about her. Impossible to button it up over the Nevra bump. She didn't worry about leashing Emily, the dog never left her side these days. Together they stood on the porch, taking in great draughts of the damp, cold air.

The days had been getting gradually longer, a few minutes gained every twenty-four hours. But this afternoon the sky was already darkening and it was only three o'clock. As if the snow was a curtain being drawn over the sky.

"Go pee, Emily," Ali urged. With the contrariness of the pregnant, she now wanted to get back inside the house.

But the dog seemed reluctant to leave the porch. She just peered out into the snow, nose quivering and ears cocked.

"Alright," Ali said, "if you won't, you won't. But you'll have to wait for Pete."

Then from afar off, she heard what the dog was listening to. The faint whine of a snowmobile approaching across the fields.

At first she felt bad about Doug, that she had to do it.
It was the rifle business that began the split between them
Because he knew of course that it hadn't been stolen two years ago,
or even a year ago. He was always careful that the guns were locked
up.

So she had to tell him what she'd done, though never why of course
And he took the blame.
But she could see he couldn't take the lying to his friend, the police
chief.
He was going to crack sometime soon.

It was too bad the way things worked out.
Doug wasn't a bad man, just unlucky.
And in this world, as Pop used to say, you had to make your own
luck.

So there was just one more thing to do, one more voice to stop.
She would destroy those boxes that were the start of all the trouble
She would bury the old story forever
The end. Period. Over.

And then it would be all smooth sailing.

She'd get the award, sell the Homes and be set for life.
She'd be respectable.
No more being scared in the night.

*   *   *

The snowmobile pulled up in the side yard, its yellow beamed headlamp marking a path on the snow. The rider, faceless under helmet and goggles, switched off the ignition and for a moment the abrupt silence echoed like a bell in Ali's ears.

Then she became aware of the barking dog, pulling at her hand. "Shush, Emily," she said, "it's O.K."

The rider got off the machine and approached the porch, pulling off the helmet. Dawn Guardian's shock of short blonde hair emerged. She wore a black snowmobile suit and for a moment looked like some attractive actress from a superhero movie.

"Hello," Ali said, surprised. She didn't know Dawn well, but had heard of course about the Guardians' recent troubles from Pete. Closer up, she could see the fine lines of strain on the woman's face.

Dawn shook off some snow which had already gathered on her hair. She looked up the steps at Ali.

"Hello," she said, smiling ruefully. "Since Doug's accident, I thought I'd never be out on the machine again, but I just had to do something physical to get away from my thoughts for a little while."

"I know what you mean," Ali said, patting her Nevra bump. "I can't wait till I can get out and about again. Just to walk normally will be a treat."

She looked a bit uncertainly at the snow which seemed to be blowing about more fiercely now. "Are you stopping for a moment?" she asked. "Would you like a cup of coffee or something?"

Dawn seemed uncertain as well, as she stared out towards the almost invisible road. The day was darkening rapidly. Ali switched on the porch lamp, which made a comforting circle of light on the snow.

"Maybe you should stay," Ali suggested again.

Dawn seemed to pull herself out of a reverie, as if she had been calculating the hazard of the snow, the distance home.

"No thanks," she said, "But if you don't mind, maybe I could use your phone to make a quick call. I realize I was kind of impulsive when I left the Rowan Tree. I'd better call the staff nurse and let her know I'm on my way back."

"Of course, go right ahead," Ali said, opening the door behind her.

She held Emily tightly by the collar. Emily had subsided but was still grumbling a low growl as they followed Dawn into the kitchen.

"Will she bite?" Dawn asked.

"No of course not," Ali said.

"Do you mind shutting her up somewhere? I'm nervous of dogs. I was bitten by a German Shepherd when I was eight."

"I guess I can put her in the bedroom."

Dawn still paced nervously round the kitchen, though Ali assured her that the dog couldn't bother her now.

"The phone's in the living room," Ali said.

She noticed then that Dawn had a cell phone wallet on her belt but she didn't mention it. The woman seemed very nervous and edgy. Ali wondered if Dawn had received some bad news about her husband, but hardly knew how to ask. She didn't want to bring up the painful subject.

Dawn kept pacing around while the kettle boiled. It seemed almost as if she was looking for something, although she paid no attention to the furniture or the other objects in the room. Then she let out an odd little sigh by the window. She'd bent down to look at Akantha's boxes.

"That's some work I'm doing for the Island Archives project," Ali explained. "Or I'm supposed to be doing," she said guiltily. "I'm afraid I've shelved the project until after I've had the baby."

Dawn didn't seem to be listening. She'd torn a carton open and had begun to haul papers out onto the floor. Ali was shocked, both at the rudeness and at Dawn's reckless treatment of the fragile material. She hardly knew what to say.

"I'd really rather you didn't do that," she began. "I haven't had a chance to catalogue anything yet and the material isn't actually available to the public as yet."

Dawn kept on rummaging. Now she was opening the second box.

"Please," Ali protested, outrage now overtaking her shock. "Those are someone's private confidential papers. Legally they've been entrusted to the Archives Project. You'll have to wait until we've examined them."

She moved towards Dawn who was now kneeling on the floor, surrounded by a pile of carelessly strewn newspapers.

"I must insist that you stop," Ali said as forcefully as she could.

Dawn leapt agilely to her feet, brushing Ali aside.

"Where are the photo albums?" she demanded.

"Pardon?" Ali asked with disbelief.

"You heard me, there must be some photo albums. They're not in these boxes, where are they?"

And she turned and gave the cartons a vicious, dismissive kick.

The winter wind is cold and wild, come close to me my darling child

"Sorry," Nuran apologized to her publicist. "I'm afraid I wasn't listening." She turned again to look anxiously out the window of the hotel restaurant. "I just noticed the snow, it seems to have come out of nowhere."

Sara Hunt, a bright young woman about Ali's age, looked astonished. "My goodness, I've been enjoying our conversation so much, I didn't notice." She keyed something into her I-phone. "I'd better check whether my train to Montreal is leaving on time."

She tapped busily on the gadget for a minute, then sighed in relief. "Yes that's alright. It's running a half hour late but it's moving. The weather news says that there's snow blowing in all along the lake though."

I could tell that with my own eyes, Nuran thought.

"And there's a warning to watch for white-outs on Middle Island," Sara continued. She looked concerned, "Maybe you should call your daughter and check how it is over there before you leave."

Nuran tried the number twice from her own cell phone. The second time, she left a message. *I'll probably be late because of the snow. Please be sure to call Pete and let him know you are alone.*

She looked over at Sara and smiled weakly. "My daughter Ali is expecting her first child."

"Oh that's lovely," Sara cooed, as she rose from her seat and began pulling on her coat. "So you'll be a grandmother. Do you know what you're having?"

"Yes, a granddaughter."

"When?"

"Soon." *Too soon. I should never have left her.*

"You'll have to send me a picture," Sara said, now anxiously scanning the window view herself. She looked at Nuran. "Maybe you should stay here at the hotel tonight. It's already three-thirty and that snow is just going to get thicker."

Nuran looked at the white swirling maelstrom outside the glass. People struggled past, bent before the wind.

Sara hovered, ready to leave. "March is surely going out like a lion. I hate to think of you getting stuck," she said. "It could be dangerous. Would you like me to book you a room?"

Nuran could hardly hear the woman. Her mind was aroar with apprehension, premonition, something approaching panic. Feelings she did not normally allow herself, but now they came rushing in with a vengeance.

I should never have left her. What was I thinking?

I have left her too often, all her life, and this is the worst leaving of all.

But something had to be done. She had to get a grip.

"Go," she said to Sara. "Go and catch your train. I will think of the best thing to do."

"Are you sure? Do stay here at least until you have some news of the weather over on the Island."

Nuran watched Sara leave, then picked up the cellphone. But again there was no answer, just her daughter's recorded, cheerful voice. In the street, a car slipped in slush and skidded to the sidewalk curb. People jumped out of the way.

She wouldn't book a room just yet. The snow might stop.

There was no need to panic, to think of Ali in labour. She wasn't due for another two weeks. And Pete would have headed home as soon as he saw the snow begin.

*　　*　　*

Pete edged out of town into the gathering storm, his emotions swirling as wildly as the snow squalls that sheared across his windshield. Why had they not investigated Lina Russell's death more thoroughly at the time? He cast his mind back to that visit to Akantha's cottage. Had there been some clue, some connection right there at the beginning. Something that he had overlooked?

But at the time he thought he was investigating a simple break in, not a possible murder. That was the way this case, or these cases had gone, one muddle after another. Until now, when he was painfully aware of the twisted mind working behind the scenes.

Outside the cruiser window, the snow was thickening. He could barely see the side of the road. It seemed that Old Man Winter, who had been hoarding his cache of snow for the past two months, had now opened all the cupboards in the sky.

And Ali wasn't answering the cell phone.

She could have gone into labour! She might have left already in the ambulance. But no, she would have had the paramedics call him.

He could hear her voice now, objecting to his frequent calls, "I'm not a clock."

But why wasn't Nuran answering either?

His heart surging with love and frustration, he threw the phone back down on the seat.

*　　*　　*

"What are you looking for?" Ali asked helplessly. "I've been going through that material. Maybe I can help you find it."

But Dawn had spotted the open album on the couch. She grabbed it up and began rapidly flipping through the pages with angry, frantic movements. In her black clothing, she looked like a ruthless, thin-armed insect, ripping at her prey.

She hadn't yet noticed the scattered letters at her feet. The letters from Adelpha.

"You're Patricia," Ali said with sudden, sick realization.

She didn't know how she knew, she just did.

Dawn didn't seem surprised at Ali's knowledge.

"The old woman wouldn't call me Dawn," she said bitterly, not looking up from her task. "She said she didn't like it. She had always wanted a daughter to call Patricia."

"She loved you," Ali said with growing repulsion. "She loved you like a daughter, yet you betrayed her! You took her money somehow and never came back."

Dawn threw the album aside, and picked up another.

"I earned that money, every penny. Two years of pretending to be interested in her stupid stories about her wonderful childhood, her wonderful parents. Besides, I didn't take everything. She still had a house, she still had a pension."

"But she died of a broken heart! She stopped eating, she never made it up with her sister. She died alone."

"Shut up, just shut up. I have to think. And stop that damn dog's barking."

But Ali was unable to stop herself, she went on in a slow, wondering voice. "Then you came here and Akantha saw you somehow. She remembered what you'd done to her sister."

The black-clad figure moved restlessly about the room, looking for more boxes. She spoke in a clipped monotone while she searched.

"It was her own fault. She saw me on the news when they announced the Business Women's Award. And that was a hell of a joke for sure, that the two of us would end up on the Island. She sent me a letter with a copy of that old newspaper article. I knew what it meant right away. No one else would know."

Dawn turned back to Ali, said fiercely. "If only she'd left the past alone. I'd moved on, why couldn't she? But, no she had to bring it all back up."

But Ali could only think of Akantha, returning to the Island after the death of her sister. To the Island, with its happy childhood memories of two little girls playing on the beach and roaming the sunny fields. Instead, living alone in her little cottage, tiny remnant of that former idyll, she had only grown more bitter. She had gradually withdrawn into the solitary life of a virtual hermit, with only her cats for companionship. The cottage crammed with decrepit furniture and boxes of old newspapers, letters and photo albums that she never looked at.

Then one day, into her solitary, cat-cluttered living room, over the most modern piece of equipment in the house, came a message from the past. On the screen of the ancient television set, was broadcast a face, an image that burned like a flaming brand on her addled mind.

Ali pictured Akantha thunderstruck, no doubt temporarily speechless, as she stared unbelievingly at the television set. At the woman who had brought her years of grief, who had left Adelpha to a lonely death.

The television picture changes as the announcer moves on to the weather. Akantha pushes herself up off the mouldering old couch and shuffles as quickly as she can into the next room. Pushing away cats, she pulls out a carton from under the bed. She tears items out, tosses them willy-nilly on the bed.

As Dawn was doing now. What was she looking for?

What had Akantha been seeking?

Dawn shoved aside a chair and crouched down to look under the couch.

"The old crone remembered my *voice* of all things," she said venomously. "I used to answer the telephone for Adelpha when she didn't want to talk to her sister anymore. What kind of person can remember a voice after all that time?"

She stood up, breathing heavily. "But of course there was more than that. When I called her, she kept going on about this 'proof' she had and I knew right away what it had to be. The only way to identify me.

Adelpha had this old Polaroid camera, the kind that rolled out the picture as soon as you took it. I told her I didn't like to have my picture taken but one day I found the camera in her bedroom dresser drawer. I took it away but she must have snapped a picture once without me noticing.

So I knew what Akantha was talking about. She wouldn't tell me any more over the phone though, she said I had to come to her place. I asked her if she wanted money but she said she would talk about that when we met. I had to go of course. I couldn't risk that she would send the clipping and a photo to the newspaper or to the police, even though I doubted that anyone would take an old woman's ramblings seriously and make a connection with that old Hamilton case."

Ali paled. "So you killed her?"

"No," Dawn said disgustedly, "I didn't kill the old bat. She was on the floor when I got there. Must have have fallen off that stepstool and gone down like a bunch of rotten old sticks."

"Was she dead?" Ali almost whispered.

Dawn shrugged. "Sure looked like a corpse. If she wasn't, she was pretty close to it. That fall was an act of God, if you want to look at it that way. But the old woman brought it on herself. She was a meddler, she wouldn't leave the past alone. I took the newspaper clipping but I didn't have time to look through all the piles of junk."

"I went back to search the place a few days later. But the neighbour's dog barked and I had to leave again."

The break-in that Pete and Nick had gone to investigate, Ali thought.

"Then I decided not to sweat it any more. There was no reason for anyone else to sort through those piles of junk and if they did, they would hardly pay any attention to a faded Polaroid picture, in some old woman's photo album. If she had ever had a photo at all."

She looked coldly at Ali. "And no one would have ever given a damn, except you, another damned meddler. I should have burned the damn shack down when I had the chance."

"So is this all the stuff?" her gesture encompassed the cartons, the strewn papers. "There must be something more, another photo album or a box of pictures."

"Maybe there isn't a picture at all," Ali said. "You said you weren't sure."

Dawn was ripping out album pages now as if she could physically obliterate the past. Ali wincing at the destruction, took a step forward.

"There was *something*," Dawn grunted. "And the old hag must have told Lina Russell about it. Lina left a message for me after Akantha's funeral, that she wanted to talk to me. I didn't need a picture drawn for me to figure out what she was after. I had a new blackmailer. Somebody else who wanted to bankrupt me and send me back to wiping behinds and emptying bedpans."

"Oh I'm sure not," Ali protested. "Lina would never have done anything like that."

"She never got the chance to," Dawn said with grim satisfaction. "I made sure of that."

Ali had to grab the back of the chair or she would have collapsed.

"*You* shot at Lina's car?" she whispered hoarsely. "You ran her off the road *deliberately?*"

Dawn was looking restlessly around the room. "Yes I shot at her. And then I was safe again".

She added with a bitter look. "Until you came along. So, unfortunately I'm not finished yet."

40

Where was he? It was hard to tell.

The windshield wipers were nearly defeated by the weight of the heavy snow that stuck in sodden clumps to the rubber blades. Pete had to put his arm out the open window periodically to help clear the glass with his soaking glove.

There were no familiar landmarks, the cruiser was crawling through a landscape of white. Like a tiny blue beetle lost in a child's snowshaker globe. When he'd first turned onto the road, he had been able to spot the occasional mailbox but now there weren't even those few markers to show the side of the road.

By the odometer reading, he'd moved five kilometers in the past ten minutes.

Only ten long kms to go.

Jane would be phoning Ali every few minutes. She was bound to get through.

If Ali was conscious, if Ali could answer the phone.

He wondered if Jane had been able to get hold of Nick. How much help could the guy be though, he'd be driving through the same storm.

And what the hell was that, roaring along behind him. Some monster with flashing blue eyes. The snowplow!

Does the driver even see me? Is he aware there is a car on the road ahead of him?

Whoa buddy!

He veered sideways as the monster roared past, spattering his windshield with great clods of snow. When he could finally see and hear again, he found the cruiser still sitting upright. Unfortunately, it wouldn't move. He could feel his side wheels spinning uselessly over the lip of the roadside ditch. He pushed open the driver's door, and ran around to the back of the car, praying there was still a shovel in the cruiser trunk.

"Hey Pete, want some help?"

Seemingly materializing out of the swirling snow, Nick appeared, grinning his goofy grin. "I hitched a ride with the snowplow guy," he explained proudly.

Pete threw him the shovel.

"You dig, I'll push."

"Bobby the snowplow guy is coming too."

Pete noticed then that the big yellow plow had stopped as well. A burly man in an orange safety parka was battling his way over to them.

"Sorry, bud," he apologized to Pete. "I didn't see you till I was on top a ya. Didn't expect nobody to be out in this."

"That's O.K. I appreciate your help," Pete said fervently. Bobby looked big enough to push the car out himself. But in the end, it took gangly Poitras too, who was plenty strong enough it turned out. The three men had the cruiser back on the road in minutes.

"Best to stay behind me now," Bobby said. "Quicker that way."

They set off following the roar and swath of the plow, its flashing blue lights a beacon in the dimming daylight. Despite the delay, Pete was heartened by the help.

"Thanks buddy," he said to Nick. "Thanks for coming."

"No problem. Now tell me what's up. Jane wasn't too clear."

Pete filled him in quickly.

"Wow!" Nick's eyes widened at the ominous news. "No wonder you're in a hurry. So what's the plan? Looks like it's just you and me, the chief is stuck over in Bonville. Jane says nobody is getting over the causeway till this stuff lightens up."

"Try calling Ali again," Pete said. But there was still no answer.

*   *   *

Ali was still reeling from the news about Lina. Emily, upset by the sounds, started to bark again behind the bedroom door.

"Tell that dog to shut up," Dawn ordered. "Or I'll go in there and make it stop."

"She'll stop," Ali promised. She went over to the door, tried to talk soothingly through it.

Anything to stall the woman, to gain some time.

Time for some help to arrive?

Time to think about what is actually going on here.

Apparently I'm alone with a murderess. Someone who has killed.

And she's just told me that, which cannot be good.

It's simply logical, now she'll have to kill me.

And it definitely looks like a blizzard building up out there

So the rescuing possibilities are pretty slim.

I wonder what she plans to do – if she has much of a plan. By now she's reckless, tipped over the edge, a multiple murderer.

All this flashed through her mind in a nanosecond.

Unfortunately a solution was going to take much longer. Too long, most likely.

Better not to think too far ahead. That way madness lies. And utter panic.

Never had she wished more urgently that she could read another person's mind.

Could this woman, not a great friend, but a fellow Island resident, actually be contemplating killing her? And how? Again Ali felt the blood enter her head, but she couldn't faint, her unborn child was depending on her.

Had Dawn brought a gun? Ali hadn't seen one, not a rifle anyway. It could still be out with the snowmobile. What weapons were to hand? Knives in the kitchen? Oh god Dawn wasn't going to stab her!

Once, Ali could have put up a good struggle, she was younger and used to be in good shape. But now, she could hardly risk the strain or she might lose the baby. And she knew she mustn't run, likely couldn't run anyway. But she could talk! All murderers wanted to talk, at least in the movies. She must try to persuade Dawn to leave her alone.

The telephone rang, Ali felt her heart leap with unthinking joy and relief. "That's Pete," she babbled happily. "He calls all the time to check how I am."

"Don't answer," Dawn warned, grabbing at Ali's outstretched hand.

Ali struggled but Dawn's grip was like a manacle, her tense face only inches away. She forced Ali back into the chair. And now the nightmare was all very real. It was if a spell had broken, as the last vestiges of hope of reasoning with her assailant faded away. The phone rang a couple more times, the insistent, repeated ringing echoing in the room. When it finally stopped, Ali felt an overwhelming loneliness. She stared bleakly at Dawn, trying to detect a spark of empathy, of human feeling. Or at least sanity.

"You can't mean to hurt me," she tried. "It's not just me, it's the baby."

Dawn shrugged. "Take it from me. It's better for the kid not to be born into this cruel world."

"But how are you going to make this killing look like an accident?" Ali protested. "You'll get caught for sure." Though she doubted Dawn was thinking logically any more.

"Oh you're going to have an accident all right," Dawn said. "You're going to fall down those very slippery back steps. When they find you, everybody will say it was too bad that you hit your head on the way down. A tragedy really."

As if her own words had decided her, she grabbed Ali's arm. "Now get up," she commanded. "*Walk!*"

She half-dragged and pushed Ali into the kitchen. At the door, Ali tried desperately to hang on to the frame.

"What are you doing?" she cried. "This is crazy!"

In the bedroom, Emily was barking frantically and flinging herself against the door. But now Dawn was utterly cold-eyed, cold-hearted. Not listening, not answering. Like an icicle. Unreachable.

Ali gave up her grip on the door frame. The strain was too great. She would have to hope that when they got out to the porch, she would have a chance to push Dawn down the steps in front of her. It would be a terrible risk to take, and it wasn't much of a plan but at this point, hope was all she had.

41

The woman looked so frightened. And yet so brave. The maternal instinct they called it.

Like a vixen protecting her kittens.

Protecting her child, though it wasn't even here yet.

Pity she wouldn't get the chance to be a mother. She might have been one of the good ones you read about in stories.

Not like the real mothers you saw in the placement homes. The cruel ones who called you names and locked you in closets if you dared to talk back. And the fathers were worse, much worse . . . .

Ali gasped as the cold air of the porch smacked into her lungs. The shock also cleared her head though, cutting like a knife through her panicked thoughts. Obviously, Dawn was not so crazy that she going to turn her back and be pushed down the stairs. Was there nothing else Ali could do to save herself and Nevra? The porch deck was slippery with the fresh wet snow, she could gain no purchase to hold herself back. But Dawn had grabbed hold of the railing with her other hand and was using the support to good advantage. Inch by inch, she was gaining in the struggle.

*   *   *

Bobby tooted goodbye on the snowplow horn and the big vehicle roared on in its noisy lumbering way. Pete rammed the cruiser through the piled up ridge of snow in his own driveway. He and Nick had debated about using the siren, then decided there was more advantage in surprise, if any.

Now, seeing the desperate struggle in the porch lights, there was no debate. They got out and ran. Only to stop abruptly a moment later. Dawn had managed to drag Ali to the top of the steps. All players seemed temporarily mesmerized, calculating what best to do.

"I'll push her down," Dawn called out. "I will, I swear it!" Her voice sounded tinny and brittle in the cold air. The porch light lit her blonde hair like an icy halo.

Pete saw that the woman was in a perilously fragile state, nearly over the edge of sanity. Beside her, Ali looked terribly pale. She had no coat and he could see that she was shivering uncontrollably. He fought down his own emotions, trying not to slip over into panic himself.

"Let Ali go," he answered, as calmly as he could. "You've got nothing to gain by hurting her. Let her go and then we can talk."

"No!" Dawn said rawly, her words rising towards hysteria. "*You're* going to let *me* go. And I'm taking her with me. We're going to walk together out to the car."

Pete glanced quickly at Nick. *Do you see any weapon?* he mouthed. *How does she think she's going to get past us, once she's off the porch?*

Nick shook his head. *I don't see anything. She's just nuts.*

Pete took a step forward. Dawn tugged at Ali.

He took another step. Ali groaned in pain or anger and moved, pulling back hard against Dawn's grip. She sagged to the porch floor. Pete started running. Dawn took one quick look at the situation and let go of Ali. Moving agilely as a doe, she vaulted over the porch railing and sprinted towards the shadowed side of the house.

Pete slipped on the icy steps, scrambled on hands and knees to the top. Then he had Ali in his arms.

"She killed Lina," Ali cried. "Oh, Pete, it's so awful. She killed Lina!"

"Is she O.K.?" Nick asked anxiously, hovering on the step below.

Pete nodded. "I hope so. But go!" he said urgently, as they heard the roar of the snowmobile starting up. "Get her!"

Nick jumped over the railing, letting out a loud oomph as he landed.

Pete bent over Ali, "Now let's get you inside and warmed up."

Moments later, Nick came running back, panting for breath, his face and parka collar soaked with wet snow. Pete had got Ali onto the sofa and covered her with a blanket. Emily, released at last from the bedroom, was anxiously licking everyone in sight.

"I lost her," Nick said glumly. "The snowmobile was already moving away when I got out there."

He slapped some snow out of his glove. "What now? We can't follow her, the cruiser isn't going anywhere in this stuff."

Pete looked up from the couch where he was holding Ali's hand tightly.

"There's only one way off the Island," he said. "Radio the chief to block the causeway." As Nick started off, he added. "Oh and ask the chief to get me a doctor on the line too, will you? We've got a baby coming."

* * *

My heart is a lonely hunter, That hunts on a lonely hill

She should be able to see the village street lights soon. It had been a rough ride, fighting the bucking machine along the slippery road, the snow lashing her raw, streaming face. Her arms and wrists ached.with the effort of holding to a steady course. Luckily there was no traffic, all the nosey old Island folk were sticking close to home on this treacherous night. And it would have been impossible to make any time along the fields where visibility was just about nil. She'd have ended up like Doug, squashed under an overturned machine.

Best not to think of any of that stuff, though. Not of Doug or the Rowan Tree or the award. That part of her life was over, a shut door, like all the others. It was time to start again. She'd had lots of practice.

A person could get tired though. Tired of the running. How old was she now – forty-two? And Pop had died when she was twelve. Thirty years ago. She didn't even know that he had died till the witch from the foster agency came to tell her. And how was that possible, that she hadn't known? You'd think that she would have felt the pain when he had left the world forever. Instead, she just went on sleeping or eating or mopping floors or whatever other stupid dumb useless thing they had her doing at the time. Sorry Pop.

She'd cried all night, quietly so no one would hear.

And that was the last time she felt sorry for anybody. Including herself. What was the point? Wasted effort.

Better concentrate on the task ahead. She'd always been good at that. It was her strong point, to get the task done. Lord, she was tired though. Bone-weary. She'd read the description once in a book and now she felt it. There was no sap left in her bones. If her gloves hadn't been practically frozen to the handlebars, she doubted she could still hang on. She was tired of driving, tired of *moving*, tired of everything. It had been another long day and she wanted only to sleep.

She was coming up on the village now. Bayshore Road looked quiet, deserted really. The street lights wavered like candles through the sleet. There were only a couple of faint snowed-over tracks to show that anyone had been along in the past few hours.

But the neon sign of the Island Grill glowed redly in the night and there were several cars parked before the motel. They'd all be watching the television in there though, probably drinking and shouting at some sports game. Nobody would pay any attention to a snowmobile going past. Besides, she had no choice, the causeway was only another few hundred feet. She had to go past the Grill to get there.

She only had to hang on for a little while longer, then she'd be across the Bay and off the Island. One last mighty dash and then she'd be safe.

She turned on to the causeway, the machine clinging tightly to the road above the storm-lashed waves beyond the embankment. Almost home free.

And then the lights came on, swirling red and white and orange. Waiting like ruthless eyes at the other end.

Blinding lights!

Jacklighting her, like a helpless doe in one of her panicked childhood dreams.

There they waited, with their shrieking sirens and their dreadful glaring lights.

The relentless pursuers

They would never go away

They would I never leave her alone.

Never

Why not just let go?

Yes, let go.

Stop fighting, end the battle.

And slip into the water's loving, icy embrace.

42

I t snowed and snowed and snowed.

All night long, without stopping. As if in apology for being late.

As if someone up in the skies was sweeping off a giant celestial sidewalk.

The last few flakes now drifted lazily down past the hospital room window.

"How do you feel, honey?" Pete asked.

Ali lay at ease with her hair spread out against the starchy, snow-white pillow, the baby in her pink swaddling blanket, held close in her arms.

"I feel as if I need a couple of months of rest."

"Too late for that, my sweetie."

"Just kidding," she laughed. "I feel absolutely wonderful!"

"You look wonderful too, my darling. You both do."

She lifted a corner of the blanket and crooned. "What an introduction to the world, my little darling! Born on the living room couch and then a wild ride to the hospital following the snow plow."

Pete grinned. "Lucky for us that Bob stopped to check in on the way back from the Point."

Ali kissed Nevra's softy fuzzed scalp. "We'll have to send nice Uncle Bobby a thank-you picture."

They'd followed the plow into town, Nick carefully driving the cruiser while Pete held his family wrapped up in blankets in the back seat.

Ali looked up at Pete and their glances kindled. "We did it," she said softly.

He held his wife and daughter close. "Yes we did."

There was a light tap on the door of the room.

"Hello," Ali called brightly, as Pete stood up.

Nuran remained in the doorway, her coat unbuttoned and her hair looking as if she'd only just run her fingers through it on her way from the motel where she'd spent the night. On her face was an expression that Ali had never seen before. Uncertainty? Shyness? But that was impossible.

"Come in, mother," she said, feeling strangely uncertain herself.

Nuran moved hesitantly into the room. "I didn't read your message till this morning," she said. "I got the first taxi I could."

She had reached the bed.

"Oh my goodness," she said in a rush. "Is this my beautiful granddaughter?"

Ali held the bundle out towards her mother's arms and the two women burst into tears.

When Pete returned a bit later with cardboard cups of tea, the three were sitting on the bed together, tears dried and smiles all round.

Nuran thanked Pete and took her cup. "So now you've delivered a baby," she said.

He grinned. "Just basic cop training. I think it was a little tough on Nick, my partner though. Actually I was pretty scared, too."

She patted him on the shoulder. "You did well. You're a good man to have around in an emergency."

Ali threw him a kiss. "He's a good man to have around, anytime."

*   *   *

Foot-high banks of cleared snow ringed the police station parking lot.

"Congratulations!" Jane greeted Pete happily, "I've sent over some flowers from all of us here. Is she beautiful?"

"She's beautiful," Pete said. "She's perfect."

"I'm going to pop in and see the little darling after work," Jane said. "Can't wait!"

Halstead looked up from his desk on which sat a box of chicken wings and fries from the Grill. "Lunch," He pushed the box toward Pete. "But you know you don't have to be here just yet."

"It's O.K. thanks. Nuran is at the hospital with them right now and I don't think there are any more babies to be delivered at the moment."

"You did well, son. I've been in the waiting room for a few births but I've never been called on to do anything more than to pass out the cigars."

Pete felt in his pocket. "Sorry, I haven't had time to pick up cigars. How about a raincheck? I owe Bobby one too."

"You can get me a beer next time we're at the Grill."

"You're on. But right now, you've got a story to tell me."

Halstead nodded, "You'd better sit down, it's a long one."

He finished a gnawed wing and pushed back his chair.

"Once upon a time," he began. "There was a little girl called Patricia Dawn Smith. She was born in Callandar, Ontario but her parents soon moved out to Vancouver where they'd heard the city was friendlier to drug addicts. The family lived on a welfare allowance, stretched even tighter because of the parents' addictions. Dawn's mother died when she was five.

Her father kept the household, such as it was, together for another couple of years. Then when Dad was diagnosed with AIDS, the authorities stepped in and took young Dawn into care, such as that was.

Nine foster homes later, seventeen year old Dawn stepped out into the streets of Vancouver. We're working on filling in the gaps but what we do know is that about ten years after that, she was working as a minimum wage, home care aide named Patricia Ennis, who was sent on assignment to the home of Adelpha Samos."

He paused.

"I can fill in this part," Pete offered. "I picked up the letters from the house on my way here and finally read what Ali had been telling me all along."

He put a buff envelope on the desk.

"Letters from Adelpha to Akantha. It's pretty much all here, or at least enough so that we can fill in the blanks. How Adelpha came to trust Patricia, to rely on her. 'The daughter she never had,' that's what she calls her in one of the letters. 'Patricia' really got her hooks in there.

Then the old lady let her take over the banking. At that point, Akantha got worried and urged her sister to check for references. Instead, Adelpha took offense and apparently cut off communicating with her sister at all. "

Hastead nodded. "Adelpha didn't know that Patricia or our Dawn, was systematically draining the bank account. She was smart about it at first and not overgreedy. We've been checking with the bank this morning and found that over the course of the year Dawn took several thousand dollars for herself from Adelpha's checking account.

Then though, she got bigger ideas and came up with the story of needing money for a stake to set up her own business. She got Adelpha to cash in bonds to the amount of $200,000 and then our Miss Dawn flew the coop. She actually drove away in Adelpha's 1975 Mercedes. The car was never found either, she probably sold it to a chop shop." He sighed. "And that was the last seen of Patricia Ennis."

Pete stood up, massaging his neck, still taut from the night's dramatic events. "So she was a thief but she didn't actually murder Adelpha Samos."

Halstead scowled. "She didn't spend any time worrying about the old woman either. Adelpha was likely more broken by the betrayal than by the loss of the money. She was alone and confused and basically seems to have lost all interest in life. Till the neighbours realized something was wrong and called the police."

"And that was the end of Adelpha Samos."

They thought about that for a moment.

Pete broke the silence. "So what did our sweet little swindler girl do next? Rob a bank?"

Halstead spread his hands. "Could be. But the fact is, we don't know. She went back under the radar for a few years anyway. She might have forged a new I.D., maybe fleeced other victims. But at some point, she bought a ticket for a Caribbean cruise."

"Where she met Doug Guardian, who eventually brought her to Middle Island."

They thought of Guardian, lying in his bed at Bonville General. The brain swelling had subsided and in a few weeks he would be out of the intensive care unit, facing a drastically altered life.

Pete sat back down. "It must have come as a terrific shock to Dawn when Akantha contacted her. She couldn't have known that Akantha had moved to Middle Island after her sister died."

"Or about the family's old island connection." Halstead said. "Though Adelpha sounds like the type of person who would get out the photo albums and talk about her family."

Pete remembered what Ali had said once. "Nobody ever listens to old people, certainly not the Dawn Guardian type."

Hastead smiled sourly. "And yet she ended up running a retirement nursing home for seniors. That's a laugh, talk about putting a fox in with the chickens! I wonder what an audit of the Rowan Tree accounts will show."

Pete looked doubtful. "I'll bet they're as clean as a whistle. The woman was done with crime. She wanted desperately to be straight, to be respectable, that's what she told Ali."

Halstead looked out the window at the pristine field, said wearily, "Yeah, she wanted it so badly, she'd kill for it."

Pete thought of the ancient television set in Akantha's cottage, Nick fiddling with the rabbit ears. How ironic, that the Bonville news was on the only television channel Akantha received. And that the woman who cheated her sister should appear on the screen so many years later, beautiful and laughing, nominated for an award. That she had been living right there on the Island, only a few miles away

So Akantha had put the newsclipping in an envelope and mailed it, sealing her own fate. A week later, Dawn Guardian left a second Samos sister to die.

"Fresh, hot coffee," Jane called from the lunch room. "Any takers?"

After the short break, they resumed their conversation.

"Then we get to Lina Russell," Pete said.

"Now there's a tragedy," Halstead said grimly, "and all based on a goddamned mistake."

Late last night, Pete had phoned the chief with Ali's information. That Lina had contacted Dawn and said she wanted to talk to her. That Dawn had assumed she had a new blackmailer.

"Of course that wasn't true," Halstead said. "As anyone who knew Lina could have told her." He cursed. "I've been out to the Rowan Tree this morning and talked to Carol, the assistant manager. She said that Lina was concerned about her grandmother's deteriorating condition. She'd read of the use of memory patches for some Alzheimer's patients and wondered if they were worth a try. That's all she wanted to talk about."

"But why would Dawn think Lina meant to talk about Akantha Samos?"

Halstead shook his head. "We'll never know now but poor Lina must have mentioned something. Akantha was one of her clients and the story of Akantha's fatal fall was in the news. Dawn would know that Lina had been the old lady's home visitor, and she was in such a state of anxiety by then, that she must have thought that Lina was coming to expose her or make a deal."

"Jesus." Pete said.

Halstead nodded. "Then apparently even that murder didn't end the threat, when she learned later that Akantha's boxes had gone to Ali."

Pete felt that awful chill all over again. When he'd realized where Dawn Guardian was heading.

"You were right about Doug too," Halstead said. "He took the blame when Dawn said she'd accidentally shot at Lina, mistaking her for the hunters. Though I wonder whether he would have gone on covering for her once he suspected it was murder."

"Obviously Dawn didn't trust him to. She was going to kill him to make sure. And she'd been married to the guy for ten years!" Pete marvelled. "Like a black widow spider or something. And she was taking a helluva risk there. What if Doug didn't die – and in fact he didn't."

"I doubt she was thinking rationally by then," Halstead said. "I guess she was hoping to get him in the hospital, at least until she could make the deal with the Royal Retirement people."

He'd found a reference to an appointment with the company in Dawn's day-book at the Rowan Tree. A call to a company official confirmed that Dawn was about to sell the homes, now that her husband was unfortunately incapacitated.

. Pete pushed back his chair, "So is someone like that, just plain bad?"

Halstead looked down at the file information that Jane had printed out.

"The woman had a rocky start in life. The parents were pretty hopeless and then they died. She had bad luck in the foster homes where the agencies sent her. So, no roots, no kindness, no security. Not much to build a life on."

"But look how she repaid the people who were kind to her, who never hurt her. Her husband, Lina Russell, what she was going to do to Ali . . ."

"I don't think she was able to recognize that Doug loved her, nobody else had. She grew up only trusting herself. She spent years scratching and clawing to get to a place where she could afford to be good. So there she was, excited, full of energy and ambition about the new project. Then she gets Akantha's letter with the newspaper clipping. She thought she was going to lose it all."

Pete shook his head. "Do you think she felt bad about any of it, do you think she felt guilty?"

"I think she was tired," Halstead said. "She wanted to go into the Bay, she wanted to end it."

He saw again that dreadful moment as he stood there at the causeway exit with the other cops, the red and orange lights flashing in the night. The shock as they saw the machine turn sharply and realized what the rider was going to do. There was no time to stop her. By the time the officers had run to the spot, rider and machine had disappeared into the frigid water. It was only eight feet deep but deep enough, at least under those conditions. It would be a couple of hours before they could even get divers with the proper gear. Helplessly he stood, staring into the blackness.

Now he straightened papers and closed up the file folder. The movement made a small sound in the room. There was still work to be done, information to be checked, reviewed and confirmed but there was no rush.

"You'd better go visit your wife and baby daughter," he told Jakes. "They're probably missing you already."

The Jakes house was busy with women. Pete supposed he had better get used to it, but today he had kissed his tiny daughter, then thankfully taken his leave.

"It gets better," Ali promised, as she waved him off. "When the admiring crowds settle down."

Today there was a most welcome admirer, their neighbour Miranda who had flown back early from Costa Rica. Tanned and vigorously healthy, she look years younger than her mid-seventies. She had brought a brightly-coloured toy parrot for the baby.

"If my dog will even let me near her," she laughed. Since her arrival, Emily had stayed close, wagging her tail about Miranda's legs and nearly knocking her over.

Miranda and Nuran seemed mutually delighted at becoming acquainted. Ali could foresee long, interesting conversations concerning the state of women's rights in Costa Rica. This morning though, passed in a cozy blur of companionship, tea and lots of admiring coos and aahs for baby Nevra.

Ali stretched out her arms luxuriously. "This is absolutely delicious, I want you to know. I can *move* again, I can *think*. I can stay awake for more than five minutes. Hooray!"

When the baby was wrapped up snugly in her bassinet and lunch sandwiches on the table, the talk inevitably turned to recent events.

"Did you know the Samos sisters, Miranda?" Ali asked.

"I knew of them, but the girls were nearly ten years older than me. They had stopped coming to the Island for the summer in my time. The house was empty for awhile and then it burned down. I guess the father sold the land at some point."

Ali shook her head. "How horribly ironic that Dawn ended up looking after old folks instead of looking how to rob them."

Miranda bit neatly into her egg salad sandwich. "It's a dreadful, evil story. I think I feel saddest about Lina. The Samos sisters had lived their lives but Lina should have had years to go."

"I don't know that Dawn Guardian was evil," Ali protested. "Her father died of AIDS. She was an unhappy foster child, constantly moved around. She was pretty and if she wasn't actually abused, life would still have been pretty scary. Pete said that her school marks were good, but I doubt that she ever had the chance to make many friends. No wonder she reverted to living by her father's survival habits."

Nuran agreed. "When you think of it, how could she have had anything but a warped view of human relationships. The people or agencies in the woman's past should bear some responsibility for the crimes."

"You're right of course," Miranda amended. "But unfortunately, it doesn't work that way. Poor woman, she had about as much chance as any orphaned wild creature."

They were all quiet for a moment, looking at the baby snug in her blanket.

Nuran bent to kiss the creamy, petal-soft cheek. "Never mind little Nevra, you are a lucky child. Your parents will surround you with love."

Ali feasted her eyes on the sight of grandmother and child, and her ears on Nuran's words. Nuran was already enmeshed in Nevra's power. How not be, the baby's sweet face would melt a stone!

*   *   *

Bedtime. Luxurious sleep, for a few hours anyway, till the four o'clock feeding. Nevra lay snug in her basinette beside their bed, Emily was back home with Miranda across the road.

Ali, in frothy new nightgown, was putting a new photo on the dresser, a picture of Nuran holding the baby.

"For Nevra's photo album," she said. She'd also popped a picture of the baby into a card to send to Pete's father. Nothing ventured . . .

To make room on the dresser top, she had to move the picture of the Samos sisters a bit to the side. Holding the frame, she frowned,

"I still wonder about one thing. I know that Akantha was a dotty old lady but how could she be so foolish as to ask Dawn to come to the cottage. What do you think she was planning to do?"

Pete, under the covers and already preparing to get what rest he could, said drowsily. "I guess she wanted to confront Patricia at last. And maybe blackmail her too, though I know my sweet wife hates to see anything bad in anyone."

Ali shook her head, "I don't believe it. What would she want money for at her age — her cats? No, I think she just wanted to see Patricia/Dawn face to face, to show her that she hadn't gotten away with it, that someone knew of her guilt. To say, you're the woman who destroyed my sister."

"Um huh," Pete mumbled.

"What this?" Ali asked, in a puzzled tone.

Something had slipped out from behind the picture frame and fallen to the carpet. It looked like another, smaller photo, but she could only see the back. She bent to pick it up. She could bend again!

She turned the photo over in her hand. The picture was of a young woman standing on a porch, watering a hanging basket of geraniums. On the strip of white plastic beneath the picture, someone had written simply. 'My daughter."

The woman had shoulder length brown hair and bangs but even in the faded colours of the old Polaroid film, she was easily recognizable as Dawn Guardian.

Ali breathed shakily. "This is what Dawn was looking for! I completely forgot about this picture in the bedroom."

Pete by now was fully awake and sitting up. "Let me see."

He took the photo from her and gave it a long look. "And a good thing you didn't think of it. Instead, Dawn kept searching the living room and bought us some time. Time for Nick and I to get here."

Later, in bed with her husband and child breathing snugly beside her, Ali looked across the room at the picture of her two 'aunts'. Her protectors.

Thank you.

She sent the warm thought out into the dark winter night.

44

The convention room at Bonville's Commodore Hotel was a festive sight, fifteen round tables bedecked with white cloths, sparkling wine glasses, and slim vases from *Fine Flowers,* holding sprigs of pussy willows and forced yellow forsythia.

On the podium at the front of the room with the eleven other nominees, sat Steph, sparkling too, in long black skirt and a red shimmering top.

"I feel odd," she'd said earlier when they'd arrived at the hotel. "It doesn't seem right for me to be here, after all that's happened."

"You have every right to be here," Halstead assured her. "You've created a business you can be proud of. "

"What's going to happen to Doug?" she asked.

"He's getting better every day," he said. "Jane's niece, the nurse said that he was sitting in his wheelchair in the sunroom yesterday."

"But what is his future? And who will run the Rowan Tree homes?"

"Actually, Carol the assistant manager will be looking after things until Doug can make a decision about whether to sell or not. She's very able and the staff are all pitching in with extra help. Apparently there's someone at the Bonville home too, who can take over for now."

He paused. "As for Doug, he'll be an invalid for some time yet. I hear he'll be going to a really good rehabilitation centre in Toronto."

"And emotionally?"

He shrugged helplessly. "I don't know Steph, how does anybody recover from that kind of shock?"

Discovering that your wife is a murderer and that she tried to kill you too.

"Mom looks terrific, doesn't she?" said Steph's daughter Livy, who was home visiting for the Easter break.

"Yes she does."

The girl looked very pretty as well. Last year she had been a gloomy Goth style adherent, from her dyed black hair to her purple fingernails. Under great stress at the time, she had been pale and wraith-like, uncommunicative even with her mother. But the months out in B.C. seemed to have done her good. Her clothes were still a little strange he thought, but at least not all black. Her soft brown hair swung lightly over rounder cheeks and there was real pride in her voice when she spoke of Steph.

At the podium, the speaker seemed to have finished her remarks.

"I think they're coming up to the awards soon," Livy said. She held up crossed fingers for luck. Halstead adjusted the complimentary red carnation in his buttonhole and crossed his own fingers behind his back.

On the platform, Steph sat primly, with ankles crossed, her face outwardly calm. An image flashed across his mind. Steph in her cheerleader sweater and short pleated skirt, no older than Livy was now. Running out onto the football field. Leaping with chrysanthemum yellow coloured pompoms into a cheer.

1,2,3,4 who are we rooting for,
5,6,7,8 who do we appreciate
Go Islanders go!

He smiled and felt his dilemma of the past months slide away.

What did it matter whether they were married or not? What did it matter where he lived, as long as his home was with her? He could always moor the *Lone Loon* somewhere nearby, as a hideaway from the poetry classes. Heck, he could attend the poetry classes.

" . . . .and the Ontario Eastern Division, Business Woman of the Year award, goes to Stephanie Bind, owner of YourPlace Retreat, Middle Island."

Livy stood up and cheered, most unGoth-like.

When a flushed Steph neared the table, award plaque clutched proudly in hand, he stood up to give her a hearty kiss.

She broke free and looked doubtfully at her daughter.

"Don't pay any attention to me, kids," Livy teased. "Kiss away."

Later though, over dessert, she asked.

"Well are you guys going to make it legal or not? Not that you have to for my sake. Dad and Theresa aren't married either, you know."

Halstead protested. "It so happens I want to make an honest woman out of your mother but she keeps turning me down."

"Don't *look* at me like that," Steph said. "Are the two of you ganging up on me?"

"You could have a lovely summer wedding," Livy suggested. "You could pose for the pictures in the flower garden of your award-winning Retreat."

Stephanie grinned. "Only if I get some say in what you'll be wearing, oh daughter of mine. Heaven knows what fashion you'll be into by then."

After the lunch, she asked Halstead, "Are you coming back with us?"

He kissed her cheek. "I'll come by later. There's something I have to do."

*   *   *

The closed casket lay unaccompanied in a room at the Bonville funeral home. Someone had ordered a vase of lilies, no doubt competent Carol, of the Rowan Tree. Halstead didn't sign the book either, but when he was driving back to the Island along the causeway, he stopped by the side of the road and dropped the red carnation from his buttonhole onto the ice. Yes, there was ice at last, a thin silvery rime that sparkled in the sun. The flower lay there, alone and cold.

Then he continued on home to his Island, to his life.

* * *

Middle Island Art Gallery, Open Thursday, Friday and Saturday 10 to 4.

Nick had looked in the window a couple of times but hadn't gone in. Now someone had seen him though, so if he didn't go in, he'd look like some kind of wierdo.

That was a good one, the cop going into an art gallery and he's the wierdo.

He thought he was hoping that she wasn't there, that he could just look at her paintings. But when she wasn't, he felt a keen disappointment.

He walked over to see the paintings anyway.

The one of the cedars and the birds wasn't there, maybe she hadn't finished it yet. But there were others, several painted in the woods. It was like being in the actual woods but different, as if the woods were in some other country. Or on some other planet. It was the colours that gave this effect, he could see.

Then she was suddenly there, behind him, rude as ever.

Demanding, "What are you doing here?" Glaring up at him, "I hope you didn't bring your gun here. This is a place for *art*, not guns."

He lifted up his arms and spread them out. "No gun, see?"

She didn't look mollified at all. Although she did look wonderful. Till now, he'd only seen her in bulky coat and hat but today she wore a black sweater and some kind of swirly gold skirt. She looked as pretty as an ornament.

"Actually," he said, "I'm thinking of trading my rifle in for a camera. I was wondering whether you could tell me some good places to take pictures."

He'd caught her interest at last. "You don't want to shoot anymore? How did this happen?"

Because I saw a baby born. I saw life begin.

But he wouldn't tell her now. Maybe some other time. For now, he would be happy just to walk around the gallery beside her and look at the wonderful pictures.

EPILOGUE

If winter comes, can spring be far behind?

Pete had stopped the car at the swamp to listen to the spring peepers. Early May and the woods and swamp had healed quickly over the scars, the veering of a car, the drag of a lurching snowmobile. A quicker healing than in the human heart.

If there's a bullet in that water, let it lie. Let it turn to rust. It's spring. Life is renewed, life rises yet again.

Soon, Old Tom Turkey and his lady friends could enjoy a summer's peace.

And next winter there would be a new story to add to the repetoire of the old-timers at the Island Grill. The story of the night that little Nevra Jakes was born in the big March blizzard.

— The End —

QUOTATIONS

Chapter Three. If seasons all were summers/And leaves would never fall.
(Thomas Hardy)

Chapter Eleven. In nature's infinite book of secrets/A little I can read.
(Shakespeare, Antony and Cleopatra.)

Chapter Thirteen. What dark days seen!/The very birds are mute.
(Shakespeare, Sonnet 97).

Chapter Eighteen. There's a certain slant of light on winter afternoons/That oppresses like the heft of cathedral tunes
(Emily Dickenson)

Chapter Twenty-Three. Frosty mornings, tingling thumbs
(R.L. Stevenson)

Chapter Thirty-Five. A tyrant spell has bound me/And I cannot, cannot go.
(Emily Bronte.)

Chapter Thirty-Six. Every why has a wherefore
(Shakespeare, Comedy of Errors)

Chapter Thirty-Nine. The winter wind is cold and wild/Come close
    to me my darling child.
(Emily Bronte)

Chapter Forty-One. My heart is a lonely hunter/That hunts on a
    lonely hill.
(William Sharpe, 1896)

Epilogue. If winter comes, can spring be far behind?
(Percy Bysse Shelly, Ode to the West Wind)

Cover photo by Karen Emmons.